Love Like That

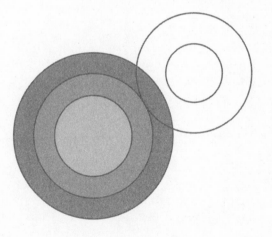

Love Like That

Amanda Hill

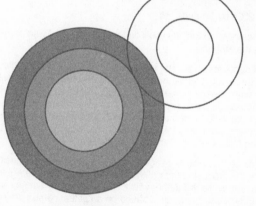

RED
DRESS
INK
™

First edition April 2005

LOVE LIKE THAT

A Red Dress Ink novel

ISBN 0-373-89518-6

© 2005 by Amanda Hill.

The poem "In the city you'll find me" is reprinted with permission by the author.

www.RedDressInk.com

Printed in U.S.A.

For Katherine and Kelli

ACKNOWLEDGMENTS

I am so incredibly fortunate to have had such wonderful people help see *Love Like That* on its journey: Thanks to Stephanie Lee, my agent at Manus & Associates, because she was its motivational force; and to Farrin Jacobs, my editor at Red Dress Ink, for believing in this book enough to publish it. To Mom, Dad, Lisa, Terry and Mimi, for their encouragement, support and love. To Tammy Jensen, my mainstay, because after hearing the story countless times, she still read every word. To Ann Phillips, for her unwavering enthusiasm. To Regina Sanchez, for her invaluable guidance. To my friends from Ventura, for their many timeless qualities that will always call me home. And lastly, a bit of gratitude to those not named who provided such unforgettable inspiration for the people who live between these pages.

In the city you'll find me

mixed beliefs in liquored drinks
confidence purchased in sleek boutiques
lost dreams in rings of nicotine
sordid nights triumphant with poetic lies
carnal pleasure anointed with tight-fisted thighs
comfort snorted in glittering lines
red lips rebel in a sea of neurotic faces
street lights flicker inconceivable wishes

hidden beneath my cheapened skin
nurturing my inconsistent sin

In the city you'll find me

—Katherine Larsen

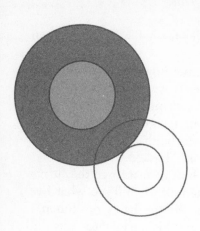

Prologue

My vomit was teal. When I first saw it I screamed and said we should call 911. I thought my insides were really that color and that maybe I was an alien. Jeremy said to shut up and relax. He said it was from the blue curaçao in the drinks. Some of it had crusted on the underside of the toilet seat.

I closed my eyes and imagined I had woken up from a four-poster canopy bed with satin sheets and lace and lush carpeting beneath my feet like a princess in a fairy tale. The faucet was leaking. Jeremy was coughing from the futon. He yelled that he had smoked too much and how could I let him do such a thing. I stumbled leaving the bathroom, and lit a cigarette.

He acted like he didn't know me. He does that sometimes. I lay down on the futon with him and concentrated on breathing as the smoke circled around us in yellowish-gray streamers. He put *Alien* in the DVD player and we watched it in silence.

"Are you going to live?" he finally asked.

"I'm not sure. It might help if you rub my back," I replied.

He scratched it disinterestedly for a few seconds, then stopped.

I remembered when we first met how we would lie facing each other and smile sleepily as we talked about all the things lovers do. Now my back was to him and he didn't seem to care. I guess because we've gotten routine. Or maybe just because we don't have to care. Maybe that is our routine.

"Can I get something to drink?" I asked.

He sighed like I'd just asked him to rearrange the furniture and got up with exaggerated effort. "I'll see what I've got, okay? But I'm warning you—it's probably not much."

He was right. The only thing in his refrigerator was this yucky fruit-soda-type diet drink. He drank half and handed me the bottle. I took a tentative sip and nearly gagged. But it was cold so I drank it.

He settled down again. "Don't you have to pick Roman up from the airport today?"

"You know I do."

He yawned. "How long's he staying this time, anyway?"

"Um…am I totally retarded, or wasn't I just telling you *last night* that he'll be here for three weeks?"

"Well…I don't know. I wouldn't say you're *totally* retarded," he replied. "Seriously, though. Three whole weeks?"

I frowned at him. "You shouldn't have a problem with it."

"I don't." He put his hands behind his head and shrugged into the futon mattress.

"Then why did you say it like that? *Three whole weeks?*" I mimicked.

"I didn't say it like *that,*" he informed me.

I sat up. "Yeah, you did. Like you're put off by the idea of Roman being here that long because you know you can't call me while he's around."

He eyed me. "Don't fool yourself, toots. Three weeks isn't even that long."

I got up to locate my belongings. "Whatever. I'd better be on my way, actually."

"Okay."

How very odd to find my roommate's shiny blue Prada pumps, which I'd borrowed on the sly the night before, in the cabinet beneath the kitchen sink. I thought the empty tequila bottle on the kitchen counter could probably explain a lot of things. But not everything.

I felt Jeremy's eyes follow me to the door before he said, "Hey."

"What?" I paused with my hand on the doorknob.

"C'mere for a sec."

I went over to the futon and knelt down. He placed a hand on the back of my neck and pulled me down for a dizzy kiss. He let go first and stroked my chin with the pad of one thumb. "Have fun."

"I will."

"Give Roman my best," he chuckled.

I rolled my eyes. "I'll see you later, okay?"

He gave me a little wave and I closed the door behind me.

The thing about Jeremy is that I can always tell he's irritated by the idea of Roman, but then he acts like it's nothing to him. And I don't really think he has the right to be irritated, anyway. *His* girlfriend lives right here in L.A. Maybe he was worried about the bigger picture. Maybe I'm always fooling myself.

Outside it was hot and bright with the end of June and someone was having car trouble in the alley. I walked down the stairs and thought for the thousandth time that someday I'm going to trip and fall down these stairs. My head will be crushed open on the cement with brains and blood pouring out and trickling down into the dirty flower bed, where we used to throw cigarette butts and beer caps before the neighbors yelled about it. They'll call the police and say there's a dead girl at the bottom of the stairs outside of their apartment. Jeremy will be questioned and will say he has no idea who she is. He'll get his camera and take pictures of my gooey head and the ooze that's seeping from the hole and

he'll hide them in a box with a lock and look at them sometimes with a guilty pleasure. Roman will wonder what I was
doing there. He'll find out. He'll find out about me, like in
that Gin Blossoms song I loved in high school.

I went into the mart next door. Figures they would be
out of my cigarettes. I encountered two crazy homeless men
on the way out. They were smelly and filthy and talking
nonsense. They asked me for money and I lied and said I
had none.

I drove home feeling gross. Raw and exposed. I usually
don't feel like that after being with Jeremy. I guess only when
Roman's coming to town later that day. It takes just a little
time to adjust. Los Angeles looked exactly how I felt. Tarnished.

When I was a little girl, my mother would bring me down
from the northern surf haven of my birth to shop at ritzy
stores Ventura just doesn't have. She wanted to expose me
to all walks of life, despite the quasi-paradise existence of my
seaside hometown that has made many a native never leave
it. We would lunch in upscale cafés and swing glossy bags
from swank boutiques as we walked on sparkling streets. L.A.
was so nice to me then. She lured me to her. Now L.A. treats
me like the grown woman I'm supposed to be. She refuses
to give me guidance. Still she leads me on.

I told myself that any girl feels tarnished coming home
still dressed from the night before—sequined jeans all wrong
for day, sultry dark eye makeup a testimony to her under-
world nocturnal activity. I said any girl would feel awful
leaving her lover's apartment with nothing but a seriously
bad hangover.

I stopped at 7-Eleven for the cigarettes. I encountered
Bruce Willis. He was coming out as I was going in. I
wouldn't have even noticed it was him if he hadn't said,
"Here you go," in that Hudson Hawk/Butch Coolidge/John
McClane voice of his as he held the door open for me. I was
unfazed. He was wearing a baseball cap and dark sunglasses.

I thought about busting out one of his movie lines on him to show my respect, but then thought he probably got that all the time so I didn't say anything. I did have to wonder what Bruce was doing getting coffee at a convenience store east of Fairfax. It's the heart of Hollywood, sure…but the Hollywood they only show in movies about snuff films and prep-school prostitutes.

There are some charming little pockets in this alarming neighborhood, though. Such as the blue-and-white cookie-cutter house where I live with my two roommates. It's a nice house for three people. It even has a breakfast nook and a little backyard with a brick patio. I pulled into the driveway as Ava's boyfriend came charging out the front door. He screamed something I didn't hear over his shoulder. Ava chased him out onto the porch in silky pink pajamas, her white-blond hair fixed in two childish braids. She hurled an empty beer bottle at him and it shattered on the sidewalk.

"Jesus Christ, Ava!" he shouted. He stood there hitching up his cords as if he'd been without pants when this fight had begun.

She threw another bottle. There was a whole stash of empties lined up on the porch railing. She threw them all before storming back inside and slamming the door behind her.

"What's going on?" I asked him. He looked funny, standing in a pile of broken glass on our sidewalk. I wanted to laugh at him.

He shook his head. "I just can't handle this lunacy a second longer. See you later, hon. It's been real." He pushed his glasses up on his nose and ran to his Saab, peeling away from the curb and disappearing down the street. I knew he'd never be back.

Ava was in the kitchen fixing cereal when I went in. My other roommate, Electra, was sleeping on one of the couches in the living room. We really splurged on them but it was a good buy. They are both red with huge cushions and you'd think you'd get tired of red but it's amazing what you can do with it. They face each other against opposite walls and there's a big square coffee table in between them with a Zodiac wheel carved into it. The walls are painted cream, not white, and the floor is paneled in wood. We have posters around of our favorite movies like *St. Elmo's Fire* and *Legends of the Fall* and the people we idolize like Marilyn Monroe and Ella Fitzgerald.

Electra wasn't alone. She was sleeping with a man. They were both naked from the looks of things, all arms and legs hanging out from beneath a lavender chenille throw.

"What's with the random dude?" I asked Ava.

"Oh, Electra wanted it last night so we took her to Crazy Girls to pick it up. She figured a strip joint would be a good place to find a ready and willing male."

"I see. So what was that scene with Tim just now?" I asked. She got out the milk. I knew it was bad but I didn't tell her.

She looked wounded. "Oh…the usual. There's always something wrong with me."

"That's not true." I looked in the fridge to find something to drink. Electra's Brita pitcher was labeled with a note that said if either one of us drank her cold water she was going to *kill* us.

"But they think so." Her lip was quavering. "You know what he said? He said our house was so dirty that he always had to go home and take a shower after he left."

I poured water from the tap and pretended that the metallic Hollywood taste of it was ambrosia. I took a look around the kitchen. Food-stained dishes were piling up in the sink. The trash was overflowing by the wall. There was an empty jar of spaghetti sauce on the counter, next to two dry stems of angel hair that had dropped out of the package. A handful of them had fallen onto the floor and been stepped on several times.

"And then he was looking at my books and saying I wasn't intellectually literate and that I should read the classics—like

I *haven't*. I said, look, for your information, I went to just as many private schools as you did," she went on. "Then I told him this is California, not Connecticut—and it's more important to impress people with what I'm wearing than what I'm reading. The next thing I knew we were screaming at each other."

I sagged against the fridge and packed my cigarettes. "Tim was an incredible snob, anyway. That Ivy League act he had going on was annoying. I never liked him."

"Yes, but I did."

"You'll get over it."

"I always do." She looked all hurt again.

I thought of something to say while I watched her douse her Fruity Pebbles with the stinky milk. "Come on, Ava. Just think of the next girl he dates and how she'll recoil with horror when he asks her to stick her finger up his ass while she's giving him a blow job."

She spit cereal into the sink she was laughing so hard. I had to laugh, too.

"How's Jeremy? Where'd you guys go last night?" she asked.

"Ugh. The Liquid Kitty."

"Oh, no. Did you drink Lolitas?"

"Lolitas and Low Lifes. How'd you know?"

"There's some bluish puke on your sweater."

"That's got to be attractive."

"Bewitching. Matches your shoes, too. Hey, those are *my* shoes!"

I glanced down. "Oh, yeah, sorry. Forgot to ask."

"That's okay. I wore your green glitter tank top last night."

Everything is community property when girls live together. At least it is with us.

I yawned. "I'm tired."

"No time for a nap. Roman's coming in at two," she reminded me.

"I remember."

"Can I go to the airport with you?"

"Sure."

She put her bowl in the sink with a frown. "This tastes awful. I'm making Mini Raviolis instead. You want some?"

My stomach lurched. "Sounds divine."

I thought about Saturday mornings when I was little as I walked down the hall. My mother making pancakes and my father reading the newspaper on the back patio, drinking coffee. The radio turned to 94.7 playing smooth jazz. My little sister and me watching *Jem* while waiting for our breakfast. No worries, no cares and no reality.

I could have carved out my own version of that life. I could be back in Ventura right now, undoubtedly married to my high school sweetheart. We would have one or two children. On weekend nights we would go to high school football games—at our high school stadium—with wink-wink plastic cups full of domestic beer. On weekend days we would brunch with my parents or his, maybe both, and then engage in home improvement or family time at the beach. And we would go to neighborhood barbecues, and we would buy our fruits and vegetables at roadside stands, and we would wish the 101 Drive-In hadn't been torn down because wow, what a lot of great memories we made there back when we *so* weren't watching movies, and we would probably be very happy.

Hometowns, though. They either suck you in or they spit you out.

I went into my room and sat down on my bed as daylight streamed through the dusty blinds and birds chirped annoyingly from the neighbor's avocado tree. I was glad Roman was on his way because just then I wished I could run away to Australia and never come back again. I took a shower. I looked at myself in the mirror. I saw long strands of wet blond hair. A smear of Mango Mandarin lotion on one pale cheek. Blue eyes puzzled by the sight of a familiar stranger.

I couldn't feel clean. I couldn't feel good.

It's not always like this. But when it is, I could just scream. Sometimes I hate this dirty city. I'm starting to hate this dirty life.

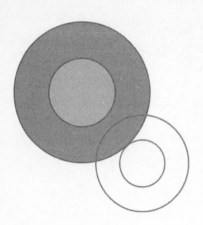

Chapter 1

Roman didn't mind that Ava was waiting at the airport with me. He's not the kind of man who would think that was irritating. He hugged us both and kissed me and it was so good to see him. I don't see him very often because he lives on the other side of the country. Sometimes he goes and lives in other countries. Sometimes I forget about the wonderfulness of him because he's gone from me so often. But when I see him I always remember right away. I'm reminded that a smooth dark midnight sky is okay, but a sky with bright glittering stars is even better.

Ava talked most of the ride home about what had happened with Tim. How she couldn't believe he would ditch her when they started off as friends. Roman was good-natured about it and listened as if he was really interested, even though I knew he really wanted to be hearing about my life and not Ava's. He's very nice to her, though. He doesn't say cruel things about her like Jeremy does, like that she's fucked up and beyond help. He says she's just a sweet, wayward kid. I think she just gets involved with guys who are friends way too often, and there are risks involved in that situation. The same thing happens every time. A guy friend, most likely suffering from lack of a consistent lay, starts thinking his girl friend is a halfway decent piece and he should probably fuck her. The girl friend assumes that means he has fallen in love with her, so she falls in love with him. Then they're not friends anymore. I could tell Ava a few things about that, and do, but she never listens, and she never learns. She says I'm a hypocrite.

She says I'm a hypocrite because I try to give advice and then I act however I want to and don't even care at all. She says I'm a hypocrite for having a nice boyfriend like Roman and cheating on him when he's away.

But that's not what it's about. I think Ava just doesn't understand. She loves eternal. No questions asked. When she's in love, there could *never* be anyone else. Even if her man was on the moon.

It's not like I *don't* love eternal. It's just that I suppose I am more guarded at first. Ava dives right in without checking to see if the water is shallow. I guess what I mean is that when I met Roman, he was unbelievable in an almost ethereal sense...like Jake Ryan in *Sixteen Candles*. I thought for sure it would never last because it just seemed *too* good. So when Jeremy, who seemed much more like the kind of guy I *should* end up with, walked into my life about three seconds after Roman did...I took a chance.

And now it's two years later. And I'm still taking chances.

Roman kept his hand on my knee while he drove us home. He's not the kind of man who would ever expect me to drive, even in my own car. We kept smiling over at each other. I felt warm and happy. It was good to have him home. L.A.'s not his home and he says it likely never will be, but I always feel like he's home when he's visiting because then he's home with me.

Electra was doing her toes in the living room when we got back to the house. She was wearing a turquoise-and-silver kimono with silky butterflies all over it. She got up to give Roman a hug. She highly approves of him. He doesn't drive her crazy hanging around like most other guys would.

"Hey, I like that new poster of Marilyn," Roman said appreciatively. Never mind the layer of dust coating the TV screen, the coffee table crowded with multiple nights' worth of discarded Del Taco trash. Never mind the array of empty bottles nobody's bothered to toss, the overflowing ashtrays. Roman only notices the new poster of Marilyn. I love how he looks on the bright side. I think that is a special quality in him.

"Thanks," I told him. I didn't tell him Jeremy gave me that poster for my birthday. He also gave me *The Exorcist* on DVD, which I suspected he purchased more for his own enjoyment than to celebrate the fact that I was turning twenty-five. He's twenty-seven already so the thrill was lost on him. The thrill usually is.

Roman kissed my neck. "Want me to make drinks, Dalton?"

"I can do it," I told him as I kissed *his* neck. I love my man. I think we are the perfect combination, just like peanut butter and jelly.

"So what's new with you?" Electra asked Roman as he settled down to relax and I went into the kitchen to fix us some drinks.

He leaned back against the cushions and looked content. "I'm waiting to hear about my next placement. I won't know anything definite until next week or so, but I've got a pretty good idea."

"Really? Tell me about it," she said. "I find your career so fascinating." Electra can be overly sarcastic, but she was actually sincere.

Roman's career is pretty fascinating. He works for the International Center for Relief and Advancement, which is a D.C.-based nonprofit organization. He and his colleagues are relief specialists who travel to nations with underprivileged economies and try to help them. Most of them have Dr. preceding their name, and a long string of impressive credentials to follow. At Roman's level they research countries to assess their assistance needs. Then they strategize and write proposals about how to go in and improve the quality of life for the people who are most affected. If a proposal is accepted, it becomes a project, and then a team is sent to carry it out. It's a far cry from event planning, which is what I do, but Roman says in many ways our jobs are similar. I think he is incredibly kind.

Roman lit a cigarette and tossed the pack to Electra. "Okay, so you really want to know? I have been busting my ass lately. I'm trying to get the director position for this next project so that Landon might finally start giving me the respect I think I've earned over the last six years that I've given my entire goddamn existence to ICRA. As it is, I'll be working out of our charming West Coast bureau during most of my visit so Landon doesn't think I'm just out here fucking around. That's the one good thing about L.A.—having an office to go to when I'm here."

I handed him a refreshing vodka tonic as I sat down on the couch with him. "That's the *one* good thing?" I asked skeptically.

He relaxed an arm around my shoulders and kissed my cheek. "Not the only good thing, baby. You know what I meant. Gets Landon off my ass if I say I'm coming out here for work and not just to see you. We both know I come out here just to see you, but Landon doesn't need to know that. If he did, he'd be imagining that all we do here is eat health food and go surfing, and that would horrify him, and then he'd give me a bunch of shit. Landon doesn't understand the concept of leisure—even if we hardly eat health food and have yet to catch a wave."

I laughed. Landon is Roman's totally demanding asshole boss. Roman says he still treats him like an intern even though everybody else knows Roman has fully reached bigcheese status. Roman says Landon is on his case all the time, which is one of the reasons he has to work so hard. He loves his work, he says, and loves working hard—but Landon says, "Don't just love it, Roman. Be *in love* with it."

"Where will you be going this time?" Electra asked.

"I put in proposals for three places in Africa."

"Africa's awfully far away," I said dubiously.

He jostled my shoulders. "It's really not when you think about it. You just get on a plane and go. Besides, I'm staying here for three whole weeks. Just to be with my baby."

I smiled. He wrinkled his nose at me as he smiled back.

"Can we go to Ruth's Chris tonight like we did the last time when you came, Roman?" Ava piped up. She was sitting on the floor, cutting out magazine pictures with pink-handled scissors.

"Just say when, *bella*."

I love that Roman is so generous without being grand or boastful about it. I love that he is so easy-breezy. He treats my friends as if they are special because he knows they're special to me. It's not like he's some walking, talking, ever-smiling human Ken. I've seen him get pissed. I've heard him yell. Sometimes he can be the *biggest* SOB. But he doesn't get put off very easily and that is really important to me.

Having Roman around was great. He would drop me off at work in the mornings so he could use my car during the day. Then he would pick me up in the evenings and we'd chat about this and that as we drove to the house. We'd cook dinner together and watch movies he'd rented for us, or read side by side in bed. I thought about how nice it was to be together, not having to worry about stupid shit like getting wasted or wasting time. It was cozy and fulfilling. When he's here, life is grand. When he's gone, life's just life. When he's not around I feel like there's no end in sight. I'm a fish in a tank, dreaming of the ocean.

"You got a nice guy there," Ava's friend Dylan Waters told me one night, having randomly materialized. Technically you could say Dylan's my friend, too, but I'm happy to let Ava take all the credit. It irks me how he'll disappear for months and then suddenly he just shows up and starts hanging around all the time, giving unsolicited advice and acting like he owns the place.

"Thanks for the tip. Now, what are you doing here?"

He was in control of the kitchen, chopping up vegetables for a burger barbecue. He handed me a piece of avocado before dragging on a cigarette. "Miss me, did ya?"

I rolled my eyes.

"She called me," he explained, with a shrug.

"That much I gathered. Now, what are you doing here?"

He laughed as he pressed a bottle of Tim's Pete's Wicked Ale into my hand. "Just shut up and drink this, will ya? It's the last of the dude's brew. He packed up his khakis and moved back to New Haven without even saying goodbye."

"I take it you're here to console her, then?" I asked, raising an eyebrow.

"You know it," he said proudly, like it was some seriously gallant act on his part. Yeah, really chivalrous. I've been observing this asshole's methods since I was eighteen. He picks people up just to throw them over.

"You single right now?" I asked, eyeing him.

"Right now I am," he said, winking.

It was a balmy evening and Ava and Electra were clustered around the patio table, wearing bright mango-and-banana tube tops and shimmery lip gloss. I pulled out a chair to join them as the men gravitated toward the grill.

I met these two during our very first week of college. We were having an "Around the World" party in our dorm where every room represented a different country and served a corresponding cocktail. My room represented the Ukraine so we were serving white Russians. You had to decorate and dress up so it was really authentic. I wore a fur hat and a sweater with fur cuffs to match. I don't really remember how the three of us bonded. It's hard to define the moment that you first become friends with somebody. They are so different from each other. Definitely the sugar and spice in my life.

In private, sometimes Jeremy refers to Ava as "Deprava." He refers to Electra as "I'llfuckya." Isn't he clever.

Roman thinks Ava and Electra are entertaining and comical. When I asked him once if he thought they were freaky and over the top, he said of course not—they're just girls.

"Dylan's *seriously* unexpected appearance better not be your solution to getting over Tim," Electra said to Ava, authoritatively. "I mean, if you've just summoned him here to dote on you, that's acceptable…but I better not see you swooning!"

"I see you swooning over Dylan and I will definitely puke," I added.

"He's going to be my date at Aunt Carlotta's wedding this weekend," Ava explained. "You know I have to bring a date or Papa will make a fuss and try to set me up with Tony Montesilvano. I do realize Dylan's hardly 'date' material, but at least he already knows the family."

Electra and I exchanged glances. Yeah, okay. We could buy that because Ava's pretty sensitive about exposing an unknown to the family. In fact, an unknown will usually run after meeting the family. The first complaint is typically the crazy priest, Father De Marco, who's always shaking a crucifix and shouting drunkenly in Italian. The Damianos brought him along when they relocated from New Jersey. Ava says they moved for a change of pace, but I *swear* I once overheard Uncle Paolo say they had to "flee" New Jersey because of that "dispute" with the Gasparellos. Now they live on a heavily guarded, walled estate in Del Mar. I mean *all* of them, and we're talking like thirty people. Ava's stepmom, Anna, used to be a showgirl at Bally's. She is only twenty-nine. Ava's father, Carlo, married her after one date. Oh, and just for the record—Ava's little brother, Luciano-Marciano, told me once that he and Anna do it in the closet sometimes when his father isn't home. Why the closet? You tell me.

"I'm going to call Josh after dinner and make sure his ass is on a plane," Electra told us. "Because if I find out he took a later flight due to some bullshit market disaster, you just better know he's not getting any kitty when we go to Palm Springs!"

Electra's boyfriend lives in New York City. She met him while he was getting his MBA at USC and these days he is a big-shot investment banker on Wall Street. Ava and I call him Mr. Big Bucks in private. Electra is supposed to move out there when she's ready, but since she's not ready, he just flies in every now and then to spend a bunch of money on her and get laid. They are planning to get married, but they don't know when and neither of them is worried that they'll break up so they don't press the issue. Out of sight, out of mind is how she feels about Josh. But when Josh is in town, hey, love the one you're with! Josh thinks Electra is all that and a bag of chips. The cat's meow. The bee's knees! He suspects nothing and thinks that his little jewel of a girlfriend is as faithful to him as the Pope is to the Catholic Church.

"Hey, how do you ladies want the burgers?" Dylan called.

"Bloody," I replied.

"Ew, disgusting!" Electra shrieked. "And here's something for you to file away for future reference, dipshit—you don't cook a Gardenburger like a meat burger, you just cook it till it's not frozen anymore."

"Kiss my ass, bitch!" Dylan said merrily.

"Kiss mine!"

"You first!" He stuck his ass out and pointed at it. She kissed the air and he went crazy laughing. Roman shook his head and winked at me over the flames.

When we were done eating, Electra went inside to call Josh and the four of us stayed outside and smoked twilight cigarettes. The sky was all violet and red. Electra wrapped the fence with bamboo and put out tiki torches last summer to feign tropical. If not for the police helicopters circling overhead and the constant rush of passing traffic out on Fountain, the ambience would be downright sultry.

Dylan gave Roman a long look. "Hey, brother, can I ask you something?"

"Sure you can, brother," Roman replied. He had a hand resting comfortably on the back of my neck.

"Is it hard for you to be away from your fine-ass woman so much of the time?"

"Please," I said, rolling my eyes.

"No, seriously," Dylan said, rolling his right back. "I want to know."

Roman looked thoughtful. "Well, of course. Why do you ask?"

"Just wondering. 'Cause you know chicks, they get lonely. And when they get lonely…well…all I'm saying is you shouldn't leave a fine-ass woman unattended for too long." He gave me a sly wink, looking devilish in the firelight. We settled into an uncomfortable silence. I shot Dylan the look of death and kicked Ava under the table.

"Bacco, tabacco e Venere riducono l'uomo in cenere," she said to Roman, knowingly. Wine, women and tobacco can ruin a man. Roman laughed.

"What the fuck was that?" Dylan demanded.

"Nothing, *bastardo*. You come inside with me now," she commanded him. "If you're coming to San Diego with me for the weekend, then we need to get packing."

"Anything you say, *bella*." He slung an arm around her neck and kissed the top of her head as they got up from the table.

I watched them go.

Roman was frowning. He looked concerned. "Do you get lonely?"

I shrugged. "Sometimes."

He nodded thoughtfully. "You should tell me these things."

I shrugged again. "It's nothing, Roman. I just get lonely. I miss you."

He kissed me. "I miss you, too, Dalton. You have to know that."

"I do."

"Promise?"

"Yes."

We kissed again. He told me he had something special planned for the weekend, in honor of our two-year anniversary. We were going away, just the two of us. I said I couldn't wait.

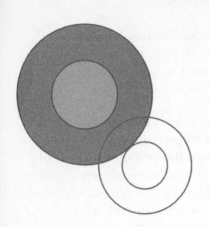

Chapter 2

I was surprised when he proposed. It came out of nowhere. It was the Fourth of July and we were having wine and cheese and crackers and crème brûlée on a cliff by the ocean on Catalina. We were talking about random stuff like what kind of cheese is in cheesecake and how it's weird that Italy is shaped like a boot and what was really going on in the movie *Vanilla Sky*. Then he got all serious.

"You know something...Dylan made a good point the other night."

"Which was?"

"Us being apart as much as we are. It's not right."

"Oh, that." I didn't want him thinking I was some baby who went around bawling about how neglected she was. "Well, let's not judge ourselves by anything Dylan has to say. He's pretty much just a big dorky asshole."

He laughed. "No, just outspoken, I think. An unexpected voice of reason."

"That's putting it very tactfully. Like saying he's one sweet son of a bitch."

He laughed again. Then he put his hand in mine and looked at me with soulful eyes. "Really, though. There've been some things on my mind that I've been wanting to talk to you about. I thought now that we're alone would be a good time. What do you think?"

My heart was pounding as I nodded. I was expecting him to tell me he was tired of things the way they were, tired of me, tired of our relationship. I was too young, too silly and lacking direction. I was never serious, completely trivial, and always broke because I made impractical purchases like my Louis Vuitton Mary Janes and those strass-inlaid Chanel sunglasses that were almost as much as my rent payment but so fucking glamorous I just couldn't deny myself. I felt jittery and nervous. What if he'd done some research and now he knew all the things about me he wasn't supposed to know? What if he wanted to tell me what a horrible person I was for acting the way I did in his absence?

But that wasn't it at all. Instead he started talking about the future and how much I meant to him and how he didn't want to lose me but he was leaving again. Not just leaving to go home but really leaving. He'd gotten his next placement. He had to be in Cameroon by August 1 and would be staying six months. He said he was afraid that one of these days someone else was going to snatch me up while he was gone. He said he was afraid that I was going to find someone else. Fireworks exploded in the black sky above, shimmering gold and pink and green on the black ocean below. He asked me if I would marry him when he got back, and said that if I wanted, he would give up his career for me.

How grand and traditional. A moonlight proposal by the sea.

"Are you sure you want to marry me?" was all I could think to say.

"Why would you ask me something like that?" he laughed.

I guess because there are two sides to every story. The

Roman me, the me he sees, is the nice Dalton. The lover. The one I would be all the time, if the mean Dalton, the hater, wasn't always demanding her share of the limelight. That Dalton has fists. She bullies the nice one into submission. She says, "Listen, when you're nice people fuck with you. When you're not, you can fuck with *them*."

Good Dalton says why. Bad Dalton says why not.

"I could see us getting married," I said thoughtfully.

"So can I," he said eagerly.

A thought popped into my head. Electra once saying our relationship is chaste.

I may tone it down around him, but I'm still far from darling. It's not like we never get down. It's not like we sit around listening to Mozart and comparing Monet and Matisse. Roman himself is not some stiff. He is a wild man. He speaks other languages and I'm not talking just French and Spanish. He lives most of his life in jungles and deserts that most civilized people wouldn't go to if their lives depended on it. He wears his hair longer like a gay man or a celebrity and isn't ashamed of it. He has a real camera, the kind that cost a thousand dollars and not some cute pink thing from Toys "R" Us with *Barbie* written on it.

We are not *chaste*. We are *classy*.

"But I would never ask you to give up your career," I said boldly. "Your work is your whole life."

He slipped the ring onto my finger. "Not my whole life, Dalton."

He doesn't call me Doll like everybody else does. As the story goes, my mom thought that my given name of Dalton was too heavy at first so she shortened it and it stuck. I guess the real spelling should be *Dal* but then people would mispronounce it because people can be stupid like that. Doll's fine with me…but I draw the line at Dolly. No fucking way.

The ring itself was a shining band of platinum, crowned with a glittering two-carat piece of ice that could catch the sparkle in someone's eye from across the room. I wore it wound around the designated finger of my left hand like a collar encircling a dog's neck. All the time fluttering my hand and watching it wink at me in defiance, representing everything I have ever, and never wanted. But I think these are things most every woman wants even if she acts like she doesn't. It's just all so confusing when it really comes down to that one final choice about your life. It's kind of strange to finally have to say, this person is The One and Only One for the rest of eternity.

To be honest, it's overwhelming. Not because I don't want him. I definitely want him. I'm just overwhelmed because the last time I saw him he was my long-distance boyfriend and now he's my future life partner. Forever.

"Can I go to Cameroon with you?" I asked.

"Well…getting the directorship doesn't exactly mean I'll have carte blanche in Africa," he told me. "It actually means I'm going to have to work like a dog. I'll hardly have time to sleep, much less show you a decent time there. And Cameroon rocks, but it's not the kind of place a girl like you would enjoy on her own."

I was disappointed. After becoming engaged…you'd think…I don't know. I suddenly felt like the only difference was me having a sparkly reminder of Roman that got snagged in my hair.

"We'll do it like so," Roman said. "I'll go and do this for six months. I'll perform so brilliantly and dazzle Landon so hard that he won't even blink when I appeal to him to let me stay in D.C. for a while, later, so that we can have a real home and life together there before I'm expected to take on another project."

"That works for me," I said.

"You're so understanding," he told me, eyes all limpid. "What did I ever do to deserve you?"

"I think it's the other way around."

"Nonsense, Dalton. I'm the lucky one here."

We were driving home a couple of days later when something occurred to me. As we cruised past the Overland exit on the 10, the one that leads to Jeremy's apartment, it occurred to me that "forever" with my future life partner is not supposed to include my current partner in crime.

But what am I, crazy? Jeremy practically hates me. He treats me like a nuisance. The same way I treat him.

We pulled into the driveway. Roman got our luggage and took it into the house, where my roommates were camped out in the living room, watching a Brat Pack movie marathon.

"I got engaged," I reported.

Electra was off her couch in a flash. "Engaged!" she screamed. She grabbed my hand and eyed the ring jealously. "Wow!"

Ava crowded in for a look. "That's a big one. A real big fucking diamond! You must be so excited, Doll!"

"Of course I'm excited," I replied as Roman poured champagne for all of us. And I really was. Excited. Nervous. Scared. Everything.

Roman extended his stay so he could be with me almost up until the last minute before having to report for his assignment. He said he was just going to quickly fly to D.C., shave and change his clothes, then catch his flight to Cameroon. He's so funny like that. He comes across so sane and orderly, and then lives his life by the seat of his pants. I've never known anyone like him before. Like as in someone who really does the things they say they're going to do. If Roman woke up one day and wanted to learn how to play the piano, he would sign up for piano lessons that afternoon instead of just talking about it forever. It's like how the Duquesnes are from Syracuse and they all go to Syracuse, naturally, but at the last minute Roman Duquesne decided he wanted to go to Georgetown and turned in his application the day before the deadline. He was expected to become a doctor like his older brother and two older sisters, but he went into international studies instead. Everybody always said he was a dreamer and a fool, and that his spontaneity would get him nowhere fast, but now he says they're eating their words because he's living his life the way he wants to and that's what life is all about. That's a good philosophy, I think. Live your life however *you* want to.

On his last night in town, we ate at a scrumptious Italian restaurant. We drank lots of red wine. We ordered plates of pasta with tangy red sauce. As he slathered pieces of warm sourdough bread with butter for the two of us, he asked me if I was disappointed that he was leaving. I wasn't sure how to respond. Every time I'm with him I know he's going to go away again. I love knowing that we're getting married, but I'm an instant-gratification kind of girl. I want everything *now*.

"It's okay," I told him. "I'd love it if you were staying…but I understand."

"It's a great career opportunity for me, you know. I think my getting the directorship means that Landon may finally be taking me seriously. It's going to lead to great things, Dalton. For both of us."

I nodded. "I know."

"It's only six months," he reminded me.

"I'm not complaining," I reminded him.

He looked at me for a moment. "Are you angry that you're not going with me?"

"I don't think I'm *angry*. Now that you mention it, though, six months does sound like quite a while. You've never been gone that long."

"You're right. I haven't," he said thoughtfully.

I didn't want to sound like some selfish bitch girlfriend who thought she should be more important than anything else in the world. I didn't want to be that girlfriend, either. So I told him, "I'll deal. There are probably some loose ends I should tie up before I go anywhere, anyway. I have had a life here for quite some time. A silly life, I know, but still."

He looked visibly relieved as he sipped his wine. He'd obviously been worried that I was going to have some big freak-out about the whole issue. "First of all, it's not a silly life. Be twenty-five and enjoy it. I know I did. Second, six months is hardly any time at all. It will fly by. And it's actually a really smart idea for you to get all your loose ends tied up, and you're a smart girl to suggest it. Think of all the time you'll have to plan the wedding, right? I think on the whole, women are probably more knowledgeable about weddings, anyway."

I didn't point out that he is cultured about every subject and could plan a nice wedding if he really wanted to or had the time. Nor did I point out that I am hardly that kind of woman. I had a vision of myself fully vamped out, walking down the aisle to "Poison" by Alice Cooper. Actually, this was the beginning of a script idea Jeremy had once. It was called *You and Me and the Devil Makes Three*. He never finished it and too bad because it really started getting good when the bride whipped out a knife and started butchering the wedding guests.

Roman smiled at me. "I think that's when things will really get started for us, don't you? When we get married?"

"Definitely."

Later that night I bid my fiancé farewell in the grand traditional ceremony of fucking. I like the word *fucking*. I like the word *fuck*. It's shocking and good for all occasions. He is gentler than most lovers have been and we have really great sex but right then it made my stomach hurt. It ached. Maybe from eating so much. Maybe because Roman was leaving. I found a focal point in a chaotic Mardi Gras poster on my bedroom wall. He fell asleep with his cheek pressed to my stomach. I played with his hair and watched the moon move across the sky outside my window.

When I drove him to the airport the next day he looked concerned as we stood in front of the terminal. It was hot and noisy out there, hardly a romantic goodbye spot. I hate not being able to go into the airport anymore.

"Are you going to be okay here?" he asked.

I laughed. "Roman, come on. I'm not exactly living in Tel Aviv."

He fidgeted. "Yeah, I know. It's just…this place. It really gets to you, you know?"

Ah, that it does. It takes a certain breed. L.A. is like a person. She's like that one certain friend who's always been such a bad influence. She makes you think you can act a certain way. Be a certain person. Put up with shit you wouldn't put up with otherwise, because of the little rewards you get from her for being so understanding of her wicked ways. But for some strange reason, you love her like that. And she loves you, and she says it's okay…it's okay to be like that, because everyone's like that.

I was really tired. I wasn't thinking straight.

I fussed with the collar on his shirt as he placed his arms around me. He clasped his hands on the small of my back. People smiled at us. People thought, oh, we were so cute. And we are kind of cute. Roman's really cute. He's got that clean, woodsy look about him like he was born to wear flannel and whittle small wooden horses on the porch of a cabin in the mountains somewhere. Like a Ralph Lauren ad. His hair is the color of café au lait. And when my man squeezes me in a hug like this, I always remember that he's a black belt in some exotic, ass-kicking martial art form.

"You just be careful out there, Dalton," he told me.

I laughed. "*You* be careful out there."

He kissed my forehead. "Take care of yourself, okay?"

"Okay."

I watched him disappear into the terminal. I twisted my ring and wondered why I didn't feel any different this time. I knew this was real. I knew it was good. But it felt just like any other time. Here today, gone tomorrow.

I bought a Diet Pepsi from a vending machine and sat on the hood of my car on top of the parking garage. The mid-summer heat shimmered over the tarmac and sizzled on my skin. At one-fifty-three Roman's plane lifted into the air, shooting toward the infinite azure sky. I waved four fingers. He was gone.

Normally on a day like this, I would return to the other half of my double life without a moment's thought. I would return to the place where what started as a hopeless fling became an even more hopeless involvement. Where my lover doesn't have hidden expectations. Where in fact he seems to have *no* expectations.

I wouldn't say Roman has expectations, either. He's not a forceful man. He doesn't tell anyone how to live their life. But being around him is like being in church. A place where you just feel like you have to be good. With him I act like someone I'm probably supposed to be. His perfect, devoted little girlfriend. His lovely, good fiancée. With Roman I try to be a lady.

With Jeremy I am neither perfect nor devoted. I don't think I'm ever very lovely or good. But I can act however I want. I can drink ten Captain Morgan and Cokes and talk gibberish and throw my clothes off and dance around like an idiot. I can confess to something horrible. I can act crazy without someone thinking I'm a psychopath, and even when he does think I'm a psychopath, he seems to like that about me.

Roman doesn't make my heart foolish and he never drives the wild, wanton beast right out of me. He is perfect and safe and intellectual and deep.

Jeremy makes me want to torture someone.

Roman is the kind of man who holds doors open for women and never says *tit* or *snatch* and most definitely wouldn't ever think of calling a woman a whore. He adores and worships his father.

Jeremy hates his father. They do not speak. He refers to his father as a bastard and a prick.

I decided to put him on hold for a while. I wanted to spend some time alone.

I wanted to cut my hair short. I wanted to spend a lot of money. I wanted to get high.

Instead, I went to a McDonald's drive-thru and ordered some fries.

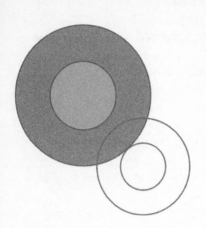

Chapter 3

I turned my calendar at work to August on the first of the month. I drew a little continent of Africa on the square and put a little stick man in it to represent Roman.

My boss came into my office and folded her arms at me. "If you're bored, Doll, I'm sure I can find plenty for you to do. As it is, I gave you a whole list of things to take care of before the day is over." She gave me a meaningful look.

"Oh, what?" I asked innocently. The list was long and uninteresting. "I was just, uh…keeping my calendar up to date."

"Uh-huh," she said, not convinced. "Now, listen. I'm going into a meeting with the rest of the partners and then I'm leaving straight for my lunch appointment. Can you try to remember to call on my cell if anything comes up?"

I nodded dutifully.

She looked at my finger with interest. "That's not an engagement ring, is it?"

I hid my hand. I was actually surprised it had taken her so long to notice, but then again, Karen is very self-absorbed. "Oh, what? Yes."

"Let me see it." She took my hand and gave the ring a critical once-over. "Excellent clarity. From Tiffany?"

As if there is no other jewelry store in the entire fucking galaxy. But yes, it was from Tiffany. I still thought it was presumptuous of her to ask.

She nodded with approval as she let go of my hand. "This is the guy who lives back east, right? Not that other clown I see you with?"

"It's the one back east. But he's not there now. He had to leave the country for six months."

She raised her eyebrows. "What *exactly* does he do again?"

The woman is fucking oblivious. "He's with the relief organization. Remember? We did their fund-raising gala two years ago? You and I?"

"I remember now. Congratulations, then. That's very exciting. We'll have to take a lunch one day to lay out some ideas for your wedding."

"Yes, we certainly will."

She left me alone after that. I swiveled around to the window and stared out at the city. When I am way up high in this Century City skyscraper I pretend I'm somewhere else, like Chicago or Dallas or Atlanta. I thought my boss was probably having her period. When she's on her period I keep my office door closed. Usually we get along okay, even though I think she's an ass.

The dossier on Karen is this: Karen Brazington, executive partner of Charisma and guru of the event-planning industry in Los Angeles. Thirty-six years old. Once married to her UCLA sweetheart, a heart surgeon at Cedars-Sinai whom she left when he became married to his career, now divorced and not speaking except through their lawyers. Currently engaged to a William Morris talent agent named Sal Lefkowitz whom she met when he contacted her, by referral, to put together his niece's bat mitzvah. Has lived in seriously high-rent Westside property all of her adult life and drives a new C-Class Mercedes in a fetching metallic silver.

Wears her hair in a shaggy, uneven cut that she gets trimmed and highlighted every six weeks with nearly religious fanaticism. Drinks flavored martinis, listens to Sting and Norah Jones, coughs reflexively when exposed to cigarette smoke and watches all reality TV shows courtesy of TiVo.

Please don't ever let this happen to me.

My job at Charisma is to be Karen's personal and administrative assistant. On my résumé it says Event Coordinator. Karen gets to do all the fun work and the big planning. She gets to have the power lunches and wear the killer suits. I get to wear the killer suits, too, but only for show. My only real purpose there is to do everything Karen doesn't want to do. My friends say I have a glamorous job. And in some ways it is a glamorous job. It is so glamorous that sometimes I want to jump out the window.

I started at Charisma right out of college. I walked into an employment agency with big plans to walk out with a corner office and a fancy title and sixty thou' annually right off. Instead I walked out with a new job as the assistant to the office manager at Charisma. I think that literally translates to "slave" because all I did then was put away supplies in the copy room, wash the dishes in the kitchen and run errands for people. Karen noticed me and made me her assistant after four months of that mindless crap. She liked me. She said I was sharp. I think what it was really all about was that she liked the way I dressed. When I first started with her, she sat me down and said, "You and me, from now on, are a team. We need to look like a team, think like a team, take care of each other like team members. So far you've got the first part down."

There are some perks. I get to go to premieres and their after parties. I get to talk to famous names on the phone. I get to go to the Emmys, the Golden Globes and the Academy Awards. But since I'm not really into all that shit, sometimes it's really just like a whole lot of unpaid overtime.

There are also some quirks. Such as the long, endless days

of trying to keep myself sane. Luckily you learn pretty early on that to keep yourself sane in the life as somebody's assistant, the trick is to waste as much time as possible when the boss isn't looking. So I wandered out into the hallway to see if anyone was doing anything. The head-honcho meeting was in full swing in the conference room. Lots of free time until they got out.

There was a deep discussion going on among my fellow minions about how everyone had lost their virginity. I joined in.

It happened when I was fifteen with the neighbor boy Charlie Porter. He was cute in an ugly sort of way, with coarse dark hair like a rottweiler and knowing eyes the color of desert sand. He was popular because he acted like a jerk and he didn't care, and kids respected that quality. He was the kind of boy who talked back to teachers and wasn't afraid of the consequences. When his parents were gone he had parties and people had sex in his parents' bed and no one washed the sheets afterward. He was forever sucking on an orange Tootsie Pop so his breath always smelled like oranges. He wore Drakkar Noir cologne and forest-green Vans and listened to Jane's Addiction and the Red Hot Chili Peppers. Total dream.

Charlie lived up the street from me, at the top of the hill, and the water from the hose when he washed his dad's car would run down in the gutter past my house with soap bubbles and leaves. We played together when were little kids. But somewhere around the start of middle school, boys become boys and girls become girls. That's when Charlie started calling me fatty and porky and piggy and his friends did the same and laughed while they rode their skateboards past my house and I hid beneath the front window and watched, ashamed. Then I would go upstairs and watch *Stayin' Alive* and wish I were some sexy dancing queen on the Manhattan show scene instead of a fleshy preteen eating Oreos and dreading the fact that my P.E. class had access to a swimming pool.

On the first day of school sophomore year he passed by me at my locker and stuck a little pink flower in my hair. They grew in clumps of orange and purple and fuchsia by the front entrance of the school, where all the most popular kids hung out before the bell rang. I was wearing black pants with suspenders. I was skinny from dieting all summer. I was starving. When I turned around he kept walking, his back to me, his arm out as he slapped hands with Pete Keller. I glanced in my locker mirror. No way. I knew that Charlie and Aurelia Sparks had broken up over the summer, but still. They'd been together since seventh grade.

In geometry the teacher asked us to pick homework partners. He passed me a note that said to pick him because my last name came before his in the alphabet and she was going to call on me first. When she got to me and I said Charlie Porter, the whole class turned around to look at me. Aurelia had a pinched-up expression on her face. She had worn her hair in the same glossy golden ringlet curls since we were little girls. I could feel my face burning. Charlie said, "Okay," like it was no big deal, like thirty pens weren't suddenly flying across thirty pieces of loose-leaf paper, penning notes to be distributed via the hallways of Ventura High as soon as nutrition break was under way.

I went up the street to his house after school and banged on the door. He answered it, eating a piece of toast with lots of peanut butter slathered on top. I could hear the TV in the background, the characters from *Charles in Charge* trapped inside of a rerun. I asked him what the hell was going on and felt my face burning again. He told me to relax about it, then threw his toast over my shoulder and pulled me up against him. We kissed and I could taste peanut butter and the faint sweetness of orange candy rolling around on his tongue. He said I could come in after that and I said I had to go home. I almost fell walking back down the hill. My mother made my favorite dinner that night, chicken and pasta with mushrooms in cream sauce, and I couldn't even eat it. She laughed and said the first day at school will do that to you. Later that night I wrote Charlie's name next to First Kiss in my diary.

He held my hand the next day walking into geometry. I thought Aurelia's eyes were going to pop out of her head. When I had tried out for cheerleading she had been one of the judges. I knew she had voted against me even though I had practiced my routines for weeks and was definitely the best choice. I heard her talking about me in the bathroom after class, as she and Liz Major stood in front of the mirror in their cheerleading get-ups, putting more and more drug-store makeup on and spritzing themselves with Le Jardin. She said, "He's only into her now because her boobs have gotten so fucking huge." Liz said, "No kidding. Remember how fucking fat she used to be?"

I knew I wasn't "fucking fat" anymore. But even when you're not fucking fat anymore, you sometimes think and act like you still are. You see the same person in the mirror. You're surprised that the most popular guy in school suddenly likes you. A real dream come true.

"Fuck those stupid bitches," my best friend Lily Lovejoy told me at lunch. We shared a bag of carrot sticks and a half pint of chocolate milk. "Aurelia's a piece of trash and Liz is just debris. You know you're not fat anymore. And you weren't even fat, you were just a little chubby. There's a difference. So fuck those cheap whores."

Lily always had her own way of putting it all into perspective. She taught me a lot about life. She taught me almost everything. *This is Lily Lorraine Lovejoy and you goddamn better believe it.* Her motto then, her motto now.

"Lily is *totally* right," Daisy Kiplinger agreed. My other best friend, she was eating frosted Hostess treats and outfitted in various forms of surfer-girl wear. I knew she was ditching fifth and sixth period to go to the beach even though it was only the second day of school. "I'd like to see that bitch choke on her pom-poms and for Liz to O.D."

Everyone started saying Charlie and I were "going out." Everyone acted like I had never been forgotten, like those dumpy in-between years had never happened, like I had been important forever. Now I joined Lily and Daisy talking shit about all the bitches who were always hanging around *our* boys. I still remembered how our boys had called me names, but now they referred to me as one of their "girls" with pride. I still remembered how the bitches had looked at me in the shower in P.E. as if I was a gruesome creature from a Tobe Hooper movie, but now they couldn't stop talking about how cute my clothes were and how we should all ditch and go to the Busy Bee Café and how I just had to go to this party and that party. At football games, Aurelia bounced around with the other cheerleaders, her hair bouncing with her, throwing hard looks my way. Everybody said she was jealous because she still liked Charlie. Liz Major came up during a break once and gave me half her Coke and asked if I had any cigarettes. We smoked together up behind the snack bar, her in her cheerleading get-up and me in my Guess jeans and an oversize Stussy sweatshirt that belonged to Charlie. She said now that I was with Charlie, everything was cool. She said now that I was with Charlie, *I* was cool. I told her that was very gracious of her, but that I had always been cool. I said it was only stupid people like her that had made everybody else think otherwise.

Charlie waited a grand total of six weeks before asking, "Can we do it?" one afternoon when we were in his room fooling around and listening to The Cure. "C'mon, Peaches," he said. "It'll be fun." I thought about it. Lily's virginity was long gone. I wasn't sure that Daisy had ever been a virgin.

"I guess," I told him. "I mean, you love me, right?"

"Yeah. I totally do."

"Okay, then. We can."

His naked skin was clammy and his pillowcase smelled like greasy hair. He was insistent and bold and I was surprised when it touched me. I closed my eyes as he dug his chin into my chest, making a bruise. My head kept hitting the Bible that was behind me on the bookcase. The Bible was on top of a book called *Naked Lunch*. After what felt like an eternity he tensed and collapsed and I felt sticky hot wetness running out of me and down onto the faded Scooby-Doo sheets.

I rode my bike home afterward with "Lovesong" running through my head and an uncomfortable dampness in my underwear. When I went to the bathroom it was all red and brown and weird in there and I didn't want my mom to see it when she did the laundry. It hurt like fire to pee and I had to squeeze my eyes shut and hold on to the roll of toilet paper as I did it.

My mom gave me a cookie as I got a can of Diet Pepsi from the fridge and told me I was getting too skinny. She said she was making fried chicken for dinner and she wanted me to eat a whole plate. I pictured great big bones of some dead chicken, covered in globs of greasy fried flour and oil, and a mountainous mass of mashed potatoes erupting and over-flowing with salty gravy. Suddenly everything sounded horrible.

I asked Charlie to the Sadie Hawkins Dance the next day. He said he was going with Aurelia.

I was so wrapped up in the loss-of-virginity round table that I forgot to call Karen with the message that her lunch appointment had been changed to Thursday. Oops. When she got back from Barney Greengrass she yelled at me to get behind the eight ball and start thinking outside of the box. She said I had to step up to the plate and take ownership.

And I thought I could get by on the ability to multitask with attention to detail in a fast-paced environment.

"You'll never be promoted if you can't even remember the smallest details," she told me with a frown.

I nodded.

"You'll never convince me that you want a future here if you can't even keep on top of the things you do now."

I nodded.

"Now, try to get me the things I asked for by the end of the day, could you?"

I nodded.

"Your first priority is straightening out that catering mess at the Hyatt!" she yelled. "Tell them we are paying bulk for lunch or we're taking our business elsewhere!" she screamed, just before slamming the door on her way out.

The idea of calling the caterers and haggling over the chicken florentine for the Women in Business luncheon down in Irvine was really unappealing. So I surfed the Internet.

I looked on www.weddingchannel.com and started freaking out because there are about a million and a half details that go into planning a wedding and so far I've only taken care of the location…kind of. My mother wants to have the wedding at our church and the reception at this old mansion in Santa Paula that rents out for such occasions. But when I told Lily I was getting married *her* mother got on the phone and said if we really want to do something special we should have the reception on her yacht. It's parked in the Ventura Harbor and was Kitty's wedding present from Lily's first stepfather, Don. He died when we were in sixth grade. He drowned in the ocean during a day of bad undertow when he was surfing. They had to drag his body out of the water. Kitty was so upset that she got married again eight months later, to a stockbroker named Al who wears lots of gold chunk-chain jewelry and shaves his head bald on purpose. Al smokes cigars and calls women "honey" no matter how old they are. Everyone loves Al.

Thoughts of all the things that make a bride crazy and annoying drove me to the *Cosmo* Web site, where I read a piece titled "A Girl's Life in the Big City." According to the girl in the article, life in L.A. is just like in the movies. L.A. men are successful and nice and vying to set up romantic dates, everyone goes to trendy bars or clubs to drink green apple martinis every single night, the rent on a stylish two-bedroom beachfront apartment is completely affordable, and one is always, but always, outfitted in really expensive sandals and sundresses. Because as I'm sure you already know, it is *always* summer here in Los Angeles. Endless Summer, just like the Beach Boys sang.

You've got to love the stigma of the feminine existence in this town. I wondered if any of the other readers thought this chick's perspective to be true to life, because I couldn't really relate to such ridiculousness at all. I drank a fattening blended coffee drink and snacked on some Cheese Nips and stressed about my enormous "minimum" payment to Macy's and heard Karen bitching on the phone to her attorney through my wall. I cranked up my music to tune her out and got back to my surfing.

I pulled up the Lonely Planet Web site to read about Cameroon, even though Roman told me all about it before he left. It had a big warning message about what a dangerous place it is. Roman's there with a group of big cheeses who have government connections. He always comes home safe. I thought if he got kidnapped like in *Proof of Life* and a man who looked and talked like Russell Crowe showed up to help me find him, Roman might be on his own.

Our meeting was fortuitous. Roman was only at that gala because Landon commanded him to make an appearance. I was only at that gala because Karen has this habit of pretending she can totally handle it and then calling me at the last minute before an event and begging me please, please will I attend, because the woman can't fucking do anything for herself. I'd planned to skip Roman's speech for a smoke break but then thought I'd wait it out because Karen was giving me the eye. Turned out he had some really interesting things to say. I thought what a smart, handsome man and knew he would never talk to me, even though I swore I had caught him looking at me a lot. The next day there were a

dozen peach roses waiting for me at work with a note asking me if I would have dinner with him. I never had any
idea that men actually did things like that.

He took me to an unknown restaurant and we ate creamy
garlic pasta and drank delicious sweet wine and he talked to
me as if I was every bit the intellectual that he was even
though he was ten years older than me and he had graduate
and doctorate degrees on a shelf at home from fancy uni-
versities like Georgetown and Oxford. I was fascinated. I was
enchanted. He lived in Washington but he spent a lot of time
out of the country ("in the field" was how he put it) doing
really nice things for really unfortunate people. At my door
he kissed my cheek and asked if he could call me when he
was in town again. He was the first man who ever walked
me to my door and kissed my cheek like that without expecting a screw in return. I said yes. He came back the very
next weekend and took me up the coast to a bed-and-break-
fast in Santa Barbara. We held hands as we took moonlit
walks on the beach and cuddled in corners of dark romantic restaurants and bade each other good-night before going
into our rooms to sleep in separate beds. He said he had to
go back to D.C. but he wanted to fly me out to visit as soon
as we could arrange it. And so became our relationship.

And now we're getting married. And I know I really
lucked out. Because with Roman I'll never have to worry
about sitting in this office for the rest of my life, wishing I
were somewhere else. With Roman I'll never have to worry
about anything.

I picked up the phone to call the caterers. Might as well
make myself useful till then.

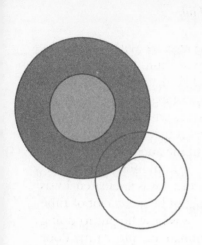

Chapter 4

I picked up Electra on the way home. She works right in Beverly Hills so usually we carpool. The funny thing is that I'm almost always the one driving. She says it's because her big red Range Rover is a gas-guzzler, but I think it's just that she likes to be chauffeured.

"Has Roman called from Cameroon?" she asked.

"He will when he has time. He said he's going to be very busy."

"Yeah, yeah, that's what they all say. You know, I can just tell when Josh has his secretary lying for him. Like he's really in that many meetings!"

A quick rundown on this one. Electra Hanover Kibbler, former Miss Teen South Carolina. All-knowing know-it-all. Want her opinion—you've got it. Don't hate her because she's beautiful.

At home we found Ava sprawled out on the living room floor. She was burning every candle in the house. She was playing Morrissey and drinking vino from a big jug. She was wearing Mickey Mouse socks and her hair was in beribboned pigtails.

A quick rundown on this one. Ava Maria Damiano, household pet and resident oddball. So sheltered growing up that she only ever left the family home to go to Catholic school. Grew up *fast* in college. Decided that grown-up life sucked and she'd rather be somebody's baby.

"What's wrong, sugar?" Electra asked. "Why aren't you at your acting class?"

"I didn't want to go," Ava replied, pouting.

"I hope to God you're not wallowing in memories of Tim," Electra told her, as she sat down on one couch and I sat down on the other.

I noticed that Ava was wearing one of Tim's old shirts. He'd left it at the house and bitched for weeks that he knew we had it even though Ava swore it was nowhere to be found. I'd kept it hostage in my middle dresser drawer, with a note attached that read, "You are one nosy fuck," in all caps just in case he went looking. When you write in all caps it means you are YELLING at someone.

"*Are* you wallowing in memories of Tim?" I asked.

"I'm not *wallowing* in anything," she replied.

"So are you moping for a reason, then, or do I have to come down there and beat it out of you?" Electra demanded. Harsh, but necessary. Ava pretends. She denies. She can go wacky just like that. It's hard to know when she's on and when she's off.

"I fucked up an audition," Ava told her, pouting anew.

"Oh, is that all?" Electra asked, none too sorry.

"It was for a movie, Electra," Ava informed her. "I would have been billed."

"As what?"

"Party Girl Number Three," Ava replied.

"Pooh," Electra dismissed. "You're Party Girl Number *One*, sugar." She got up from the couch. "Now howsabout I turn off this depressing moaning and put in something we can sing to? That'll make you feel better!"

"You don't even care," Ava grumbled.

"Sure I do!" Electra said, turning on my karaoke microphone. I think I have a serious problem because sometimes I'll use it when nobody's home.

"But you're just trying to make me forget about it," Ava complained.

Electra started dancing around the living room, singing "Back in Baby's Arms."

"I'm serious," Ava told me.

Electra climbed up onto the coffee table, really belting it out. She always dresses like she's going clubbing. In her shockingly low-cut red pants and seriously scandalous red spangled tank top, it was like watching Shakira but hearing Patsy Cline.

Ava's good at depression, very good—but not even she could help herself. She laughed hysterically. In all honesty, it's pretty easy to placate her.

I drained a bottle of Coors Light (who the hell bought *that?*) I'd found way in the back of the fridge. It had no label and that meant it was free to anyone who wanted it. Electra labels everything because if she doesn't, she thinks we'll eat her food. I would never eat her food. She eats the grossest shit I've ever seen. I don't even know what half of it is. She has cheese that looks like Kraft Singles, but when you read the label you see that it's really fake veggie cheese made from a bunch of supposedly healthy crap. I don't think anything that color can truly be healthy no matter what it's made from.

Electra collapsed on the couch and fanned herself with a *Lucky* magazine. "Any calls, Ava?"

"Just Jeremy. He said to call him, Doll."

"I don't know why. He called me at work after he talked to you," I told her.

"Typical."

"Yes, and how typical of him to come running as soon as Roman's touched down on foreign soil," Electra said, her voice decidedly snotty. I knew she was just jealous that she didn't have anyone to come running just then. Except for brief moments of kindness or hilarity, Electra really only wears one face. Not much mystery there.

Ava jumped to her feet and slipped and slid over to me across the smooth floor in her socks. I let her fall into me and take my hand in her dainty way. She turned my finger this way and that, trying to catch the light with the diamond. "Are you going to keep seeing Jeremy, Doll?"

"I'm going to keep hanging out with him, yes."

"He sleeps over, though."

"Yeah, but it's not like we're screwing every time. I just... need that."

"Need what?"

"Him. His company."

"Then why are you marrying Roman?"

Ava pretends like she's dumb but she's really not. A space-case for sure, but if you watch *Jeopardy!* with her she busts out with every answer and you get embarrassed that you didn't know half that shit when Ava of all people did. Ava thinks you have to pretend to be dumb to get what you want. Sometimes it works.

I pushed her off me. "You know why I'm marrying Roman. I love him."

"But you love Jeremy, too...don't you?"

"But I love you, too...and I'm not going to stop seeing you, am I?"

She frowned. "I guess it's kind of the same thing."

"Yeah, and you can't just give up a bad habit just like that," Electra contributed. "Like smoking. You know it's unhealthy but you do it, anyway."

"Are you going to quit?" Ava asked me.

"Eventually. When I get tired of waking up with a bad cigarette hangover."

Electra cracked up. It's nice to have her empathy some-times. I welcome the change.

I know Roman would *never* have an affair. Never! But he's

over saving the citizens of Cameroon from a bleaker fate. I'm here. *Huge* difference. Excuses, excuses.

"Hey, while we're on the subject of Stupid, what does *he* think of you being engaged, anyway?" Electra asked curiously.

"He said good luck, but he meant it sarcastically."

Ava put her head on my shoulder, all dreamy. "It's all so romantic, this separation. That you have to wait to be reunited and when you are, you'll be getting married! It's just so romantic!"

"Yeah...I know it." It's so romantic, I say all the time. Our relationship is just pure romance. A real fantasy. It's such a fucking fantasy that in the two years that we've been together, I think I've only seen him on fifteen separate occasions.

I patted Ava's head. "Why don't we get you out of that old shirt and go to Barney's Beanery? Maybe it would do you some good to get out of the house."

"Okay," Ava agreed. She got up. "You come too, Electra."

"I will." Electra watched her leave the room. She looked impressed. "That was pretty nice of you, Doll."

I shrugged. "Yeah, well...I'm feeling magnanimous."

We raised our eyebrows at each other. Then we laughed.

I called Jeremy before we left and told him to meet us. I was looking forward to seeing him. He's not the world's easiest person, but we connect. Maybe because I suppose I can be pretty difficult, too. Sometimes we don't give each other even one inch. Electra says we are so close that we know each other's every fault, and so we get defensive with each other. She doesn't know *everything,* but she is right about him knowing my every fault. I tell him things I could never, ever tell Roman.

At the Beanery I hung out by the bar, sipping pale ale as Electra and Ava played pool. There was a big swarm of guys around their table. Ava practically has *Come fuck me over* written across her forehead and Electra can't go anywhere without having men accost her. She loves that. It gives her more power as a feminist because she can say they're only interested in her body. Well of course they are. She doesn't have her fucking IQ tattooed on her forehead. And even if she did…with that body no one would care.

"What do you think of that one?" she asked, taking a break to talk to me. She pointed her pool cue in the direction of a pretty boy in a pair of tight jeans and a baby-blue muscle shirt, hair all gelled to perfection.

"Gay," I replied.

"The fuck! He's not gay." She licked the corner of her mouth. "His name's Troy. That's manly enough."

"I still say no guy with a body like that and hair like that is straight in West Hollywood, Electra."

"He's a model," she said, shrugging. "The one on the Calvin Klein billboard outside the Beverly Center. You know, in the underwear?"

"I thought he looked familiar."

"I'm going for him," she said, narrowing her eyes.

"Just be careful!" I shouted after her as she pranced across the bar. The last time she tried to woo a gay guy she really frightened the poor fella. It was a traumatic experience for us all. I think she's convinced that she's so beautiful she can turn homosexual to heterosexual like it's simple chemistry. It's annoying to be around that, but I grudgingly respect such blazing self-confidence.

I waved as I saw Jeremy come in. He walked over to me and tousled my hair. Then we hugged. He stood next to me and we chugged pints as we watched the scene.

"So who's Harlot O'Hara's newest conquest?" he asked.

I aimed my glass in the pretty boy's direction. "What do you think?"

"Gay."

I laughed. "That's what I said!"

He took my hand and examined my engagement ring. "Looks fake."

"Oh, come on."

"It does!"

I pulled my hand away. "You could congratulate me, you know."

"Congratulations."

"Thanks."

He shook his head. "Marriage, man. It doesn't seem like you."

"Why not?"

"I don't know. You're all goofy and shit. You're all over the place."

"What a strange thing to say!"

"You're the strange one, toots. Want another beer?"

I studied his features as he leaned over the bar to order us two more. He has a big nose, I think. And his hair is so dark you can see where the hair on his face is going to pop out even when he's just shaved. He has deep dark eyes that are blue and gray like the ocean on a stormy afternoon.

Sometimes I kid myself and say that Jeremy is the love of my life. Sometimes I want to murder him. He's cold and critical and not very supportive. But the way he makes me feel…I just can't explain it. I can't even explain it to myself. He makes me feel so good. He makes me feel like I am not alone. He makes me feel safe. I don't tell him these things.

Electra came back looking smug. "He's not gay. He's coming home with us."

"Good for you."

She eyed Jeremy while his back was turned. "My God, Doll, what is that shirt he's got on? He looks like he just got off his shift at the hospital."

In reality he writes copy for the Associated Press. He tells people he's a reporter but it's not like he's scooping stories, really. He just takes the words and feeds them into the computer and then later they show up under someone else's byline and never Jeremy Flowers.

I nudged her. "Let's bail soon. I want to go after I drink this last beer."

"I'm almost ready, too. I'm eager to introduce that pretty boy to my bed." She laughed as she sashayed off.

I watched her go. She's a funny girl. She would never feel an ounce of guilt over anything she does when Josh isn't looking. Do I feel guilty? Of course. But like I told Ava. I need Jeremy. I can't explain just how or why. I just know I do. Maybe it's that he can relate to me in some twisted way. We both want the best we can get, but even when it's great, we're never sure if we've got it. We both want to get some-where, only we're not sure just where.

Or maybe it's just that I adore him in a very strange, mys-tically irritating way. Maybe it's as simple as that.

"What an awful fucking world," Jeremy was saying later as we watched the late news and it seemed like everything was about killing and kidnapping and terrorism and hate crimes. He was lying on my bed with me and taking up most of the space. He's a big, tall man so he's allowed to do that. I'd say just a little taller than Roman but much paunchier.

"You're not kidding."

He turned on his side and looked at me.

"What?" I asked. Two picture frames had already gone over on my desk from Electra's sleigh bed knocking against the wall. She and the pretty boy were shouting from her room. I couldn't count all the times I'd heard, "Oh, yeah! Uh-huh, that's right! Give it to me, baby, give it to me!"

"Nothing. Just thinking about you and my girlfriend."

Jeremy's girlfriend is named Pristina. I laughed my ass off when he told me that. He rolled his eyes and told me to get an encyclopedia and that really insulted me. Apparently Pristina's of Eastern European descent. Whatever. I could give a fuck where she came from. And I certainly don't need to get an *encyclopedia*. I'm quite positive *he* didn't know the intricacies of the Federal Republic of Yugoslavia before

Pristina told him of how she was named for her parents' birthplace in Kosovo. He won't even play against me in Trivial Pursuit because he knows I will kick his ass in every category except Sports & Leisure.

She sounds exotic and interesting, but trust me. She's not. And she has a mustache. She really does. I saw this infomercial recently for this roll-on hair remover. You just roll it right on and your hair wipes right off. I thought about ordering one and having it shipped to her.

He seems to find her unattractive, but then acts as though she is the loveliest woman in the world. He seems to dislike her personality, but then acts as though she is the most delightful woman in the world. I can't really figure out why he stays with her. But if I were to ask, he'd just shake his head at me like I so do not get it.

She works as an in-house nurse to a very sick and very wealthy old man who has been hanging on to life with an iron grip for years now. She is there five days a week and sometimes six. There are several other nurses who attend to him as well, and all of them are secretly hoping that he will remember them in his will. The whole setup reminds me of this porno movie I saw once where all these nurses were helping these con artists conspire to steal this dying man's money, or something like that. They spent most of the movie giving one another oral sex. I can't remember how it ended. I was probably too busy giving oral sex myself.

"So what are your deep thoughts on Pristina and myself?" I asked.

"Well, I've figured out her big problem. She's too goddamn demanding."

"I'm sure."

"You know what your big problem is?"

"What's that?"

"You have no feelings, Doll. No emotion. You're so fucking apathetic. That's what your problem is."

"I think I have a lot of feelings," I informed him. "Just

'cause I don't go around crying and giggling all the time doesn't mean I have no feelings."

He gave me a look. "Are you even happy about being engaged?"

"Give me a little credit. If you really want to know, I am very happy. I'm just not going to go on and on to you about it."

"Why not?"

I gave him a look. "Jeremy."

"Doll."

"I'm just not going to sit here and spew my engagement bliss to *you*. Get it?"

"I guess." I noticed his breathing was deep and uneven. "But can I ask you something?"

"You know you can."

"How are you so sure that marrying Roman is the right thing to do?"

I turned on my side and propped myself up on an elbow, so that we were face-to-face. "Because he's a wonderful man who wants to give me everything and share his life with me. And I love him."

He gazed at me. "I wish it were so easy for me."

"What do you mean?"

"To want to share my life with just one person."

"Oh."

"Don't think that means that you're the reason I don't want to marry Pristina," he added quickly. "I wouldn't want to give you the wrong impression."

He's not my favorite person. He is so my favorite person. Somehow I'm never busy when he wants to do something. When I first started bringing him around, Electra listened to him preach and do his number for about ten minutes. Then she decided to hate him. She said she'd never met somebody who had so little conviction. She said in a really sick way, we were great together.

He calls me almost every night. And we don't even have

to say a word sometimes when we're with each other. We just breathe and it's fine like that.

"You want to have sex?" he asked.

"Sure."

"I'm bored," he told me, right in the middle. "I can't finish."

"Then don't."

He took my arm and examined it. "Your skin is practically alabaster, Doll. You need to hit the beach...get a tan."

In L.A. everyone is supposed to be tanned. It's part of the image that you live your life under the sun. Everyone is supposed to be beautiful, too. Sometimes everyone *is* beautiful.

Jeremy's hair gets oily really fast and so does his face. He snarls when he's angry and his lip curls up and his teeth bare like he's a big cat hissing at prey. He wears stupid shirts and he's a jackass and a real jerk. He lectures me. He tells me I'm boring in bed. He's beautiful.

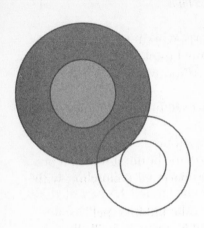

Chapter 5

"I need a date, Doll. I need to book the church," my mom said on the phone the next day.

"Aren't you getting a little ahead of yourself, booking the church already?" I asked, glancing at the calendar. Yep, still August. For some reason the stick man was wearing a grass skirt. "Roman's not coming back until February."

Karen rapped on the wall. "You have to book the venue the first thing—haven't I taught you anything?" she screamed.

"March," I said into the phone.

"Okay, I'm looking at the calendar. The 8th and the 15th are both good."

"How 'bout March 15?" I heard my dad say in the background. "That was the day Julius Caesar was assassinated."

"Oh, be a little more macabre, Arnold!"

"No, I like that," I said.

"March 15 it is, then," my mom replied. "Now, honey, are you coming home at all to see Maddy before she has to go back to school? She's getting back from Europe next week."

My sister is nineteen and will be a sophomore at Stanford.

She has spent the summer in Paris, working as an au pair to some French family to pay her way. I think that's really weird. I spent the summer in Paris once and was totally fine to let my parents pick up the check.

"I'm really busy, Mom. I don't see myself coming home anytime soon," I replied.

"You're not that busy!" Karen shouted.

"Well, you're going to have to come home at some point," my mom informed me. "To do marriage counseling with Reverend Nelson."

"Christ, Mom, you have got to be kidding me!"

"I am," she laughed. "Reverend Nelson says he'll allow for just one session when Roman gets back."

"Better thank Grandma Jane for that one, Doll," my dad said in the background. "She slipped a big donation into the collection plate last Sunday with your name on it."

"You still have to come home at some point," my mom said.

I haven't been home in months. I can't cross the county line without some childhood monster jumping out at me. I see them at all the old haunts—Coastal Cone, Santino's Pizza Parlor, Foster's Freeze. Only now the little demons are all grown up. Still, I remember them and they remember me. No matter what I do or who I become. It's like a creepy Never-Never Land.

I popped into Ava's salon to have my hair cut after work. Normally I would avoid senseless, excessive trimming, but with Ava being the receptionist and making my salon appointments, I can never get out of it. In her salon, they play nothing but techno and everyone has colored streaks in their hair like cotton-candy pink and bubblegum blue and apple green. Ava may be a "starving" actress of sorts, but not really starving because her father keeps her in large amounts of cash. She only keeps that job for the social interaction and the deal on color.

She needed a ride home but she had to work until six, so

I went down to Aldo and bought a pair of expensive black slides. Then I went over to The Limited and got a few new sweaters. Sometimes it's sweet liberty to spend money you don't have—almost like you're living someone else's life. Then you get the bill and oh, no—you realize it really was you and this is your life.

"Guess what?" Ava giggled as we drove home listening to Madonna's *Immaculate Collection*. She had fresh lavender highlights and a cheeky glow. "Dylan likes me. And I like him."

Last night while we were out Dylan left this very keen message on our answering machine. He played the whole song "Ava Adore" and hung up when it was over. If you listen to the lyrics of "Ava Adore" you'd realize it's a song about some seriously messed-up love.

But what a smooth move, really. That's the way a big dorky asshole cajoles you into falling for him, by impressing you with his smooth moves. I told you I was onto his methods.

"Oh, *shit!* Don't think I didn't see this one coming! The fuck!"

Ava had just broken the news to Electra.

"Ava…not *Dylan*," Electra pleaded, when Ava told us he was on his way over. We were having Baja Fresh on the patio in the backyard and a homeless man we call Fret was standing on the other side of the gate, in the alley, asking us if he could please have some money. We call him Fret because when people say no to him he goes back and forth with his hand in his mouth, saying, "Oh, dear, oh, dear."

"Get out of here before I call the fucking police!" Electra finally screamed, throwing something at him. It was that limp green onion they always wrap up with your burrito. He ran off before she could chuck the slice of lime that comes with it.

"Electra, that was mean," Ava told her, frowning.

"Well?" she asked haughtily, throwing her hair over one shoulder. Electra has the longest, shiniest brown hair ever. Stunning. She is fucking gorgeous.

"Well, you shouldn't be so mean," Ava lectured. "The man is homeless!"

"Yes, and I work for a living," Electra replied, spooning up some of her rice. She eats a burrito from the center and never touches it with her hands. Her mother's family name is on a bottle of whiskey. Her father's family name is on a pack of cigarettes. Electra doesn't like it when you talk about all that. She thinks it's gauche for people to go around flaunting their wealth. Now check out those monogrammed Gucci slides of hers, and the matching bag.

"Back to Dylan," I said, pouring more margarita into my glass from the pitcher on the center of the table.

"Yeah, why *him?*" Electra demanded.

Ava looked thoughtful. "He says I'm a star in his sky."

Electra looked at her as though she were pitiful. "Oh, *please*. Must we go through this galactic debacle again?"

And the whacked-out milk lecture starts in five, four, three, two...

"You need to learn that women are like dairy products to men, sugar. They're fresh before use, and spoil quickly. Women friends are like *milk*. Something substantial to drink if there's not an appealing alternative in sight—like a Coke. Right now you're like an unopened carton of milk to Dylan. And man, he's gotten *thirsty*. So he wants to drink you because you're *right there* and there's no Coke and he's fucking thirsty! That's all it is! So fine, but when he trashes you, don't be surprised. You won't even go to the recycling bin because milk fucking spoils! Hello!" Electra shrieked.

"You're totally stuck in the Milky Way, Electra, and besides—I'm not trying to alter the course of the universe," Ava informed her. "I just like him."

"Yeah, well...he'll stop thinking of you as his fucking *star* as soon as you start thinking he's pulled down the moon!"

Ava looked to be considering this. "Can I ask you a question?"

"Sure," Electra said graciously.

"What makes you the authority on absolutely fucking everything?"

"Oh, ha ha, really funny!" Electra bitched as Ava and I collapsed into giggles. "Let's have a gathering, then. I can't handle Dylan on his own. Doll, you call some people."

I called Jeremy even though I suspected he was with Pristina. He was. He told me over a bunch of restaurant racket that he may come over later because she was on call. If Pristina were kidnapped and held for ransom and I had a lot of money, I would put it all into mutual funds and not even feel guilty.

I hung out in the living room with Andy Whitcomb, who is my best guy friend. We grew up around the block from each other and have been pals since our moms were in our elementary school PTA. I even took him with me to college, which we attended at Chapman University in Orange. Andy is just like me. And just like me, no way in hell was he moving back home after graduation. So he lives nearby, just off Third Street near the Beverly Center. Everyone thinks he's gay because he works in couture at Nordstrom and his apartment is beyond Pottery Barn. Fashion sense aside, he's not gay at all. He is actually a real sleaze. When he talks about the female sex organ he calls it "trim." One time he was hooking up with a girl and he found a hair on her nipple all long and dark just like it was a pube. Instead of ignoring it he bit it off with his teeth. When I heard that story I laughed for an hour. Andy gets laid *a lot*.

"Do you want to be in my wedding?" I asked him as he strummed his guitar and I looked through a Victoria's Secret catalog for a pair of sexy boots I just know I saw in there. *Have* to have them. Ava and Dylan were making out on the other couch. I am a total voyeur. I kept sneaking glances at them.

"Yeah, sure," he replied. "But there is no way in hell I'm wearing a dress."

I rolled my eyes. "I'm sure you can wear a tuxedo just like the other guys, Andy. Only you'll have to stand on my side."

I know this is the kind of thing everyone will ooh and ah over and think is the most adorable thing they've ever heard in their entire lives.

He nodded. "I'll do it, then. Hey, you know something funny?"

"What's that?"

"This'll only be the second wedding I've ever been in."

"The reason behind that, Andy, is that the majority of your bozo friends will be lifelong confirmed bachelors," I predicted.

"Let's hope so," he said. "But don't you want to know what's so funny about it?"

"Enlighten me."

"The other wedding I was in was Dan's. Remember? Ha ha ha!"

Andy is cute but too much of a scamp. He has brown hair and impish brown eyes and a wiry build like a soccer player.

"You're a fucker," I told him, glaring.

"I am and I won't deny it," he practically giggled.

He was referring, of course, to Dan Michaelson. My high school sweetheart. Though our breakup took place years ago, we have sustained a heinous feud. This feud spreads out over time and geography. It has invisible, toxic tentacles.

"You've got to admit it's kind of ironic," Andy laughed. "I mean, wasn't the original plan for you and Dan to get married at the same time? To each other?"

"Yeah, when we were *seventeen*," I said, starting to get itchy. I feel sick talking about Dan and Andy knows it. "Anyway, you just take that Dan shit and shove it. Now, promise you'll really be one of my bridesmaids?"

"I promise, Doll. It'll be a great honor." He winked at me. "Want me to play 'Jane Says' for you?"

"Sure." He thinks it's one of my favorite songs because my favorite grandmother, my father's mother, calls me Jane.

She doesn't like my first name at all. Dalton is actually my mother's maiden name, and since my mom was an only child and had no cousins, there was nobody to carry it on in the traditional way. Grandma Jane said Dalton was an awful name to give to a cute little baby girl and she was going to call me by my middle name, and always. Grandma Mary, my mother's mother, said there was absolutely nothing wrong with the name Dalton and that she would never understand why Grandma Jane had to be so hateful about it, especially because everyone got in on that Doll thing, anyway. Only a few people call me Dalton as it is. My mother when she's *very* angry with me, my father when *he's* very angry with me, and Roman. He says Dalton is a noble name and that he can't say Doll with a straight face, it's so ludicrous.

Anyway, it's not one of my favorite songs, really. It's just one of the only songs Andy can play and *definitely* one of the only songs he can sing without making you want to run for cover. Case in point—he finished singing "Jane Says" and started belting out "Everlong." Oh. My. God.

I zoned and pretended that instead of an ICRA project director, Roman was a famous musician away on tour and I would soon be joining him. We would ride in a big bus all across the country with a hot tub in the back and drink champagne and when he gave a concert he would dedicate a special love ballad just for me as I watched from backstage. In the song he would refer to me as "My Girl," just like Jim Morrison. When people asked about his love life in interviews he would say he would never dream of going anywhere without taking his girl with him. I would make tank tops out of concert T-shirts with the band's name on the front and wear them with jeans and a leather jacket as I posed next to him for press photos. I would hang out with fashion designers and models. Fans and groupies would hate me and say they wouldn't know what Roman even saw in me.

Jeremy showed up around midnight. Ava and Dylan had retired to her bedroom and Andy had joined everyone else outside. I didn't know who half those people were. That happens a lot around here. They were being too loud.

"Wow, am I glad to get away from that," he said, flopping down on the couch beside me.

"*That* being Pristina?" I asked.

He pulled his hands down over his face. "Her friends are such bitches. It makes me love coming over here."

I gave him a skeptical look. "Why, because my friends aren't bitches? Come on."

"No, because nobody here cares. Anything goes and you may get shit for it, but nobody really minds. Around her friends I have to act totally different. I have to act all...I don't know, like I have to carry her purse and shit."

"Oh."

"Do you mind if I go see who's outside?"

"Go for it."

I watched him leave the room. What a strange creature, really. And what a pushy broad, that Pristina!

Dylan came out of Ava's room with hooded eyes and a lit cigarette hanging out of his mouth. He put his hands on his hips and peered at me, shirtless. Dylan is not unattractive. He's sexy the way all scoundrels are. He doesn't work out, you can tell, but he has a solid, manly body. He has green eyes.

"Hey, would you ever carry a girl's purse?" I asked him. "Like, if you were dating her?"

"Fuck no," he replied. "What kind of sick dude would ever want to date a girl like that?"

My point exactly.

Jeremy returned with two bottles of Heineken and handed me one. I guessed the beer stash was dwindling because Jeremy knows I hate Heineken and will only drink it as a last resort. He turned on the TV to see if there were any good movies on.

I watched the way his shoulders hunched forward as he leaned onto his knees to change channels. His face was earnest as he observed the activity on the screen. I wonder if Pristina thinks she's a lucky girl. I hope she does. I know I'm a lucky girl because when you strip away all of the foolishness and weirdness and constant bickering between us, it's actually nice to have a friend like Jeremy. It's nice to have a friend who would rather come keep you company than go home and be alone…even if to keep you company means that you're both being adulterous.

We slept quietly in my bed that night, on sheets printed with fish, holding each other in a comforting embrace. Occasionally he would wake up and kiss my neck and stroke my hair. Sometimes that's all you need—to have somebody there—to get you up the next morning and make you think about how sweet it feels to have warm blood in your veins and hot breath in your lungs and a whole life that's all yours to live and live and live.

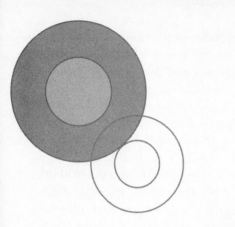

Chapter 6

After checking the mail each day for two weeks, I was excited to find a postcard from Cameroon waiting for me on a Friday afternoon. On the back it said simply, Love YOU! This was a sign that a package of strange foreign goodies would soon be coming my way, with a long handwritten letter.

Roman doesn't send e-mails. He says that such casual communication is at the root of today's relationship problems, because you just go ahead and type what you're thinking. He says when you speak you stop to think about what you're about to say. He says e-mail is cold and harsh. I ask him, Don't you go ahead and write what you're thinking with a pen? He says no. He says you carefully craft every sentence because there is no backspace, no delete, and so you don't want to make a bunch of mistakes. Mistakes make a letter look messy.

And his letters are certainly beautiful. I feel like they should be read in a special place, so on occasion I have driven seventy miles up the coast to read them by the Point. It is one of my favorite seaside spots in all of California. I get out of the car and feel the Pacific wind on my face and smell the salty air that reminds me of being a little girl coming home from the beach, with wet towels in the back of the car and sand in my ice cream and a song on the radio about a girl named Peg done up in blueprint blue. Then I pop in on Lily and we go eat at Yolanda's and make big cheesy pigs of ourselves and try to bargain for the big juicy black olive that comes on top of the enchilada plate. Then we go to Baskin-Robbins for a pint of mint chocolate chip, and take it home to her mother and Al, and her mother gives me a "cold soda for the road" which is never name brand because Kitty can be cheap like that, but it's delicious all the same.

I decided to call him.

"Baby! Is everything okay?"

"Fine," I replied. "I just got your postcard. Thanks!"

"Too bad you can't send me yourself by mail like that," he said. "It would make things a hell of a lot easier for me over here."

"I could send myself by plane," I joked, only half kidding.

"Yeah, but I'm so busy here you would never even see me. So how's everything going, Dalton? Making wedding plans?"

"Yeah, I'm on it. Booked us a church and everything. Unfortunately, we have to go to marriage counseling with Reverend Nelson when you get back. Just once, though."

"I think we can handle the critical cleric our way. Let's get tossed before we go and then argue the whole time just for fun," he suggested with a laugh.

"Now you're talking!"

"Listen, Landon's coming in on an early flight. He says we're just having breakfast but I know he's really coming to review me, so I have to get back to bed."

"Okay. Miss you."

"Miss you, too."

That night I took Ava and Electra to the opening of a new club on Sunset, the reigning celebrity "It" girl's Monaco. Charisma had put together the premiere party and the free alcohol flowed like an endless river. Sometimes I love this plastic town when I'm wasted. I love how everybody is somebody even if they're nobody. I like painting on a whole new face and wearing black-on-black sparkles and teetering around in to-die-for shoes with to-die-by heels. I like how everybody's pretty, and important, even if half the time they're making shit up or really glamorizing their lives so they won't seem inferior to anyone else. Everybody does it. Even me! It's all part of the act.

Ava and Electra brought their new handbags, but I was without because Jeremy was with Pristina. If Pristina needed a transplant and I was a positive match, I would run away to Mexico and let her search for another one while I was wasting away in Margaritaville and loving every second of it.

He called around eleven the next morning. I was watching *Friday the 13th Part V: A New Beginning* and painting my toenails glittery green. Sometimes Jeremy and I prank-phone-call each other by leaving clips from our favorite horror movies on each other's voice mails at work. These are like our love letters. Electra says we are sick.

"What'd you do last night?" he yawned into the phone.

"I got loaded."

"Oh. I hung out with Pristina."

Big news. "Oh, really, how was that?"

"Typical."

"Figures."

"You want to do something today?"

"If you want to come over, we'll figure it out."

He came over while the movie was still on and I was still in bed. I was wearing white flannel pajamas. He got in bed with me in his clothes and pulled me close. We were soft and warm together.

I closed my eyes and put my hand down his pants. He put his down mine. We didn't say anything for the longest time. In the background people screamed and hollered as they were hunted down and murdered in innovative and amusing ways. He was wearing Woods by Abercrombie & Fitch. I turn into absolute jelly when he wears that.

"I was thinking about you last night…when I was with her," he breathed into my ear.

"Oh, yeah?"

"Yeah." He moved his hand down.

"And what were you thinking?"

"I was thinking about how Pristina always shaves."

"That's not thinking about me. That's thinking about Pristina."

"I was only thinking it because you don't shave sometimes."

"I'm not trying to impress anyone."

He sighed into my neck. "I was just *saying*. I guess it's okay how you don't shave sometimes."

"Thanks." I ran my fingers up and down his back, underneath his shirt. "I really feel like I need your approval."

"You're so touchy sometimes, Doll. It's a wonder I even stick around!"

He stuck to me, anyway.

"You ruined my pedicure," I told him, after. I wagged a foot in his face so he could see. I was reclining against the headboard. I was smoking a cigarette. He was sprawled across the bed on his stomach.

"Tragedy." He crawled over me. He picked up my nail polish off the nightstand. He flicked on the stereo. I'd last been listening to my favorite homemade eighties CD compilation. We're talking some serious classics by the likes of Toto, Gerry Rafferty and Juice Newton.

"You have some seriously gay taste in music," he told me. He took one foot and began painting.

"You're so generous with your compliments."

"That was probably the best sex I ever had. Now, hold still."

"You're tickling me. Really?"

"Uh-huh. Now, come on, stop kicking."

"I'll try. I thought I was boring in bed."

"C'mon. When did I say that?"

"You know you said it."

"I think I remember saying that I was bored. That's not the same as saying you're boring in bed. You take everything so personally, Doll."

"So I'm not boring in bed?"

"I can assure you that you were highly entertaining just now."

We went down to the Third Street Promenade and walked around looking at the freaks. There's a guy down there who does a whole concert using just utensils. He is very talented. He probably makes three hundred dollars a day from people's tips alone. I think he probably uses it to buy a sack of weed.

"I dislike Santa Monica," I told him, after we'd each bought a pair of Lucky Jeans and a bag of books from Barnes & Noble.

"How come?"

"Because it tries to be all chic and upscale but really it's gross and dangerous."

He patted my head. "I think you'll live."

I'm not always sure how I feel about fate, but sometimes I think there was some weird twist of it when Jeremy showed up in my life. He was working for this courier service at the time. He was trying to get someone at a studio or an agency to read his script—big surprise, because everyone in L.A. wants to work in the Industry. Everyone is a writer or an actor. Everyone has their own production company. And *everyone* has written a script. Even if they collaborated on it with a friend. Or if they haven't, they have this *great* idea for one. Everyone just knows they have what it takes to be the next Hollywood *wunderkind*. That's usually why they came here in the first place. I think the quest for fame drives people mad. Just look at Ava.

Anyway, one day I was at a client's for a big meeting and he delivered a bunch of shit. The receptionist had gone out to pick up her car from the detail shop and Karen had told the clients I could sit for her and answer their phones, I didn't mind. The clients were delighted. I was not. I'm not a fucking receptionist. But it is my job to do whatever Karen wants me to do. If she tells me to lick her asshole, I should pretty much have to do it without complaint. As it is I'm down there kissing it every single day.

I signed for the shit and thought the delivery boy was hot. He asked me how long I'd been working there and I said about ten minutes. He laughed and introduced himself. Jeremy Flowers. I laughed and introduced myself. Doll Moss. He said with our last names we could start a hippie revival band. I said that was pretty lame. He asked if I was a receptionist by choice or if it was my career aspiration. I asked if he was a delivery boy by choice or if it was *his* career aspiration. He explained about his script then and told me how he had only been living in L.A. for a little while so far. He was from Miami. Karen screamed at me to quit flirting and pay attention to the goddamn phones.

He asked me if I wanted to have sushi with him and I said I would love to even though I hate and detest sushi. I ate two plates of California rolls at the restaurant and ordered a rum and Coke. He ate seared ahi and drank sake.

He lived in a crummy apartment in the Valley. We listened to U2 and drank Michelob Light and watched *In the Mouth of Madness*. I was impressed beyond belief to find that selection among his formidable cult horror collection. We got high and started making out and his mouth was the warmest place I had ever been. We did a lot of kissing, for hours and hours, just kissing and kissing and kissing. He had a tiny twin bed and since there was hardly any room for both of us to spread out he clutched me against him all night long. In the morning I wore his jeans and one of his flannel shirts and we noticed we both had the same Vans even though his were blue and mine were burgundy, and we laughed as we walked to get bagels and cream cheese.

"God, you are so much fun!" he told me.

"So are you!" I returned.

"You totally *get it*," he said.

Because I totally got it, I didn't even have to ask what he meant by that. All I knew was that he got it, too.

We shook our heads in marvel.

"I should tell you something…I kind of have a boyfriend. But it's not all that serious," I told him. "It's a long-distance thing. We've only been seeing each other for a few months. I don't even know how long it will last."

He shrugged. Then he laughed. "Oh, no. Did you think last night was a date?"

That's when he told me about Pristina.

I hate Pristina.

"I'm taking Pristina on a cruise," he told me now as we drove home from Santa Monica.

"Wow."

"We're going to go on one of those three-day Mexico trips."

"Sounds delightful."

"You pay something like three hundred bucks and you get everything free except alcohol."

"Better take some extra money, then."

"I've told you Pristina barely drinks."

"What an upstanding girl."

"You don't even know her."

"And I wouldn't want to." I blew smoke out the window.

He stopped at a light and looked over at me. "She's working tonight. Want to go see Tom Cruise's new movie?"

"Sure. Ava and Dylan will want to come with us, though."

"That guy's a fuck. A total joke."

"He has his good points."

"Like what? I just can't figure out what Ava sees in him."

"He takes care of her and protects her. He always has. She likes it when people treat her like a dainty, delicate little flower."

"That asshole treats her like a dainty, delicate little flower?" he asked skeptically. "More like he's her pimp and she's his ho. I think she could do better than that."

I sighed. "Listen, Jeremy...it doesn't matter if a guy comes across as a fuck or a joke or a nice, kind man. Because you're all the same inside. You all want the same things. Tits and ass."

"That's bullshit. I'm not like that. That's why I have a girl-friend. If I were just about tits and ass, I'd be out playing around."

"Uh-huh." I wouldn't necessarily say he's about tits and ass exclusively, but I do love the hypocrisy.

I turned up the stereo and we were silent the rest of the way. I tried to picture Cameroon. I tried to picture Roman in Cameroon. But I've never been to Africa and all that came to mind was a scrubby wheat-and-sage landscape I might've seen in a movie.

Our movie was at the Cineplex Odeon at Citywalk. During the show Ava and Dylan snuggled. When Dylan's with Ava, no matter how stupid he acts, she smiles the whole time. She is radiant. I like that he can do that for her. As it is he's a jackass and I sure wouldn't want him, but if he makes her happy, I guess that's all that really matters.

We went to Tony Roma's afterward and ordered all kinds of beef and ribs and steaks.

"So, Dollface," Dylan began, eyeing me. He had an arm around Ava on their side of the booth. "I been meaning to tell you that's a nice rock."

"Thanks." We had ordered a bunch of yummy sides with the meat. I was loading up on mashed potatoes and corn.

He took my hand across the table. "The clarity is out-standing. Roman's got good taste."

"I know it."

Dylan's green eyes were beyond sly as he focused his gaze on Jeremy. I put some space between us on our side of the booth. I had a feeling that if I asked Dylan to pretend he'd never seen anything down the road, he'd say, "Sure. Suck me off and we'll negotiate."

Ava pried Dylan's fingers from mine. "Eat," she commanded him.

"Does Roman pay for everything when you go out, the way a man *should?*" he asked, undaunted. Ava hadn't taken a penny out of her purse all evening. My grandmothers would say Jeremy and I were going "Dutch treat."

"Yeah, Dylan. He does."

He grinned as he gnawed on a rib. "Don't fuck it up, honey. That's all I have to say."

"Why don't you mind your own fucking business?" I yelled.

"Hey, my friends' business *is* my business," he replied. Then he winked at me.

Dylan's a real cracker head. But at least he's real. He's not afraid to say what's on his mind. I've always had a grudging respect for him because he calls it the way he sees it and doesn't care if other people find that offensive. I know he's going to screw with my roommate and then put the blame on her by saying she knew what he was about all along. But at least he doesn't put anybody on.

"That guy's such a cock!" Jeremy told me later.

I thought about how Roman would never say that Dylan is a cock. He'd say that Dylan is clever.

We lay in the dark and he fell asleep to *The Shining* as it glowed on the TV screen in the darkness. I stayed awake and thought that a few months is hardly any time at all when you really break it down. I've waited for a dream like Roman all my life. So a few months is nothing. It will fly by, just like Roman said.

Still, I looked at Jeremy as he snoozed beside me and had to consider a few things. I've always known that he was special to me in some depraved, unexplained way. But I never really started to worry about the implications behind that until this engagement. If I told Jeremy tomorrow that I couldn't be with him anymore and waited out the next few months without him, would I feel good about my decision or would I miss him? Both. I'd feel good for making such a wise decision and awful because I *would* miss him. I would feel like I might have thrown something away too soon—before I really stopped to think about just how much it meant to me.

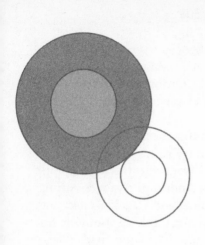

Chapter 7

"I want to tell you all about Paris," Maddy said dramatically, over the phone.

"Tell me everything."

"Well, first let me confess to something horrible."

I was guessing she'd probably smoked a cigarette. That is the extent of Maddy's wrongdoing. Love that kid. Just don't really understand how Sister Christian and I can be related sometimes.

She lowered her voice. "I didn't really go to Paris to work as an au pair. Well, I did. But there was another reason."

"What other reason?"

"Gabriel," she whispered. "He goes to Stanford, too. We met last year in the Bible Club. Anyway, he was going to Paris to work as an au pair so that's why I did, too! And we spent *all* summer together!"

"How come you never said anything until now?" I asked. "Down with J.C., moonlights as a nanny, isn't ashamed to wax French—he sounds downright dreamy."

"Sis, you are such a b-i-t-c-h," she said, spelling it out.

I laughed. "So? Why so secretive?"

"I didn't want anyone getting any ideas until I knew it was serious," she told me. "And it is! Our love is beautiful. He's even moving into an apartment closer to campus so he can be closer to me!"

"Why don't you just move in together?"

"You are just a teaser today, aren't you?" she giggled.

When we got off the phone I went into the living room and flopped down on the couch. Andy and Ava were sitting on the other couch, eating peanuts and Cracker Jacks and watching baseball on TV. I zoned out, thinking about my little sister and how different we are. I had my first college boyfriend my first week of college. Of course, it sounds like Maddy and this Gabriel kid are actually dating. My first college boyfriend would say, "You gonna be at the party?" and I'd say, "Yeah," and he'd say, "Cool." Then together we'd fight the masses at the keg line, talk about nothing and stumble back to his dorm room to have drunken sex.

Maddy is majoring in some sort of science, biology or chemistry or both, so that she can go into clinical research to cure cancer or AIDS. She keeps a 4.0. In high school, she was on the girls' softball team and the girls' volleyball team and she was ASB president. She ran the French Club and ran everyone else out of the National Honor Society. She went to the Netherlands on a foreign exchange—and you know while she was there she never touched an ounce of smoke. On weekends she and her friends did homework and watched wholesome movies and listened to holy music and helped my mom cook lavish dinners and desserts. She did not get drunk at parties. She did not take up smoking because it was cool. She did not fool around just to see what it was all about. She was a charter member of the church's youth group.

She hasn't changed one bit.

In high school, I ditched all the time. I ran across the street to smoke at nutrition break. I did my homework for third period in first period. I made my biology partner do all the work in lab. I wrote notes during class. I lied about having my period in P.E. so I could lie out and get a tan during swimming. I said I had to go to the bathroom to get excused but really I would just go down to the quad and hang out. I would flash the football team from the parking lot while they were practicing after school. Lily and I got busted for taking over the PA system at lunch and playing "I Want Your Sex" and "Me So Horny" for our boyfriends. And I once got kicked out of my youth group because I said that Jesus probably found some 'shrooms and had a hallucination about God telling him that He was His son, and then came out of it and formed a very successful cult. My father had to come pick me up and he tried not to laugh when the youth pastor told him of my blasphemy. On the way home he said that there probably hadn't been an abundance of 'shrooms growing in the sands of Israel and that perhaps I might want to lay off the substances myself before going to church.

Can't really say I've changed much, either.

Maddy wears a little gold cross around her neck. She never takes it off. When she prays, she fingers it and closes her eyes.

I had one of those, too, once. When my mom asked what happened to it, I said oops, it fell off while I was on the Sky-diver at the county fair. The truth? I stood over the edge of the pier and dropped it into the ocean. I hated that neck-lace. I hated feeling like I was in some exclusive club, wear-ing my forced beliefs around my neck. I said in some countries you can get murdered for what you believe in. My mom said that didn't happen here in the U.S. of A. but she understood what I was getting at. Grandma Mary, who had given me that precious trinket, looked at me with steely eyes after that. Grandma Jane thought the whole thing was hi-larious. She and Grandma Mary are always competing for us. Maddy has always been Grandma Mary's favorite.

My mother says Grandma Mary turned to the Lord be-cause all her babies died except for my mom. I don't see how that makes any sense. My mom says people get their strength from God when bad things happen. I say if God is the creator of the universe and the master of all things, then wasn't it *He* who took the babies away from Grandma Mary? Grandma Jane says that religion doesn't matter because God's gonna do what He's gonna do, and all you can do is wait for it to happen. She says even if you're a Jesus-freak, the guy's gonna screw ya. Plus, Jesus did die for our sins so shouldn't we at least have a little fun? I am Grandma Jane's favorite.

I got a new necklace to replace the cross, one I never took off—not even to this day. Dan gave it to me because I was really into sorcery at the time. I bought spell books and a Ouija board and wore flowing skirts and costume jewelry. The necklace has a charm that is a tiny little dagger on a long silver chain. The blade is silver and the handle is marcasite and it fits inside a matching sheath. When Grandma Mary saw it she said it was fitting for a girl like me. Grandma Jane said, Just what the fuck are you implying, Mary?

Dan and I broke up our senior year, just before the prom. I asked Mason DeWitt to take me because I knew it would make Dan sick to see us together. Dan and Mason had been foes ever since Dan transferred to our school sophomore year and couldn't play first base because Mason was already the star first baseman. Afterward we went to party in Mason's hotel suite at the Doubletree. I was so drunk I could hardly stand. We had spent almost the entire prom drinking screwdrivers in the limo. Every time he kissed me I wanted to barf. I wanted Dan.

Mason pinned me down and told me I knew I wanted it. He didn't even take off my dress. He just shoved it up so he could stick it in. I let him do it without a fight, but I was pissed off because I thought he was grotesque and there was no way I would have consented to the act if I weren't so wasted. I listened to the music. Pearl Jam's *Ten* CD was playing. I still love the lyrics to "Alive" because I think

they're hauntingly romantic, even though that song still reminds me of that night and missing Dan. Dan was there
with my own foe. That bitch. We were wearing the exact
same dress.

I got so mad thinking about Dan being there with Aurelia Sparks that I wished I could stab her. I stuck my dagger
in the back of Mason's shoulder instead. He screamed and
jumped off and ran around the room naked, touching the
wound and screaming even louder when he looked at his
fingers and saw blood. He got dressed and ran out into the
living room and told everyone that I had stabbed him with
Dan's goddamn necklace. Aurelia made a big to-do and got
a washcloth and wiped up the blood. She told him he was
probably going to need stitches. I told everyone he was a
rapist. The guys rallied to figure out who should kick his ass
and Dan took the initiative. I loved and hated him. Aurelia
drove Mason to the hospital after that because, after Dan, he
really did need stitches.

Dan drove me home. He told me he wanted to get back
together. I said yeah maybe, if only he hadn't gone to the
prom with that bitch. He said how unfortunate, because he
would love me forever and I told him how unfortunate, because I would hate him for all eternity. Then I got out of
the car, slammed the door, went upstairs to my room and
cried for hours. I was so glad I was graduating so I could just
get away from that town once and for all. When my prom
pictures came back, my mother framed one and put it on the
piano. It's still there. I can't look at that picture without fin-
gering my necklace and thinking about Mason and his stupid stitches. That Monday at school he went around telling
everyone I was a violent psychopath in case they didn't already know, and that I had probably picked up a few things
from watching so many stupid horror movies. He started calling me Pinhead like the villain in *Hellraiser*. I wish it were
Dan in that fucking picture, standing next to me in my pretty
red dress.

★ ★ ★

"You ever think about stuff?" I asked Andy, after the Padres lost to the Yankees and we were sitting on the patio, just kind of hanging out.

"What kind of stuff?"

I pulled my hands through my hair. "Stuff like that you might have—maybe should have—done differently. Or things you left unresolved. I don't know."

"Yeah," he said thoughtfully. "I probably should've nailed Daisy."

I shoved him. "That's *not* what I'm talking about. I'm talking about when you think about your life, and your past in relation to your future. How it applies...or something."

Andy climbed into my lap. He put his arms around me. "It's 'cause you're getting married. That's why you're thinking about that kind of stuff."

"Is it?"

"Naturally, Doll. Getting married is a big deal."

It is a big deal. It's a really big deal. I am special. I am worthy of someone's affection. I am worthy of *Roman's* affection. It matters that he said he wanted to marry me. That's something my father said to my mother. That is sacred.

So why do I feel like such a downer sometimes? Why do I feel like such a creep? I guess because like that stick figure fifteen-year-old who looked in the mirror and still sometimes saw a fat girl, this bad, bold woman looks in the mirror sometimes and sees a total fraud. I hide behind the fuck-all, fuck-you exterior that is me. Yet that's the only me I ever want people to see. The bitchy, ballsy, brave Doll Moss who does whatever she feels like. The one who fucks up with pride.

Roman doesn't see me that way. He sees me as special. Different. Lively. My personal favorite—*saucy.* But *why?* Maybe because he brings out the best in me.

That's why I love him. Roman is definitely great, a true wonder, but that's not it. It's that in all his amazement, he sees something amazing in *me.* He doesn't take me at face value—

a party professional, a mall-walking champion, a flesh-and-blood movie database. Sure, he has to appreciate those things because they are my landmarks. Still, he goes further. He goes beyond. He travels into the great, vast Valley of the Doll, and finds Dalton there.

Andy kissed my cheek. "You'll figure it all out."

I smiled at him. Not because I thought his comment excused me from all missteps, past and present. Because Andy doesn't try to pull me in any direction, he just holds my hand.

Ava came outside. She was wearing a T-shirt just like the one Madonna wore in the "Papa Don't Preach" video that reads Italians Do It Better.

"What's up, *donnaccia?*" Andy asked her.

"Don't call me a hussy! Why did I ever teach you my filthy words?"

"Aw, get over it, *bella*. Let's all go have dirty martinis at The Standard," Andy suggested, sticking his tongue out.

"I don't feel like it," I told him, pushing him off my lap.

"Come on," he whined. "Let's just *go*. There's nothing else to do, right?"

"She just doesn't like The Standard," Ava reminded him. "Not since that time she got kicked out for talking shit to the bouncer when he wouldn't let Jeremy in 'cause he was wearing that brown striped shirt that looked like a bowling shirt."

"We could go to Skybar," Andy told me.

"Or the Ivar," Ava added.

"Maybe Star Shoes?" Andy suggested.

"Maybe House of Blues?" Ava posed.

"Perhaps a more secluded haunt…like maybe Bar Marmont?" Andy laughed.

"I'll only go to Coach and Horses," I declared.

"I knew she couldn't resist our forces," Andy said, giving Ava a high five.

We all went out and had a groovy time. I made a mental note to get it together and stop acting like such a sourpuss.

I've got awesome friends, an awesome fiancé, two legs, long blond hair and one damn impressive DVD collection. What more could any girl ask for?

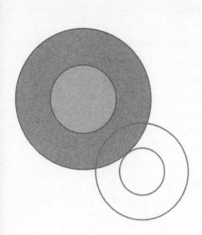

Chapter 8

"Doll! I told you we had to leave *now!* What the hell are you doing?"

"I'm coming," I said to Karen as I joined her by the elevators. She gave me the most reproachful look I have ever received in my life. Apparently I wasn't as worried as she was about being late for the Women in Business luncheon.

"So now that you're getting married, what does that mean for your future with Charisma?" she asked as we merged onto 5 from the 10. She kept the windows rolled up and the air-conditioning on at a freezing level.

"Huh?"

"I mean, are you moving to Washington? What are you doing?"

"I don't know," I replied, just to be irritating. "I don't know" just drives some people up the wall. I like that.

"Well, he's not moving to LA, is he?"

"He doesn't really like L.A. He says it's Paradise Lost."

"That doesn't tell me very much, Doll."

"'Where peace and rest can never dwell, hope never comes that comes to all'...you know?"

She gave me a sideways glance. "I'm being serious."

"So am I. No, Roman is not moving to L.A. Yes, I'll be moving to Washington after we get married. Which means my future with Charisma is looking pretty sketchy."

"Well, that's too bad. I had big plans for you." She looked disappointed.

"You did?" I was genuinely surprised.

"Yes. But don't think that just 'cause you're leaving you can slack off for the next few months. We have a busy season ahead of us."

I looked sideways at her. "I wasn't planning on it."

"Good, because I really need your help. Oh, so did I tell you who Sal just took away from Debbie Weinberg at Creative Artists?"

I was looking out the window with my chin in my hand. Whenever Karen starts talking about Sal's clients, I tune out. It's not that I don't enjoy celebrity gossip now and then. It's just that most of the time I really couldn't give a flying fig. I don't care who's suing tabloids, who makes incessant demands on hotel management, who lives in a posh crib and certainly not which A-list darling signs with Sal.

"Really? That rocks," I said absently.

"Yes, and they were so pissed when she left," she laughed.

By the time we arrived at the Hyatt Regency in Irvine, it was obvious that Karen thought Sal was the mastermind behind Hollywood's every success story. All that boasting about her betrothed put her in a mighty mood. She gave me an order the second we walked into the hotel.

"Get me an iced tea, would you, Doll?"

I nodded and set off to find her an iced tea. A cute bartender waited on me. I love Orange County. It is a virtual buffet of tasty men. I could feast for days in that Disney domain, enjoy a thousand of those delicious O.C. Dreamsicles. They know they are all that and more. This tends to put a smirk on their faces, a swagger in their walks. Unfortunately, it's those characteristics that make them even more desirable.

"What's your name?" he asked, giving me that sly eye.

"Doll."

"Really." He drew the word out into three syllables. Reh-he-heally.

"What's yours?"

He threw a slice of lemon into the iced tea and put a lid on it. "Mike."

"I fucked a guy named Mike once."

He looked taken aback. Then he said it again. "Reh-he-heally."

"Yeah." Sometimes I just come out with random shit like that. It's very liberating. "But I suppose there's always room on the list for one more."

"I'm working," he told me, winking. He handed me a straw. I reached for it and he pulled it away. I hate it when people do that.

I grabbed it before he could do it again. "So am I."

I knew I looked good 'cause I'd taken one of Ava's suits. She has the cutest suits ever. She wears them when she's pretending to be a businesswoman. When she's pretending to be a businesswoman she rents a Lexus and drives it all around, listening to Kenny G and wearing big sunglasses. She goes to fancy restaurants and sits at a table drinking white wine spritzer and looking at fake documents from her briefcase and checking her watch as if someone is late. Usually this kind of behavior gets her an afternoon date with a businessman, after which he goes back to the office with only a secret smile to explain the lipstick on his collar, the perfume on his skin.

This suit had a short skirt and a short jacket to match. It was periwinkle. I was wearing sexy black Kate Spade pumps, also Ava's.

He caught up with me in the hallway. "Were you serious back there?"

"Did you think I was?"

"Well…hoped was more like it."

He couldn't have been any older than twenty-two. Memories of carefree college life flashed through my head, back when this neighborhood was mine for the taking and I dated Newport Beach bums and Costa Mesa garage-band rich-boy punk wannabes. I was overcome with paranoia about it being the last chance in my entire life to be with a youngster from O.C. I decided to go out with a bang.

We ended up doing it in the kitchen. We were in a big pantry. We did it standing up against a big pile of bags of potatoes. They were very uncomfortable. He had his tongue pierced and a tattoo of some Chinese symbol on his shoulder.

"I'm going to come," he told me, licking my ear.

I also hate it when people do that. Who cares? Big deal! What do you want, a medal?

He had spiky hair with dark roots and blond tips. Afterward we smoked a cigarette. He sat on the concrete floor with his arms wrapped around his knees and his hands clasped. He peered at me with hooded eyes.

"You do this sort of thing often?" he asked, his voice dubious.

"No. You?"

He shook his head. "Can I call you?"

"I live in L.A." When you live in L.A, the guy had better like you *a lot* if he's going to drive *all the way* up from O.C. He may even have to love you…if he's capable.

He seemed undaunted. He shrugged and took a long drag, tapping his feet. "So?"

"I'll give you my number."

I wrote down a phony phone number on a book of matches that read Hollywood Bail Bonds. Then he said, "Oh, shit." His break was over. He kissed my cheek quickly and was out the door.

"Fine speech, isn't it?" Karen asked when I slithered back into the banquet room. Just the day before she had been reading the speech and looking up every ten seconds to yell, "Who wrote this shit?" Maybe yesterday she was just mad about her zit. When she gets a zit she runs out to the dermatologist and makes him inject it with some sort of medication that will make it disappear. When I get a zit I squeeze and pick at it. I make a big scab.

I nodded.

"Did you get my iced tea?"

"Oh, fuck," I said without meaning to. "Karen, I forgot."

"No problem. We'll just cruise by a Starbucks on the way home and you can go in and get me a chai latte." She looked at me. "You look good. Very refreshed. What have *you* been doing?"

"Nothing. I went for a smoke."

"Really? I can smell it. I wish you wouldn't do that around me. You know I'm allergic." She raised her chin and folded her arms as the speaker wrapped it up.

I wandered outside and lit another one. Having sex like that was kind of a dumb thing to do. It's not like I'm some sex-crazed maniac who just had to have some sex right then. Sleeping with strangers isn't even that interesting. It can be mysterious, puzzling and decadent—but then again, so is a shot of hot, glittering Goldschlager. But who really ever drinks Goldschlager, anyway—at least past the age of twenty-one? So why did I do that? I guess I just took an opportunity and went with it.

I looked at the water splashing into a fountain. The drops looked like diamonds bouncing off a glass surface. I frowned at my reflection as I leaned over the pool. For such a smart girl I sure am stupid sometimes. Opportunity is not getting it on with a young, hot stranger just because you can. That's the kind of opportunity that broke up Dan and me way back when, the last time I fucked a guy named Mike.

Opportunity, in reality, is what I have with Roman.

★ ★ ★

Jeremy called while I was standing in the kitchen that evening, mulling over my life. I was drinking a bottle of Ava's precious Newcastle. I knew I would get shit for drinking it. Trading clothes isn't the same as offering a bottle of Michelob Ultra in place of a Newcastle.

"Hey," he said, sounding melty. "Do you want to have dinner?"

"I could eat." I drew a turkey on the cover of Electra's new *Cosmopolitan*.

"Are you hungry or not, Doll?"

"I told you…I could eat."

"How was your day?"

"Fine. I had to go to Orange County."

"Ew, I hate Orange County! I hate it!"

"Where do you want to eat?"

"Let's just get Baja. I'll pick you up."

"Okay. See you."

He came to pick me up but he made me drive. He drives a Volkswagen Cabrio and it really embarrasses him. It didn't start embarrassing him until Dylan was kind enough to ask what he was doing driving a chick car. He says he just likes my car better. I've pointed out a hundred times that my car is old and outdated. It was the shit nine years ago, but now it just looks like a piece of shit I've been driving for nine years. He says BMW never loses its meaning.

The people at Baja Fresh know what I'm going to order every time, but Jeremy always gets something different. I always get the Baja Burrito with chicken. He got the Chicken Torta and we went outside to eat. They were shooting a movie at Coffee Bean and all the crewmembers were at Baja Fresh on a break. They kept tossing around words like grip and spec and SAG. Ava has a SAG card. This is known as a big accomplishment in the Industry. SAG stands for Screen Actors Guild. Notice how it rhymes with GAG.

"Blah blah blah blah," he started telling me, chomping on

a handful of chips. Jeremy will eat any kind of snack food you put in front of him. Even saltless pretzels. Yuck. "Blah blah?"

"Huh?"

"You're all out of it, Doll. What's going on?"

"Just thinking what's the purpose of life and what does all of this mean and what's my role in it…stuff like that."

He sat back in his chair and rubbed his belly. "Go on."

I took a deep breath. "I just feel…not grown up. Like I'm still doing stupid things all the time. I need to get more serious…or something. I need to start taking things more seriously. My existence and what I want it to be…I guess."

"I can understand that. I go through that all the time."

"Can I tell you a secret?"

"If you can't tell me, then I don't know who you *can* tell," he replied. Then he nodded, looking intrigued.

I told him about my escapade with the bartender. His eyes bugged out of his head.

"Doll! Are you fucking crazy?"

"I don't know! I just suddenly started getting all paranoid like, Oh my God, I'll never get to do anything so wild ever again if I don't do it *right now.* Isn't that awful?"

"I just have to wonder! I could never do something like that."

"Why not?"

"Just because." He shoveled my chips from my basket into his.

"Why do I always feel like I'm the guy here?"

"You have a real hang-up about women and men. Women are just women and men are just men. And you banging some stranger in a pantry for kicks has nothing to do with you being a woman and me being a man."

I gave him a look. "Oh, don't act like you have all these ethics and I don't. If some hot young girl lured you away from work for a wicked encounter you would do it. Even if you and Pristina were *married.*"

He shuddered and made a noise from the back of his throat. "Yeah, well…we're not. Besides…we're not talking about me."

"But I *want* to talk about you. 'What if' scenarios involving strangers aside…I want to talk about why you do what you do with me when you have Pristina."

He sighed. "What is there to say, really?"

"There's lots to say. We just never say it."

"I guess we don't. But if we did…" He left the thought hanging before he went on. "Why should we talk about it now? You're engaged, Doll."

"I *am* engaged. That's why I want to talk about it now. Because suddenly there are facts to face. Such as…have you thought about the end of us?"

He stuck his chin between two fingers and frowned at me. "Yes."

"And?"

"And I don't like it. I don't like having to face that issue. We've always had a good time together without a lot of pressure. We've always had other people in our lives so we've never had to wreck our situation about the whole 'what next' argument. I like that about us. We don't have to worry about the future, so we can enjoy what's now."

"That's right. It's now. Only now we have to worry about the future."

"We have a nice arrangement, Doll."

"Yes…we have had. But it will eventually have to end…or change. We've finally come to the part where that much is obvious. And we obviously can't stay in this place after my wedding."

His frown deepened. He didn't reply.

"You know what I'm getting at, Jeremy. We say we're friends but my friends will all be invited to my wedding. So, should I invite you, too?"

"Don't be retarded."

"Maybe I'll just make you my best man."

"You don't get a best man. You get a maid of honor."

I nodded. "I know that. And there is a guy in my wedding party, you know."

He rolled his eyes. "I know. The groom."

I rolled mine back. "No...I mean Andy is one of my bridesmaids."

He threw his head back and hooted. "That's so gay!"

I lit a cigarette and the people next to us made faces and started talking shit. It's practically illegal to smoke in L.A., even outside. If someone murdered you for smoking around them they would probably get off easy. The police probably wouldn't even arrest them to begin with. They would probably be commended.

"Really...what the hell are you doing here?" I asked him.

"Eating dinner. I like your nails. Did you get acrylics?"

"I always have acrylics," I reminded him.

"Well, they look great when they're fresh and new like that."

"Thanks. But don't keep doing that," I warned, giving him the eye.

"What?" he asked innocently. He took the cigarette from my fingers to take a drag. I've always found that to be his sexiest move. Commanding in an unspoken way. I could have jumped him right then and there. If he only knew what he did to me just by being his irritating self. That's why he fucking irritates me so badly. I hate him so much I can't stop wanting him.

I snatched it back. The people next to me coughed and coughed like they were dying. I blew smoke right at them. "Changing the subject so we don't have to talk about you."

"If I didn't give you a little something to wonder about, you would never even want to know," he replied, raising an eyebrow. Then he took my cigarette away once more. And I let him.

When we got back to the house there was a small gathering in progress. Our college friends Lionel and Rose were over, and of course Electra's pretty boy and Dylan, too. Li-

onel is skinny as in he is a beanpole, and he is a total chau-
vinist asshole. Rose is chubby as in she is a butterball, and is
quiet and sweet but gets on my nerves. I don't like how she
is always trying to con and coax me into gaining weight.
Electra says I'm paranoid and Rose is doing nothing of the
sort—she's just being thoughtful when she offers to go get
Wendy's while we all have the munchies.

Jeremy's take is that I have no empathy for Rose. What
the fuck? I have plenty of empathy! I just don't want to be
tempted like that. Like how sometimes he threatens to go
away and never come back, and I think that would be dread-
ful but also the very best thing. Because he tempts me, and
I get weak. How can I get over it if he's always here? He
won't leave even when I am awful to him. No matter how
awful I get. And the more awful I am, the more I want him
to stick around. It's terrible. And wonderful.

"We're going in my room," I said when Pretty Boy invited
us to join them.

"Oh, no, not until you order us some more beer," Dylan
informed me, tsk-tsking as if I'd committed a felony by
drinking that one without replacing it. Ava says she can't believe it's taken them all these years to figure out how they
feel about each other. Dylan says, "Get me a beer, bitch."

"Let's wait for the beer so we can take some in your
room," Jeremy suggested after I'd ordered them two twelve-
packs to make up for my heinous crime.

"Come have a hit from the bong, Doll," Pretty Boy of-
fered.

I didn't feel like hanging out with any of them. My
roommates seemed skanky, not stylish, in their flashy en-
sembles. Dylan's backward baseball cap bearing the Angels
logo was a mocking reminder of the sinful behavior I'd in-
dulged in down south. Pretty Boy was just too pretty. And I
can never understand why Rose and Lionel can't just drop
off our preordered portion of their weed and then be on
their merry way. Rose and Lionel only moonlight as deal-

ers. By day, they're both teachers at a swish private academy. I think Roman and I may have to consider homeschooling the Duquesne wee ones.

"Crap," Lionel said, eyeing me from underneath a cap of unwashed blond hair. "If you're getting married then I guess I'm all out of excuses."

"Give me a break," I told him, after taking a hit. "That is so lame."

"Really," Electra agreed. "I mean, Christ, how long has poor Rose been hanging on and getting nothing out of it."

"Hey, she gets plenty."

"I'll bet," both Electra and I said.

"We may as well cut off our balls and let you keep them in your purses, huh?" Lionel said, winking at the other guys.

"You know that's the ticket," Dylan agreed.

"Amen, man," Jeremy said.

"Right on, brother," Pretty Boy added.

"Go fuck yourselves," Electra said.

The beer arrived just in time. Jeremy and I grabbed a few and escaped to my room, where we played Led Zeppelin and lit candles and felt each other's bodies in the eerie flicker of firelight. *Babe, I'm gonna leave you.* Jeremy's eyes were dark and black like nothingness. His hands were strong over mine on the mattress. I was high and creepy. I wondered if Pristina ever felt the way I did. I wondered if she ever felt Jeremy and thought she was feeling heaven. I don't even know if I believe in heaven. But if I had to pick a place that resembled paradise, it would be here with him. We have our own world. One where I would probably stay if he really wanted me there. Only I don't think he really does. *What is and what should never be.*

Later that night I cuddled up to him while he was asleep and cried. He woke up and asked me what I was crying about. I said everything. He retrieved my stuffed bunny rabbit, the one I've had since I was a baby, from the floor and wedged it in between us. Its name is Kee-Kee. He kissed me on the forehead and drifted back to sleep.

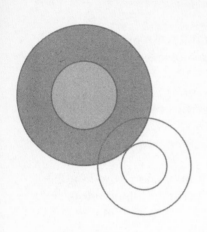

Chapter 9

The calendar said it was September and so far I had established who the members of my wedding party would be and that we would have the ceremony at my family's church and the reception on Kitty Lovejoy's yacht in the Ventura Harbor.

"I bought you these," Karen said, coming into my office with a stack of wedding magazines. She put them on the desk with an expression on her face that told me they were heavy and that I should have been carrying them. "I can't stand to see a wedding go unplanned, Doll."

Her wedding is coming up. The weekend before Thanksgiving. I've done most of the arrangements, pro bono—love that expression. Now let's just hope she won't ask me to serve at the reception.

I flipped idly through one of the magazines. "Thanks."

She came around and perched on the edge of my desk, looking at the picture I had turned to. "Will dinner be sit-down or buffet? What kind of music will there be?"

"Uh…the wedding march?" I asked.

She rolled her eyes. "Come on, Doll. You know you have

to have Pachelbel's 'Canon' when the bridesmaids are walking down the aisle. A string quartet maybe? And what about music at the reception? Will you have a DJ or a band?"

"Maybe *you* should plan my wedding," I told her.

"Well, what about Roger? Is he in on it *at all?*"

Karen forgets sometimes and mistakes Roman's name for Roger. I never correct her because I think it's pretty funny, actually.

I shook my head. "Nope. Not at all."

She folded her arms and looked suitably horrified. "Honey, you are taking next Friday off to go home and consult with your mother. You have to get moving on this."

"Why?" I asked, putting my hands behind my head and feeling belligerent. "What if we just go to Vegas and make a day of it?"

"Oh, no," she said, shaking her head. She looks so much like Christine McVie. Sometimes I imagine her swinging and shaking and singing "You Make Loving Fun." Then I try desperately not to laugh.

"What do you mean, oh, no?"

"Those who are blessed enough to call themselves Charisma event planners would never do such a thing! It's practically sacrilegious to our business!" she shrieked.

"I'm not an event planner. I'm an event planner's assistant. It's not like I can even work toward a promotion here."

"Yes, but you are establishing residency in Washington. You think they don't have events going on out there?" she asked, raising a perfectly tweezed eyebrow. "Come on, Doll. We're talking about a place where schmoozing is a sport. Where they all get together at fetes and galas, because to them networking is as second nature as walking."

I didn't point out that I've never seen her walk any farther than the parking garage.

"And don't you sit there and tell me you're just some event planner's assistant. That insults me. I happen to be the best event planner in L.A. For me to say what I'm about to say, that you have talent in this arena, is like Sal telling an ingenue that she's a good actress. So use it, Doll. In Washington, you'll *have* to use it. You'll have to plan Roger's dinner parties, won't you? I know how those Washington people are. All high society and shit. And shit, why didn't I think of *this*? Roger could even decide to go for the White House someday! Then you'll be the First Lady!"

Of course she only equates Washington with the White House. Still, I could picture Roman in the White House. Myself the First Lady, more important. Yeah, I'd wear something downright scandalous to the Inaugural Ball.

Karen went on. "I was also thinking about how you've done so much for me for my own wedding…without even really having to do it for your paycheck…." She tilted her head to one side. "I would be happy to help you out. Lend you my expertise, as it is."

"You'd do that for me?"

"Of course. You do a lot for me, don't you?"

I couldn't argue with that.

She placed a hand upon my shoulder as I flipped through one of the magazines. "And by the way, Doll, believe you me—if Sal suddenly had to go live somewhere new I'd just go and set up shop there without thinking twice about my position here at Charisma."

"You would?"

"Yes. Because I'll always make something of myself and for myself no matter where I am." She patted my shoulder and left me alone with the magazines.

I drove home that day thinking about what she'd said. It's not like I'm dying to spend my life planning other people's special events. It's just that the truth is, if I had to pick a career, I'd stick with this one because I really do enjoy it immensely when you get to see the finished product. And I *know* there are a lot of events going on in D.C. But I also know D.C. is only Roman's layover city—the one where he waits while planning his next great escape. And I can't help but wonder about my future with Roman's work always being more important than mine. What will I do, really, when we're running all around? I think anyone with a brain and even the slightest smidgen of ambition would have these concerns. It'll be great…I know. I just have moments of insecurity about how I'm going to spend the rest of my life. Knowing there will be a marriage does not fill up all the spaces. It fills up some, but I can't help but frown when I wonder about the others.

But it's not just the career thing. It's the marriage thing, too. What if it's not as wonderful as I foresee it with Roman? What if we end up in the same old situation as every other couple, just trying to make a living before we die? I see other girls my age, and younger, and older, all clamoring to meet Mr. Right, and I wonder what they're trying to accomplish, really. And when they do accomplish what they think they're supposed to accomplish, is that the end? Is love enough? Do people get bored? Wherever Roman and I end up…I guess it will be great. Won't it?

My mother always says that together we are pretty as a picture. Yes. Oh, we're so pretty. But take away the picture and what else is there?

I know it will be great but…I start to wonder if when we get married and I give up my own career and my own friends and my own city and everything else that's mine, I will feel empty and slighted and think I was always just following the wistful notion that the grass is always greener. I wonder if when we get married and he whisks me off to some other place and I've got nothing but him when we get there…if I will wish I had everything back again. Everything that was mine.

Dylan took Ava to Las Vegas for a weekend so Electra and I were on our own. I pictured them stumbling around and having a real *Leaving Las Vegas* time of it. Even I would fear such madness.

We went to Cat & Fiddle for early evening cocktails. We sat in the courtyard in the fading daylight rays and drank Bass by the pint. We talked under the shady trees and the twinkling outside lights. She wore red lace and I wore black lace because you never go anywhere in Hollywood without wanting to be noticed, trying to get noticed, but we put off the vibe that we were to be left alone.

"So where's Stupid this weekend?" Electra asked.

"He took Miss Piss on her ridiculous cruise."

"I'm sure it's a thrill a minute. I wonder how she got the whole weekend off from nursing just to go to Mexico with her jackass boyfriend?"

"No shit. I wish *she* was in the hospital."

"So what's up, Doll?"

I told her about how sometimes I got worried about giving things up for Roman and everything he was offering in exchange.

"You are truly tortured by your duplicitous soul," she said. "You think you're going to miss out when you give *all this* up for Roman?" she asked me, throwing out her arms. She laughed. "Please, Doll. We're living in a wasteland. And I can't say New York is much better, but the idea of it might improve with a ring on my finger. Don't you think?"

"If that's what you want." I sipped my beer.

"Well, of course it is. Josh is handsome and smart and successful and he treats me like a goddamn queen. And that is what it's all about, as far as I'm concerned." She gave me the eye. "I'm not going to marry some *underwear* model like my pretty boy. Just like you're not going to marry some *loser* like Jeremy."

"Harsh."

"If it slithers on its belly, it's probably a snake. Anyway." Her face took on a reminiscent look for a few moments. "It was great when Josh lived here, wasn't it? Remember all the fun we'd have going to visit him at USC and going to crazy parties and shit when we were barely legal? Most important, though, I had a boyfriend. But what's the point of having a boyfriend if he's not around? There's no one to take you out, no one to have sex with, no one to talk to when you want to talk about something. The phone and the Internet just don't do it for me."

"Get a vibrator."

"I have one, Doll. Besides, I hate it when people say that. A vibrator doesn't kiss you. Or talk to you. Or take you to see a movie. Honestly."

"I know what you mean. I hate it when people say that, too."

She put out a cigarette and leaned back in her chair to give me a meaningful look. "Josh is just being very smart, don't you think? He probably doesn't want to propose before he thinks I'm really and completely ready. He knows I don't want to throw my life away on some good-looking attachment that turns out to be a big farce a few years down the road. Like what happened with Shoshanna and Preston."

Electra's parents are divorced and they loathe each other with a venomous hatred. This has hardened her to the idea of everlasting love. She always calls them Shoshanna and Preston, like they're acquaintances instead of parents. When Electra was younger, Shoshanna had a really scandalous affair with Preston's brother, Uncle Bobby Lee, and Preston was so disgraced he had to move to the *North*. This really affected Electra for two reasons. The first was that Mama was so bad she turned Daddy into a *Yankee*. The second was that Shoshanna was always so forceful about raising Electra to be the perfect genteel lady, just like her, and then turned on her own upbringing to swindle both sides of the family. Where Electra comes from this is a big no-no because your family name is sacred. Both the Hanovers and the Kibblers can trace their bloodlines all the way back to before the Revolutionary War, when the Carolinas were colonies.

She looked moody. "You know what? The fuck. Shoshanna's just a high-and-mighty charlatan, is what it is. Thinking about all that just takes me back to the days when Shoshanna would try to compete with me for guys *my own age.* When I couldn't even take a summer boyfriend in Myrtle Beach or she'd be all over that shit. Dirty slut!"

"Is Myrtle Beach just like *Shag* in modern times?" I asked absently. Electra talking about her mother could get pretty fucking relentless. I know I can be an awful person but I could never say such hateful things about my mother. Not even if she was anything like Shoshanna, which she most definitely is *not.*

"Oh, you're *kidding* me. I won't even dignify that with a response." She sighed and took my hand, examining my ring for the hundredth time. "Anyway...my parents and their horrendous show aside...I'd sure kill for one of these, Doll. As soon as I get one of these..." She sighed again.

"Whatever happened to all of your big political aspirations? First woman president and all that? You were such an activist in college. You used to be so idealistic."

"Didn't we all? And I'm still idealistic, I'm just not unrealistic about my ideals anymore. Nobody gets into politics because they want to make a difference. They get into politics for power and money. I'm already empowered and I already have money. Josh has lots of money. When we get married, I won't even have to work if I don't want to. Of course I still *will.*"

"Oh, of course."

She gave me a long stare. "Look, Doll...I've known you long enough to know the kinds of things that are going through your head these days...and I've got to tell you... you'd be a *fool* to choose Jeremy over Roman, even if he were offering." She narrowed her eyes at me. "But so what I guess...because you never do what anybody else tells you to do, anyway. At least not until *you* decide it's the thing to do."

I thought about that. She was right.

She shook her head. "Can you imagine poor Josh if he ever knew about my indiscretions? He'd be crushed to think another man had touched me!"

"How would you feel if Josh had a female version of Troy?" I asked curiously.

"He'd have to kiss his balls goodbye 'cause I'd chop the little fuckers off," she said matter-of-factly. "And then I'd push him over the fucking Brooklyn Bridge and be done with him!"

"Really?" I asked.

"Hell *yes.* Nobody cheats on *me.*" She tossed her hair like an indignant pony. "And *you?* How would you feel if Roman had a female version of Jeremy?"

I thought about it. "Awful."

"I'll bet!" she laughed, loving it. She picked up her pack of smokes and shook one into her hand. "Yeah, I guess I can wait for my ring. I'm in *no* hurry to move to New York as it is. Yankee hellhole!"

"Oh, come on."

"Come on nothing, Doll. Taking a bite out of the Big Rotten Apple makes me want to spit out a whole mouthful of bad memories. It always reminds me of visiting Preston there after the divorce. I swear I must have gone to every fucking tourist attraction in that entire city just because he thought he had to keep me entertained. And we always had to have dinner and go to shows with his ladyloves and they were always the biggest skanks." She shuddered.

"New York's not that bad," I told her, looking down my nose.

She gave me a look that said of course it was, what was I, stupid or something? "Don't tell me like I don't know. *You* complain about *L.A.!*"

Electra can always get me. I wrinkled up my nose at her and she laughed.

"I know New York will eventually happen. I'm dealing

with it. I'm dealing with the fact that I will not only have to live on the same side of the country as that whore Shoshanna but also on the same fucking *island* as that goddamn asshole Preston. I'm dealing with the fact that I will eventually have to call myself true to Josh and Josh alone. But until then I'm having fun. Besides, men are harmless. It's not like they're beating down the door to marry me before Josh bothers to propose. They're just a bunch of horndog pigs. They don't even care that I'm smart or anything like that. It's all about my body and how they just want to get a piece of my little cat." She was always saying that. She was always saying she had to be twice as smart just so guys could learn to look past her hot look and get to know the real Electra. Oh, you poor thing, we were always telling her. Must be so hard!

"What if you were in love with someone else?" I asked.

"I would never let myself be so foolish. I love Josh just fine. Love's not the problem with us, anyway. It's just our distance and my fear of commitment."

"But what if there was someone else and he made you crazy and weird and happy and angry and excited and delighted and hateful all at the same time?"

She rolled her eyes. "Who needs love like that? You can't live a normal life when someone makes you feel that way. It leaves no room for anything else and you end up acting like a big jackass all the time. Like take Ava, for example. She can fall in love with anyone. And they all make her insane because she loves them all like that."

"I think that's her biggest problem."

"That's her gift, Doll. Her capacity to love. It's almost unconditional."

"Do you wish you could be like that?"

"Are you fucking kidding me?" she demanded. Then she laughed. "Start planning your wedding, Doll. Because if you don't, I'm taking that ring away one night while you're sleeping."

Chapter 10

My hometown is probably one of the most beautiful places in the world. There are moments at sunset when you feel that you've discovered Shangri-la. And moments at sunrise that make you understand every word of poetry that's ever been written. It's like a secret little hideaway. The city itself, nestled between the beach and the hills, has a very small-town feel to it.

Going back is always completely wonderful...and completely awful at the same time. I am young there, always. But I hate that, because I will never be young again. I don't want to be. I don't want to be old, either! At home, memories dance on every corner...down every street. Everything's the same...but different. It's the most comfortable place I can imagine being, though to be there always makes me strangely uncomfortable until I almost can't wait to get back to seedy, greedy L.A. Electra says people regard their hometowns the same way they regard loved ones who have abused them.

I headed north on the 101 with Ava that next Friday, on Karen's command that I go home to discuss the wedding

with my mom. I took Ava because she was moping about
Dylan and how it was way different before they got *involved*.
He promptly returned her calls. He brought her little treats
like cigarettes and gum. These days he acts cocky and wags
his finger at her when she gets on his nerves. He acts with
her the way he has always acted with females. Like the fucking *bastardo* Ava knows he is.

We stopped at Foster's to get strawberry-banana shakes.
Aurelia Sparks was there and she was about eighteen months
pregnant. I couldn't imagine ever having to see anything
more vomitous. We stood in line right behind her. When she
turned around and saw me standing there she blinked as if
she couldn't believe it. I could believe it.

She just stared at me with her big brown eyes. Her nose
and cheeks were freckled, left over from a summer spent
every day in a backyard or on a beach. She was wearing a
yellow jumper and white Keds. She was holding a huge
chocolate-dipped ice-cream cone. Aside from being
grotesquely pregnant, she didn't look so good. Even her
ringlets looked droopy. I knew I looked fabulous because I
always go home glam. I knew to her, I probably looked like
a movie star. Ava definitely looked like a movie star. Ava practically *is* a movie star.

How satisfying.

"Hello again," I said.

"Hi there," she said, totally bitchy. Then she stuck her
nose in the air and went flouncing off with her ice cream
and her spawn.

"Who was that bitch?" Ava asked as we drove away.

"Aurelia Sparks."

"No!"

"Let's just get over it," I told her, turning onto Foothill.
"Like, right now."

My mother's car was in the driveway when we pulled in.
She teaches the morning history periods at Buena High and
must have just gotten home. Outside, the house is white

stucco with a red tile roof. Inside, it is like an Ethan Allen showroom. All safari-style British Classics, to honor my parents' meeting place in the Serengeti. My mother was doing some missionary work and my father was in the Peace Corps. I like to imagine how that was probably meant to be, even though I have a hard time believing in that meant-to-be shit. I mean, let's get real—nobody ever thinks an ugly person is someone they're meant to be with. It's pretty romantic about my parents, though. Imagine their surprise to find out, in Africa, that they were both from the same town in California? The only reason they'd never crossed paths was because my dad was a few years older than my mom and they kept missing one another as they moved into different stages in life.

Ava and I floated through the house on the delicious aroma of chocolate chip cookies baking in the oven, and wound up in the kitchen. There's a nice view of the city and the ocean and the Channel Islands from the kitchen windows.

"Where's Dad?" I asked, after hugging my mom hello.

"Afternoon classes," she explained.

My dad's a Russian lit professor up at UCSB. I think it's cute that my parents are both educators. So does everybody else.

"Hi, Margaret," Ava said, kissing my mom's cheek and getting two cans of Diet Pepsi from the fridge without asking. Ava and Electra know my family so well that they're like extra daughters in our home. My parents don't mind. They're very easygoing.

"So how are my beautiful girls?" Mom asked as we got settled. We had dropped our overnight bags by the front door, just like I used to drop my backpack there every day after school. When we went upstairs later, they would have miraculously been moved to our rooms. My room at home is still the same as I left it. I still have my daybed and three whole bookshelves of *Sweet Valley High* books, every last numbered one of them in place. And don't forget all the posters of James Spader—my fave! Ha ha ha!

"Doing fine, just fine," Ava replied for the both of us.

"Any new men in your life, Ava?" Mom asked mysteriously.

"Oh, kind of," she said, shrugging. "I'm seeing Dylan."

"Oh, not that deadbeat you girls ran around with in college?" Mom asked disappointedly. But she wasn't really disappointed.

Ava nodded. "He's different now."

"Well, I should hope so! Goodness!"

Personally, I couldn't really say he was all that different. After college he moved back home to Anaheim to live and eat for free at his parents' house, which he still does to this day. What he makes in cash he gambles away in Las Vegas every chance he gets, if he hasn't spent it all on booze and toys—you know, important things like hockey skates, snowboards and cutting-edge electronic devices. And he works in loan processing. He says he's the one who seals the deals, but I like to imagine he's actually just the data-entry clerk who punches in the numbers on the computer once everything's been signed.

I met my mother's eyes and she raised an eyebrow. I raised one back.

The timer buzzed then and the cookies were done. I took one before it cooled and burned my tongue on the chocolate.

"I talked to Kitty and she's going to get in on a lot of the planning," Mom told me.

"Kitty knows everyone in town," I told Ava. "She can work the best deals."

"Good, 'cause there's lots left to do," Ava told Mom.

"Well, we'll help, won't we?" Mom replied, winking at her.

After a few hours of lolling about, we devoured a home-cooked meal of meat loaf and mashed potatoes. Then Ava and I dropped over to Kitty Lovejoy's house. Lovejoy is Kitty's name from her first marriage to Eddie, Lily's father. Kitty kept Lovejoy as her name because she says you should either keep your maiden name or change your name just once because it's a pain in the ass to change your name as many times as you get married. Kitty and Eddie got divorced when he decided what he really wanted to do was be an adventure photographer. Kitty and my mother refer to Eddie as a man-boy. That means he is unaware that he's supposed to act like an adult even though he is one. He hasn't been back to the States since Lily was fourteen. He and Roman would get along *great*.

"Fucking A darling, I thought you weren't gonna show!" Lily screamed, throwing the front door open. She was wearing her uniform of jeans and a sweater, with Ugg boots. She grabbed Ava by one hand and me by the other and dragged us to the car, talking all the way.

"Daisy got your e-mail and said of course she'll be in the wedding," she told me. "She's living somewhere in Central America. Panama, I think."

"Doing what?" I asked. Daisy and I don't see each other much or even talk a lot because she's a bit unconventional and it's hard to track her down. She's always on the go and only comes home when she's out of money.

"She's on a *job*," Lily replied, making quotation marks with her fingers.

We exchanged glances. Daisy's jobs have ranged from limo driver to singing blues in the nude, and I think in this case she's doing something illegal, possibly smuggling. Kitty and my mother have always said that Daisy is "really out there."

We sang along to "Boys of Summer" and "Cuts Like a Knife" on the classic rock radio station. It was good to be together again.

We drove to a liquor store to get beer and went to the beach house, where Lily technically lives even though she's always up at Kitty's just hanging around. Lily doesn't really do anything at all other than just hang around, actually. The beach house is still decorated exactly how it was when Kitty and Eddie bought it in the seventies. The carpet is orangish-red and the walls are papered in plaid. The couches are covered in nubby oatmeal material and the walls are hung with paintings of Ventura from a long time ago. The kitchen has pink tile and a linoleum floor, and the fridge is green. We had a wild party there once when Lily found the key while Kitty and Al were out of town visiting his parents in Atlantic City. All there was to drink were a stash of Al's handle bottles of Popov vodka and a bunch of Sunny Delight Kitty had picked up at Price Club for some reason. I smoked Capri 120s at the time and thought my extra-long cigarettes were the height of cool. The cops busted us all when the neighbors called and my mom had to come get us from the police station. I thought she was going to die of embarrassment when word got around town, but she didn't. She just said, "Oh, to be a teenager again."

We sat on that same patio in deck furniture that had been there ever since I could remember and talked with *The Virgin Suicides* soundtrack on the stereo inside. In the beach house we always listen to classic rock or disco because it seems fitting. We listened to the waves crashing on the beach and watched the moonlight play on the ocean.

I tilted my head back and looked up at the starry sky. In L.A. you hardly ever see stars. Not the celestial kind, at least.

I listened to Lily tell Ava what it was *really* all about. Lily talks like she's been alive for hundreds of years. She's so all-knowing. It's funny. I knew Ava needed somebody to listen to her who wasn't tired of hearing it. So I kept quiet and let them talk. Dylan, Dylan, Dylan. Blah, blah, blah. The stars were starting to blur.

I was jolted awake by the ancient beige Princess telephone ringing from the kitchen wall. No cordless in the beach house.

"Should I get that?" I asked.

Lily shrugged. "I'm sure it's just Charlie. I told him you were coming up tonight. He and the bozos are undoubtedly getting blasted at Winchesters and want us to join up."

"I want to see the bozos!" Ava cried. "I love the circus!"

"In that case, why don't you grab the phone?" Lily suggested. Ava sprang out of her chair and scampered off into the house.

"Oh, great," I said, groaning.

"What?" Lily griped. "We went to breakfast at IHOP this morning. He asked when you were coming up next. I said tonight, actually. And he said, cool. Let's all do something."

"Okay, fine—but if Dan's with them, forget it," I told her.

"Please, Doll. Dan's bitch wife never lets him leave the house these days and you know it. Now, just what is the problem, truly? You've been quiet all night. Jeremy?"

I shrugged.

"As long as you know where that stays, it's not a problem. Besides, Roman is probably off getting it with a bunch of other girls," she laughed.

"Why do you say that?"

"He's a man, isn't he?"

"Still…I highly doubt it."

I don't think he was ever that type. I don't think he was ever the kind of guy who screwed a girl and then threw her out of his room or his house. How would that have ever been possible? My sweet romantic man? He's incredibly attractive and desirable and I know he's had many girlfriends. He had this one girlfriend for a long time who worked for ICRA, too, and traveled to Brazil and Nicaragua and Senegal with him. Her name is Emmaline and I know they still talk but it's not like he still wants her. If he mentions Emmaline, it's in a casual way like when he's saying something like, "This one time when I was with Em…" to tell a story. We agreed we wouldn't talk that much about our sexual pasts because does it really matter once you've met The One? No, it doesn't. When he's here, when he's in front of me, he's all I see.

When I'm with Jeremy all I can do is look at him. Smell him. All I want to do is touch him. Taste him. And Roman seems very far away.

Roman *is* very far away.

Ava came back. "It was Charlie. I'll drive."

I felt apprehensive as Ava drove us to Main Street and parked outside of Winchesters. I knew why when I saw various familiar faces crowding the patio. I hung outside to have a cigarette as Lily took Ava into the bar.

"Peaches," Charlie said a moment later, bumping hips with me.

"Please," I replied, wrinkling up my nose at the nickname. He started calling me that in reference to my "fresh delicious boobs." Too sweet for me! You could say it was endearing that he'd never stopped, if the mention of it didn't still call to mind a serious case of having been fucked over. Charlie and I were forced to be cordial, even friendly, due to the fact that we were classmates, neighbors, and above all members of the same small social circle. Always a pleasure.

He slung an arm around my neck. "I like it when you bring Ava to town. There's just something about a girl with blue streaks in her hair and a denim jumpsuit on."

"Don't be getting any ideas."

"Well, she *is* cute. Not as cute as you, though."

"Yeah, that's me. Adorable."

He cleared his throat. "So how 'bout a smoke for me?"

I muttered grudgingly and produced a cigarette for him.

He lit it and tossed the match into the street. "Heard you're getting married."

"That is correct."

"He good enough for you?"

I rolled my eyes. "Come on, Charlie."

"I'm being serious."

"How grand. Tell me all about it."

He was quiet for a moment. In his silence I detected the coming of one of those quintessential moments that only happens now and then in life, and always when you're least expecting it. He moved to wrap his arms around me. I stiffened instinctively. He put his cheek against mine.

"I'm sorry," he finally said, voice low in my ear.

"For what?"

"For everything, Peaches. For what happened after we…
you know. I was stupid and…I just didn't know how to handle it at the time. I was all tripped out."

"I was thinking about that recently."

"Were you? What were you thinking?"

I shrugged. "Just a broad recollection of the whole situation."

"Do you think we remember the same things?"

"Obviously…if you felt the need to apologize."

He rubbed my back. "I'm so sorry, Peaches. I'm so goddamn sorry."

And that was that. And for some reason the fact that he'd
finally come clean made me feel clean, too. I didn't feel hostile toward him anymore. He was just Charlie. I pulled him
closer and really hugged him. "Thanks."

"Yeah, well…you know."

"You do realize everyone in that entire bar is now outside watching this?"

"I'm sure. So just how many people do you think would
fall over the railing and onto the sidewalk if we started making out right now? I'm guessing at least fifty."

I pushed him away, laughing.

He winked at me. "Now, listen. Are you having a band at
your wedding? Because if you want my band to play the reception, we'll do it for free."

I raised my eyebrows.

"It'll be my gift to you," he bargained. "Besides, I'm afraid
you won't invite me otherwise and I really want to be there."

"Well, are you any good?" I asked him.

"Come hear us sometime," he told me. "We play all over
the area."

"I'll do that," I told him.

"I hope so." He kissed my cheek and walked back inside.
And out of his pocket fell the wrapper from an orange
Tootsie Pop.

Lily came outside a moment later. She ran the toe of her Ugg boot over the concrete of the sidewalk in an imaginary arc. "So what'd he have to say?" she asked.

"He said he was sorry."

"Fucking Charlie. Ten years later!" She held her stomach and giggled.

My best friend—I love her. She's just so easy. And she's funny to look at. She's very skinny. Her face reminds me of that Muppet, Janice, the one who was always smiling and nodding, her eyes perpetually closed. She even has that same stick-straight blond hair, so straight it is literally limp. She knows she's funny to look at. She doesn't give a fuck. We've been friends since we were tiny tots.

"You know what else? He wants to play my wedding reception."

She cracked up, stomping her foot. "Now that is rich! Fucking Charlie. But you'd better do it, Doll—else Andy'll think he's entitled and you definitely don't want *that*." She put her head against mine. "You know something? Tomorrow we're going to get together with Kitty and Margaret and talk for hours upon hours about a bunch of useless wedding crap. So I suggest we go get as drunk as possible."

"You think tremendous hangovers will help?" I asked dubiously.

"I'm looking for any excuse to get out of it," she laughed. "I mean, I'm really happy that you're marrying a nice man who will give you a very nice life, but that doesn't for shit mean it's something I'd ever want to do!"

Chapter 11

I made a massive shopping trip a few days later, which is something I can really only do right after I get paid. Grocery shopping feels therapeutic. You can do a lot of thinking while you wander those bright aisles. I like buying things I don't even really need like Nescafé Frothé and peanut butter chips just because.

I bought so much shit that I think the next time Fret comes around I will just give him some groceries. He will thank me and say bless you, child, and then throw them away because he doesn't really want food, he wants money, for alcohol. I can understand that. If I were homeless and a bum I would just want to get drunk all the time, too. As it is I want to get drunk all the time.

Roman got me on the phone as I was finishing up.

"Isn't it early in the morning there?" I asked. "Like two or three?"

"Yes. But I can't sleep."

"How come?"

"Because I'm thinking about you."

I folded up a bag and shoved it in the recycling bin. "I hope you're thinking good thoughts."

"I am. That's why I wanted to hear your voice."

I had an inkling to ask if that was true, then why wasn't he calling more often? I knew what the answer would be. Busy.

"How's everything going?" I asked.

"Busy, baby, you?"

"I can't decide on our wedding color."

"What's the problem?"

"Well, I see my bridesmaids in black."

"Okay. So what's the problem?"

"People may say it's morbid."

"Nonsense, Dalton. It's elegant."

"But are you sure you wouldn't rather have baby blue?"

"How come?"

"Because baby blue's your favorite color."

"But I'd rather you have what you want."

I smiled again. I was glad he called because when I talk to him, I remember why I like the idea of him so much. He reminds me that I won't always have to wait to go grocery shopping until I get paid. That I won't always have two other girls in my business every single day, and that I won't always have to be in theirs in return. He reminds me that adulthood is not scary, but exciting. He reminds me that life is good, and that it always will be. He reminds me that I will one day soon share grocery shopping, and everything, with someone who cares—like I do.

He told me about the project and I told him about the wedding. He told me he had gone to a dinner with all the big cheeses and the United States ambassador to Cameroon. I told him I might get to meet the vice president on his next trip to L.A. because he was speaking at a conference at the Century Plaza Hotel and Charisma was putting it together. He told me about the mountains and the rain forests there. I told him the Santa Anas were blow-ing and it was still nice and warm. He said Love YOU! and we hung up.

Ava came home from work and brought me a Gatorade and a pack of cigarettes. What a thoughtful little dame. We sat outside together, enjoying the evening.

"Andy's coming over," she told me. "He's bringing dinner."

"Oh, good."

"He's going over lines with me later on. I have an audition for a part on *The Bold and the Beautiful*."

"What's the part?" I asked. You are only a real actress if you go to auditions. You shouldn't say you're an actress otherwise. I find that so annoying.

"Some long-lost relative of the Forresters."

"Impressive. You didn't get the audition through Suzanne, did you?" I asked.

"No, I did not," she said, rather haughtily.

"Just asking."

Suzanne is my least favorite of Ava's friends. Her father is a producer or some shit like that for big-budget action movies. Having grown up where and how she did, Suzanne knows all the inside garbage that goes on in L.A. She knows about all the whackjobs and the perverts and the sick crazies. So she knows the kinds of things they do and the kinds of things they want and for this she is able to make lots of cash having girls fuck dirty old bigwigs for money. She is a *madam*. Some of them do it because hey, if you've ever gone mad for plaid and spent your entire paycheck in Burberry, it's not a bad way to make a grand. Most of them do it because they're hoping it will land them an audition or a part. As if some important director or agent is going to get spanked and, in the process, come to the conclusion that he has unearthed some undiscovered treasure. Then again, Suzanne's girls do show up on TV quite a bit. Blackmail?

"I met the casting director at the salon," she went on. She was wearing turquoise pants and a lavender tank top that said *bella* across the front in rhinestones. Someone at the salon had put one dark streak in her hair. "She came in to have her roots done while I was chatting with Sing about her baby and somehow we just started talking and it came out that I'm an actress."

It *always* comes out when someone's an actress. It's like, "Oh, you dropped your lipstick. Let me get it. I'm an actress." Or, "I love your pretty shoes. I'm an actress."

"I'm really glad you didn't get that audition through Suzanne," I told her.

"Dylan says I'm too good to do that kind of shit," she told me, shrugging. "He said if he ever hears about it again he'll *kick my motherfuckin' ass.*"

Andy brought over a big platter of baked ziti from Micelli's. The ziti was gooey and cheesy just the way I like it. We lit candles at the table and set out place mats and clean silverware. Some of our silverware has food crusted on it because it didn't wash off in the dishwasher. Electra always tells us we have to scrub, *scrub!* She says it's not like in Cascade commercials where the dishes go in with sauce all over them and come out crystal clear.

"I'm concerned about what the bridesmaids will be wearing," Andy told me, as the conversation shifted to wedding and we devoured a tiramisu for dessert.

"I thought you weren't wearing a dress," I replied.

"I'm not. But I still need to *know,*" he replied, sticking his tongue out at me. "For instance, what color are you thinking about?"

"Black," I replied.

"Black!" Ava exclaimed. "Black is for funerals."

"No, black is formal," Andy explained. "You should know. You're from Italy."

"I wasn't *born* in Italy, *culo.*"

"Yes, but you have seen *The Godfather,* haven't you?"

"You just make no sense to me, Andy. What does *The Godfather* have to do with anything?"

"You tell me."

Ava poured more Chianti for the three of us. "Anyway. The dresses?"

"I see a shorty baby doll with pleated crepe falling down from a wide ribbon sash just under the bust," Andy said prophetically. "Tied in a big bow in back."

"I don't know if I like that," Ava said dubiously.

"Well, it's not your wedding, is it?" I asked.

"You're mean and awful," she told me, kissing the top of my head as she got up to clear the dishes. She came back out a few minutes later, worried, and assured me that she'd been kidding. I smiled and told her I knew.

I suppose all life is a routine, no matter how much you try to mix it up. Such as, I seem to find myself in this routine about once a month or so where Ava wants us to go shopping together and it is literally an all-day affair. We look at L.A. like it's a big Monopoly board. Then we go around it. The Grove. The Beverly Center. Century City. Rodeo Drive. The Westside Pavilion.

Much like a night out in Hollywood, shopping like gangbusters always reminds me of just exactly what the problem with Los Angeles is. It's the home of the rich and famous, sure—only you usually feel like you're the only one who is neither. So you spend all of your money trying to run with the rest of the crowd, and you end up broke, and then you get depressed because you know you're just faking it. You're not really part of the scene and you probably never will be…even when it seems like you're right in the middle of it.

It's funny how some people just crave it and will do anything to get there. I suppose that's what happens when you see something every day…you either start to hate it, or desperately want it. Like how Ava wants it. I think she's in love with the scene because it's so magical and unreal. Maybe she craves the stability of a phony existence after the instability of her life's reality. Everybody's always been of the belief that when Carlo brought the family out from New Jersey, he brought the family "business" right with them. When you ask just what the family "business" is, the Damianos say "imports," wink-wink. Ava will neither confirm nor deny our speculations but I *know* we're onto the truth. Carlo has *mobster* written all over him. We're talking pinstripes. And guntoting "friends" named Giannini and Angelo, who never leave his side. And whenever we've been down there visiting, he's always had his "associates" sneaking into the house for a "meeting" in the dead of night.

Or maybe I just have a totally overactive imagination. The fact remains that the family's pretty mysterious, and Ava's life's been pretty fucked up. Ava's mom, Jenny, died when Ava was in seventh grade. The rumor is that she drank herself to death. Ava says she doesn't remember her mom being a serious lush…she just remembers that she liked to party all the time. That is a *frightening* thought for someone who never sees the bottom of a glass. Apparently Carlo was so busted up about Jenny letting the bottle take her to the grave that he couldn't even look at another woman for years—at least, until he saw *Jubilee!*

Our last stop was the Beverly Center. Ava's checklist said we had yet to make any cosmetic purchases so we went trying on lipsticks and eyeshadows at the Lancôme counter at Macy's.

"I have that," I said, as Ava rubbed some Hanky Panky on her hand.

"Oh, do you? Can I borrow it?"

I nodded. She would end up owning it but who cared, it was only a lipstick.

I got a bottle of Trésor and three eyeshadow duos and six lipsticks and we went out into the mall.

We got Mrs. Fields cookies from the food court and walked around eating them. Whenever we get Mrs. Fields we buy four because if you do that you get two free. It's such a good deal.

I wanted to go into Guess and Club Monaco and Bebe and spend a pile of money, but I didn't think it was such a good idea. I still have my mother's credit card and she never says a word so I feel guilty as hell when I use it, but the truth is, I use it all the time. One time I even charged a plane ticket to Hawaii. It was when Roman and I were first dating. He said he was going to be in the neighborhood over the weekend and asked me if I would meet him at this really well-known restaurant he liked. When I asked which one he told me the name and I thought that couldn't be right because I had never heard of it. I looked it up on the Internet and it was in Honolulu. So I bought a ticket and flew to Hawaii and took a cab from the airport to the restaurant, and he was sitting there waiting for me at a table as if it was an everyday occurrence. He had a fantastic hotel suite overlooking Waikiki and we drank champagne and talked about what we would name our kids if we ever got married. He gave me real emerald earrings that he bought in Colombia. They came from a mine. They remind me of that song "Kumbayah" that you sing around the campfire. I wear them with everything, no matter what color it is.

I saw Jeremy and Pristina coming out of Express. She had two big shopping bags in her hands. You can spend a shitload of money in Express on absolutely nothing.

Pristina has long dark hair and long arms and legs like a spider's. She's always wearing shorts. Her legs are horrible. They are unshapely and grotesque. Her ankles are too skinny. If she was my nurse I would probably die just looking at her.

She was wearing no bra. I could never go without a bra. Jeremy says he doesn't like big tits. He sure likes mine.

I pretended I didn't see them even though I knew Jeremy saw me and I knew he knew that I saw him. We walked right by each other. Ava smacked Jeremy's ass.

"What the fuck?" Pristina screamed, stopping in her tracks. "Did you just slap my boyfriend's ass?"

"Who? Me?" Ava asked, looking around.

Pristina folded her arms and tapped one foot. "Uh, *yee-ahh?*"

Ava shrugged. "I'm sorry but no. You must have imagined it."

"I saw you do it," Pristina insisted, glaring.

"You're very bizarre," Ava said sympathetically. She shrugged again and jerked her head at me, like we should go.

"I'm gonna kick that bitch's ass!" Pristina sputtered to Jeremy as we walked off.

"No, you're not. Drop it. I'm thirsty. I need a Coke."

"Why did you do that?" I asked Ava as we headed for the escalators.

"It seemed like a funny thing to do. I wanted to see if she'd say anything."

"She's a raving lunatic bitch," I said, getting on the escalator to ride down. Ava held my hand. We were going to put our shit in the car before we came back up to go to the movies. We were seeing some new movie with Nicolas Cage. Ava loves Nicolas Cage. I think he looks like a dead man.

"Have you ever met her?"

"Nope. Just seen pictures, and sometimes I run into them like just now."

"She's ugly. She looks like a horse."

"Neighhhhhhhh!" I replied, making Ava laugh.

There were four different postcards in the mail when I got home. All of them were pretty, scenic shots of Cameroon wildlife in the Parc National du Waza and said Love YOU! on the back. Roman writes it like that because you can't do italics in handwriting. I guess that means I'm The One and Only One. That's sure nice to know.

I decided to spend the evening in and write him a letter. It was cozy being home alone. I thought it might be good to appreciate some me time. After we get married, I'll be sharing a bedroom for the rest of my life. I'll have to roll up my horror movie posters and pack up my disco ball and peel away my glow-in-the-dark stars. And that's not a bad thing... but alone time and your own space is still really good when you have it.

When I finished the letter I sealed it up with some pictures from our trip to Catalina. I put on Fleetwood Mac and lolled on my bed, my sock feet pressed against the wall on a black-and-white poster of Madonna from like seven or eight years ago, where she is sitting at a table dealing tarot in a revealing satin gown, and it simply reads *Spain* across the bottom.

The doorbell rang. I got up to answer it.

It was Jeremy. "That scene at the mall today was really over the top," he told me, illuminated by the porch light. He was wearing a puffy leather jacket and his hair was gelled. He looked good.

"Pristina's delightful. I don't know why we don't all hang out."

He walked past me and into the house. He stood looking at me for a long time. Then he took my hand. "Let's go for a drive."

We drove out of the city not saying anything. He went north on PCH to Malibu. After a few miles he pulled over and shut the engine off. The ocean swish-swished, the only sound in the blackness of the night.

"You know something, Doll?"

"What's that?"

"It's not like I even have a lot of room, here. Do you know what I mean?"

"I think so."

He turned sideways to face me. "It's like this. If I were to suggest right here at this moment that we do away with Roman and Pristina and just see where this leads us, what would you think about that?"

I twisted my engagement ring. "I wouldn't think you were serious."

"But what if I were?"

"I don't know. Are you?" My heart was pounding.

He fell back against his seat. "I could be. But *you're* not. You're the one who went and got engaged."

He said it as if he were a little boy and had just found out that his best friend was going to be away at camp all summer. He sounded dejected and disappointed.

"What did you think?" I asked. "That the four of us would just go on like this forever? That Roman and I would never take the next step, or you and Pristina never would?"

"Pristina and I *haven't*."

"Now you're upset about it?" I asked, surprised. "You were acting like you hardly cared the last time I tried to bring it up. You know… 'We don't have to worry about the future so we can enjoy what's now'?"

He made a long, angry sound from the back of his throat. "Doll…come on. Why was I supposed to get into it and lay it all out there when I was sitting there feeling like you'd never really even thought about it? At least not until recently."

"You can't assume that I never thought about it," I informed him. "It's just that you and I have always had a backdoor relationship. I wasn't going to say no to him just because now and then I've considered wanting more from you."

"Aha, there—you said it." He sounded pleased.

I shrugged. "We spend a lot of time with each other. I would have to be made of stone if I said I never had sweet thoughts."

"Awww…you're makin' me blush!"

"Fuck you, then."

He took my wrist and squeezed it. "If you've ever wanted more than what you were getting from me, then why not say it? Why wait until it was too late?"

"Because you would have held it against me. You'll hold this entire conversation against me someday, because that's just how you are. You turn things around."

He looked down. "No I don't."

"Yes, you do."

He relaxed his hold but didn't let go. "We'd have a great life. You could take over Charisma and put Karen to work as *your* assistant. I'll go by Jeremy Blood and become a name-brand sensation—bigger than Wes Craven! And of course I would get your input on all my scripts. We could take *Friday the 13th* back to Camp Crystal Lake!"

"I think with passions like that we'd end up putting each other in the grave." I had to laugh at what he'd said, though. Dalton Blood? Everyone would say they knew it.

"Yeah, probably. But before we turned all Sid and Nancy, don't you think we'd have a great life?"

"I'm sure we *could*. But it's a moot point, don't you think? If it were ever a possibility, why spend almost two years acting like Pristina's probably The One and I'm just some side-kick for all the in-betweens?"

"Probably for the same reason you did the exact same thing with me and Roman."

I got out of the car. I leaned against the door and lit a cigarette. He turned on the radio. "A Girl Like You" by the Smithereens came on.

He got out and came around to my side. He took the cigarette from my fingers.

"What do you want?" I asked quietly.

"It's hard to say. The smart thing at this point would be to drive you home and then leave your house and never go back again."

I nodded.

"But I'm not going to do that," he told me. "Until you say that's what *you* want."

We sat up late when we got home and watched eighties movies on TBS, laughing when the cussing parts were replaced with hilarious phrases like "witchen" instead of "bitchin'." And later, into the early hours of the morning, I lay awake in an embrace I'd only ever found with him, my eyes open, seeing what-ifs. Jeremy can be the biggest, most ununderstanding fuck on the planet when he's grumpy. He makes me act like a psycho. But there's also that part of me that only ignites in his presence. So what if I was wrong about Roman and Jeremy could be The One? The thought was too strange to think about, when I was so accustomed to holding him at arm's length.

It's not about getting away with something. It's not about going out with a bang. It's about this strange place where I don't have to be anything but me, and someone keeps coming back for more. It's about the puzzling concept of someone being both the best thing and the worst thing that have ever happened to you…both at the very same time.

If he'd been serious on the beach, I don't know what I would have said. I really don't. I've always hated the fact that he has Pristina—that she's first in his life and I'm second. I've always wished they would break up so that I could have him all to myself…even though I know that's ridiculous. Even so, there's something about Jeremy that's so me, so right, so fitting.

But I'd be crazy to give up what I have with Roman because he's all those things, too. I like how Roman and I can accomplish it without having to be so deranged about it all. Sometimes that's the nicest thing about us.

Chapter 12

I was in the shower one lusciously warm October morning when Dylan came in and took a piss without even knocking. My room is connected to Ava's by the bathroom we share, and what a pain at times like this. I stuck my head out from behind the pink curtain and glared at him.

"What?" he asked.

"You don't know?"

He flushed the toilet. I screamed as the water went burning hot. He laughed his cocky laugh. Heh. Heh. Heh.

"Get out!" I yelled at him.

"Why? Nothing there I haven't seen before," he smirked.

"Oh…you ass!" Okay…it's embarrassing but true…and part of the reason he can get under my skin so easily. I know he thinks he's all that just because he's seen me naked. We hooked up numerous times in college. Aw, forget it. We did more than hook up. It was *enormous* is all I have to say. I wonder how he doesn't break little Ava in half.

He leaned against the pink sink and folded his arms. "I want to talk to you."

"I want to talk to you, too."

"About what?"

"Your receding hairline. You can get help for that, you know."

"Heh. Heh. Heh. Very funny, bitch. Now, what about that knob you got sleeping in your bed right now?"

I turned off the water. "Hand me a towel, would you? And then go fuck yourself!"

He pulled a fluffy pink one off the rack. "I thought we were friends, honey."

I wrapped the towel around me and stepped out as he grinned maddeningly at me. "Sure, we're friends. But I'm not going to tell you my innermost thoughts all the same."

"Why? Ava tells me all of her innermost thoughts."

"Fuck off," I said, elbowing him out of the way so I could stand at the sink. He moved to block the door.

"Well?" he asked.

"Well, what?" I got out my face lotion. "I don't have to tell you shit."

"But I'm not leaving till you do."

"Dylan, you just get out of here!" I screamed.

"What the fuck, bitch, you got PMS or something?"

I met his knowing leer in the mirror. "Jeremy happens to be my friend. I can't just cut that off like it's no big thing."

"Why not? I could." He gave me a sly wink.

"Yeah, I'll bet. Now, do me a favor and move your ass."

He pressed his back to the door. He wiped a smudge of lotion off my nose. "I'm only looking out for you, Dollface. You fuck this shit up and I won't feel one bit sorry for you. So don't come crying to me when you do, the way you used to come crying to me in college."

"Well, you don't have to worry. I don't think I'd come crying to you at this stage in my life, Dylan." I gave him a pointed look. All the times I'd gone to him crying were all the times he'd put the moves on me! Fucker!

He shrugged. "You never know. Anyway, I think Roman's

a whole lot better than that piece of shit you run around with while he's gone, anyway. Roman treats you right. That poon just uses you for entertainment purposes, the same way you use him."

"And I'm supposed to value your opinion?" I asked.

"Yes. To be honest, I'm surprised at you, Dollface."

"I'm surprised at you, Dickless," I countered.

"Now we both know *that's* not true. Why you so surprised...because I care?"

I shoved him out of the way and stood dripping in the doorway to my bedroom. "Take a good long look in the mirror, Dylan. That's the only person you care about."

"You don't know the half of it." Heh. Heh. Heh.

Electra's boyfriend was visiting. Josh is a big talker. He's the kind of guy who always has to be telling some story that everyone *has* to listen to. He smokes cigars. He is the center of attention. He calls girls sugar and sweetheart. He is Mr. Nice Guy. Mr. Man. Mr. Big Bucks. To be honest...I don't really like him all that much. I never have. He's smarmy. He's good-looking and he fucking knows it. I hate men like that.

He stood in the kitchen frying bacon. He said he was going to make us the best breakfast we had ever tasted. I thought it was pretty ballsy of Josh to cook dead animal flesh when his girlfriend is such a militant vegetarian.

"I'm taking you ladies to Vegas the next time I come out," Josh told me as I sat at the table and smoked a cigarette and leafed through a catalog. Our mailbox is always stuffed full of them. Ava orders something new almost every day.

"We'll stay at the Venetian," he decided. "For New Year's."

I switched to a magazine. Electra subscribes to absolutely everything. I came across an ad for a new nail polish. A sparkly turquoise number. I thought I might seek it out the next time I was in Rite-Aid.

"How's Romes, Doll?"

"Good."

"He been eaten by cannibals yet?" At this original comment, Josh cracked himself up.

I put my magazine down and gave him a surly look. He was wearing nothing but jeans, button-fly unbuttoned, and a Tennessee Titans cap turned backward. "Are you making fun of Roman living in Africa, Josh?"

"I was just joking around, sweetheart," he said jovially as he went to work whipping up omelets.

"Yeah, but what you said was stupid," I told him.

"Easy there, sugar," he said soothingly. Then he chuckled. So annoying.

Jeremy came out of my room and rubbed his eyes. He got a box of cookies out of Ava's cabinet and sat down with me, munching on them.

"Coffee, brother?" Josh asked him.

Jeremy nodded. He always drinks coffee almost the first thing. He's like the walking dead without it.

I studied his sleepy morning appearance as I lit another cigarette. He held his fingers out as if he wanted it so I gave it to him. Josh chuckled at us and said something like, "You kids," when in truth he is only three years older than I am, and one year older than Jeremy. I wonder what Josh thinks of me and Jeremy. If it ever makes him doubt Electra's fidelity.

Electra pranced out in red satin harem pants and a sparkly white tube top, her long hair pulled up in a genie ponytail. "Josh! Do I smell *bacon?*"

"It was already dead, sugar," he told her.

She raised her nose. "Well, don't everybody be eating for like five hours. I told Rose and Lionel we would meet them at one."

Jeremy slurped coffee. He gave me the eye. I gave it back. Josh chuckled again.

We went down to the Yardhouse for the day and Josh paid. We got a big table out on the patio and everyone fussed over us because Josh is such a big talker and big spender. He was over the top. We're talking a Stetson and matching cowboy boots. Josh is originally from Nashville. When he gets tired of climbing Wall Street he wants to move back and become a country and western singer. Roman says Josh is a character.

Jeremy got up to call Pristina. She was working the whole weekend.

I drank a black and tan and played with my tongue while the guys talked. There's a space between two of my teeth and I like to stick my tongue in it. Roman says my teeth are very sharp, like a tiger's. Jeremy says my teeth are nice but that I shouldn't smoke so much. I've started using whitening toothpaste but I don't think it's working.

Electra got into a fight with the guys about girl power. It all started because Josh was telling us some story about how Electra had conned him into taking her to a romantic comedy because she was standing in a demi-cup bra and boy-shorts at the time.

"That was an underhanded thing to do," he told her.

"Why?" she asked.

"Because, sugar, you know I'm putty in your hands when you're on display like that."

"But why should the other guys have to know about it?" she asked snottily.

"Because, woman, you're fucking hot and we want to have a visual, okay?" Dylan told her. "It makes the story better."

She tossed her hair. "You guys are so cheap." Not that Electra would balk at such a compliment—even such a misogynistic one. Let's face it—you'd rather hear that you're hot and that guys want to picture you standing around in your underwear than hear that for them to picture you like that conjures up a bad case of the dry heaves.

"Hey, if I like my sugar in those thingies they call boyshorts, does that make me have gay potential?" Josh asked, frowning.

"Nah," Dylan replied. "I like those boyshort thingies, too. They make Ava's ass look fully *ripe*."

"So what was the point of the story?" I prodded. I hate

it when people don't get to the point. Josh never gets to the point. "Is that the end?"

"The end is that I have to go see this stupid fucking movie," he laughed, and the guys joined him. "Because Electra wants me to take her. I'm talking about sacrifice. Pissing on my values for my sweetheart."

The waitress set down a tray of tequila shots. Electra shoved him. "It's not like you aren't torturing me right back with what I agreed to do."

Josh handed her a shot glass and a lime. "Consider it part of your education, sugar, on the many differences between my sex and yours."

"Well, what is it?" Dylan demanded. He had one hand on his pint glass and the other on Ava's thigh. I knew the perv was having shallow dirty thoughts about Electra in her underwear. In college he tried various times to be with her and she always shunned him. He's never gotten over it. I know he fantasizes about it still. Ava says she is in *love* with Dylan. *Love*.

Josh chuckled and held up a pint of beer with one finger pointed in no particular direction. "She has to sit through three Bond movies, all my choice. I'm thinking *Thunderball*, *Octopussy* and *Dr. No*."

The guys clapped and laughed appreciatively.

I frowned. "What's so bad about that? I like James Bond. You can't get any campier than Roger Moore in *Moonraker*."

"Yeah, but, Doll...it's hardly the same thing with you," Josh told me like it should have been obvious. Like I was one of them. He went on, conspiratorially. "Anyway, I don't get chicks talking about clowns in movies like they want to have their babies."

Lionel was shaking his dirty blond head. "Chicks are just dumb like that."

Electra sucked the juice out of her lime and gave Lionel a dubious look. "Oh, *excuse* me, Lionel? You guys are the ones who are fucking pawing and licking at *Maxim* and falling out of your fucking La-Z-Boys over the Dallas Cowboys cheer-leaders. *Bro*-ther!"

"Amen, brother! Yeah!" Dylan hooted, slapping his palm to Lionel's.

I wanted to tell them to shut up already. Instead I ordered another black and tan.

Electra cracked up. "You're so stupid. You Neanderthal men are totally worse when it comes to idolizing members of the opposite sex in the media. I mean, if you could wave a magic wand and make Rose look like Jennifer Lopez right now, you'd do it, wouldn't you?"

Lionel shrugged. "Maybe not Jennifer Lopez. That bitch has seen her better day."

"All right then, Salma Hayek?"

Josh slung his arm around Lionel and nodded his okay. "Come on, man. It's Salma Hayek. Admit defeat. Even if I do have to say she looked pretty bad in that movie where she had that one big eyebrow. Aw, you know what? I'd still do Salma Hayek even with one big eyebrow. Wouldn't you, brother?"

"He can't answer that on grounds that Rose won't suck his dick for a month if he agrees," Dylan added. He and Ava smooched and made me want to be sick.

"Oh, I don't care," Rose said in her breathy voice. I knew she really did.

Roman told me once that when Josh and Lionel got started on their "men rule the world" thing he liked to just sit there and keep out of it. Roman thinks women are lovely. Delightful. Deserving of serious respect. You shouldn't talk about them like that. They are mothers. They are protectors. They are givers. It's not like he's never been one to debate and defend his beliefs. It's just that arguing feminism with chauvinists gets you absolutely nowhere. It's like having a theological discussion with Bible-beaters.

"Electra, let's just face the fact that you're an ass," Lionel told her. "Because really, puh-leeze. You act like you have all this power over us when it comes to sex, but who sits around with their friends and cries about wanting love and romance and boyfriends and husbands? Oh, you! Gee, I don't know where we get off thinking that men are in charge!"

Electra's eyes were scrunched up into little slits. "You're such an ignoramus, Lionel. You should be living in Utah with three wives and three times as many guns."

"Three wives? I could go for that," Dylan said, nodding slyly. "One for cleaning, one for cooking, and one to suck my dick!"

"Are you kidding me? I'd have all three of them sucking my dick—fuck the cleaning and the cooking!" Lionel laughed.

Electra folded her arms and shot dirty looks at all three of them. "You guys are sad. Really sad. I feel sorry for you."

"Electra, you just have to admit that it's a man's world and that it always will be. We may want the pussy, but we always get the pussy, and all you bitches do is flaunt the pussy, so we'll look and ask if we can have some and you'll feel like you have some sort of purpose here. And don't tell me you don't flaunt the pussy because if you didn't, you wouldn't be sitting there with half your tits hanging out of your top like they are." Dylan winked at her and raised his glass before taking a hearty drink.

"I may flaunt the pussy," she informed him, "But that does not mean it's a man's world."

"Give it up already," Lionel said, rolling his eyes.

"Now, don't get your panties in an uproar, sugar," Josh said, squeezing Electra's shoulder and planting a kiss on her forehead to placate her. "It's all in good fun."

"Yeah," she mumbled. "Some fucking fun!"

Jeremy came back to the table. "What'd I miss?" he asked me.

"Nothing new," I replied.

I'm so glad I don't have to clamor to marry a jackass. Really. I'm so glad I'm marrying a good, moral, well-educated gentleman who would never say such rotten things and mean them. Roman is one in a million.

Still…it must be fun to play that card now and then. Because I have to admit that if I could be a man for a week, I'd jump at the chance. And then I'd be the biggest asshole on the planet and do anything I pleased, just to see how glorious it must feel to rule the world.

Chapter 13

I woke up in the middle of the night to tell Jeremy how much I hate myself sometimes. He sat up in bed and listened, nodding occasionally. He didn't say a word.

I guess everybody feels this way sometimes. I guess we all feel small and scared and worthless now and then.

I would say these things to Roman...but I just can't. Roman thinks I am strong. He thinks I can handle anything. If I told him that sometimes I start thinking about the dirty life I've led he would be surprised. And most important, he would probably walk right out. He wouldn't want to be with a girl like me, if he knew the kind of girl I really am. He couldn't possibly love a girl like me. He's too perfect and good. And I am bad.

I'm glad he doesn't know, though. I'm glad because that way he doesn't look at me and see a whore, a sleaze, a vapid, jaded mind-fucked nothing. A ridiculous layabout who gets wasted at every opportunity, spends all of her money on material wants, and uses pop culture as philosophy. A girl who thought she could just "hang out" with another man for fun, until she realized how much that other man was so much more to her than just good times.

I'm glad Roman sees the me I want to be, the me I know I can be, when this life isn't always dragging me down. I wouldn't feel like it was dragging me down if it hadn't gotten so complicated. It used to be very simple. I had security without boundaries. Now I feel like it's time to really crack down and be an adult, whatever that means. Only it's difficult when it feels like hardly anything has changed. I know a lot *has* changed. I'm just never sure if *I* have. If I'm even trying. If I even have to. I *know* I have to. I want to. It's just that sometimes I get sidetracked.

I'm glad Roman is *stable.* I need that kind of stability because I am so unstable. With a guy like Jeremy, a guy who lets me go on being a nobody, a guy who doesn't care about my sins or my scars or my secrets, I could spend my entire life here.

I told him about feeling like I'm maybe a big disappointment. I talked about being a shallow, vindictive, insipid, worthless piece of trash. He listened and nodded. Not agreeing with me, but acknowledging that he heard me.

I keep a picture of Roman on the desk, on the shelf above the computer. In the picture he is standing next to a huge fish he caught, a swordfish or whatever that big kind of fish is, and he looks proud. I took it when we went on a fishing-boat trip off the coast of Maryland when I went out to visit him once. I spent most of the trip watching the fish get gutted and cleaned and beheaded. It didn't make me sick at all. It made me want to become a medical examiner so I can do autopsies, like Agent Scully was always doing on *The X-Files.* It seemed like Agent Scully did an autopsy in every episode.

Sometimes I feel like both he and the fish are watching me. The fish is the only one who hears me, though.

"You should tell Roman these things," Jeremy told me.

"I can't."

"Why not?"

"What if he doesn't like me anymore, after hearing them?"

"*I* still like you after hearing them, don't I?"

I put my head on his shoulder. "Will you be my date at Karen's wedding?"

He kissed my hair. "I'll have to see if Pristina's working that weekend."

Karen gave me a big account all my own. She said since she was taking almost three weeks off for her wedding, there was no way she would be able to handle it. The account is for the City of Angels Annual Christmas for the Children Gala. We get a lot of business right before the holidays. Big corporations want their company party planned, big fund-raising operations want their annual ball or dinner planned, and the list goes on and on.

Christmas for the Children is a charity that brings needy kids and gifts and donations together. I think that is really beautiful. If I'm going to believe in charity, it is something that will help kids. Kids have it easy in many respects, but they have it rough, too. Especially underprivileged kids. I think Santa Claus is the dumbest notion anyone ever invented. I wasn't buying it from the get-go. I knew even as a tiny tot that it was impossible for a man to fly a sleigh all over the world in one night, even with the different time zones. And no way Santa's elves were making those Mattel-brand toys I would find on the hearth on Christmas morning. And no way I got that shit based on my good behavior. Santa wouldn't have even had to check his list the first time because I was always naughty and never nice. And I knew for certain that Santa never visited the really poor kids in school. They never explain that in *The Night Before Christmas.*

I would get truckloads of Christmas presents. There would be stacks and stacks of neatly wrapped gifts underneath the tree, all lovingly taped and beribboned by my mother's hands in glossy papers of red and green and snowflake and reindeer prints. Every year I do Christmas Angels to try to give some of my good fortune back. I do three or four because I think one is not enough. I buy the kids the most expensive things on their lists. I know material things don't solve problems, but when it comes to needy kids and Christmas, I think presents probably help.

I endured Karen's Carly Simon through our mutual wall as I outlined some plans. I penned a date in my calendar for the press release. The charity was planning to sell at least five hundred tickets and maybe a thousand, so I went through Karen's big binder on ballrooms in the area. I called around to check on prices for the dinner and bar statistics. I remembered Pretty Boy saying something about having a friend who was moonlighting in a popular Westside jazz band, so I got his e-mail address from Electra and asked if he could get me some primo contacts. I called our satellite broadcast contact to see what they would charge if we could get a fair amount of big celebrity names, which I knew we could, because all that ever takes is a phone call to Karen's fiancé.

"What are you doing?" Karen asked, coming into my office. "I didn't hear you say you were going to lunch and it's past two."

"I've been busy." I gestured to the stuff spread out on my desk.

"I'm so glad you're taking this one off my hands," she admitted, looking critically at a French-manicured fingernail. "I know you'll do a great job."

"Thank you."

She picked up one of the wedding magazines she'd gotten me and opened it to a page I'd marked. "Is this the dress you've picked out?"

"Something along those lines. My mom's coming on Saturday to take all of my bridesmaids and me out looking. She said to have some ideas ready."

"That'll be fun," she said absently.

"What does *your* dress look like?" I asked curiously. She has refused to let anyone see it because she's so worried about people stealing her style.

"Well…now that I've seen what you're considering…" She looked over her shoulder as though there were hordes of other women standing out in the hallway with pencils and pads of paper, ready to sketch. She closed the door.

"It's sleeveless," she told me. "And the bodice is beaded but the skirt is just white satin. It's long. It's Vera Wang. I mean Vera Wang actually designed it. For me. I know her. Personally. Like, we're friends."

"Lovely."

"And then some. Just wait till you see it!"

Her dress is the only thing I *haven't* seen. It's a fact that she's been cramming that goddamn wedding down my throat for more than a year. No wonder I was so reticent about putting my own together. I feel like I just did!

"I'm going shopping," Karen sighed, putting the magazine down. "I need to get out of here for a while. Do you want to go?"

I knew we'd end up browsing the designer clearance rack at Neiman Marcus or Saks where clearance still equals holy-shit-that's-too-expensive on my pissy salary. "Thanks for the offer…but no," I told her.

I sent Jeremy an e-mail asking if he wanted to do something on Saturday night. He wrote back that he was spending the whole weekend with Pristina. I rattled off a scathing e-mail about how much that bothered me and clicked Send without thinking twice.

My mom brought Lily when she came down for our dress-shopping extravaganza. Poor Maddy had midterms so she had to miss out. Andy came with us just to be cute. He fake pouted and said if he was going to be in this wedding party and didn't even get to wear a pretty dress, he at least got some say in how the ladies looked. Everybody wanted to pinch his cheek and love on him.

We went to a big fancy bridal boutique in Beverly Hills that Karen had insisted was *the* place to go for a bride my age. You got a private salon for modeling gowns and your very own designer to help you choose the dress of your dreams. The velvet couches were mauve and the silky carpeting was lilac and they served mimosas in crystal flutes and cappuccinos in white ceramic mugs and tasty little muffins and other sweet breads in festive wicker baskets.

I'm actually pretty easy to shop for and my mother knows this, so she suggested we get the bridesmaids' gowns out of the way first. My mom is a tolerant shopper. That means she'll do it because she's nice, but you can just tell she doesn't really enjoy it. I noticed her popping a couple of aspirin as the morning got under way.

The girls ran this way and that, squealing and shouting. Andy declared himself judge and jury based on his supreme fashion expertise—coupled with his keen knowledge of what makes chicks look the hottest. He made them model for us so he could make a good decision, and after seeing about fifty different dresses and listening to Electra and Ava squabble over lace versus shimmer and how strapless beats a halter neck any day, I wanted some aspirin, too.

The winner was a shorty black baby-doll number with a pleated crepe skirt dropping down from a wide ribbon sash just under the bust…which tied in a big bow in the back. I knew instantly that Andy had put his stamp on this look long ago by secretly combing girlie glossies. I knew he had chosen this dress because he knew it was what *I* would have chosen. He winked at me as if to say, *See, I got your back*. Electra was satisfied by the leg exposure, though the threats went flying that at *her* wedding, we were goddamn wearing lavender and we were going to like it! Ava said she had really wanted something poufy and pastel, all Disney fairy tale but could admit that she did look awfully sultry in black. Lily doesn't dress up, ever, but she just shrugged and looked at me like fuck it 'cause I only have to wear it once.

"Now you," my mom said proudly as my friends went to work.

"You have to get something with little pearls," Electra informed me as the designer stood by with a fat glossy book cataloging pages and pages of bridal creations. "Pearls are classic. Elegant. Bridal."

Ava shook her head. "No, sparklies! You want to glitter from afar."

Andy placed a finger to his chin. "You look best with some cleavage. But not spilling out of there like some cheap whore."

I gave him a look. "So inappropriate sometimes, Andy."

Mom squinted. "A full skirt. Nothing too contemporary."

"Yeah, none of that slinky mermaid-looking shit," Lily agreed. She was perched on the back of a sofa behind Electra, playing with her hair. "That's just god-awful."

The designer took notes, and when we were finished hemming and hawing, she brought out three dresses for me to try on. Everybody waited in the salon and chatted and relaxed while the designer helped me in the dressing room. I never realized that putting on a wedding gown is such an ordeal. What is super-seriously fucked up is that apparently they only keep samples on-site in size four or smaller. Then they clip the thing to your bustier with clothespins so all your fat spills out in the back. Way to encourage a diet. Fuck it, I'll never give up beer.

I knew the first gown was it the second I put it on. My mom had already said no, I was *not* getting married in our church in a ruby-hued dress called Temptation. I settled for ecru—which is a fancy term for cream. I thought white would be just a little too much, all things considered.

The gown had a fitted satin bodice, strapless, covered in patterns of Swarovski crystals. They sparkled down onto the skirt like gentle starbursts. The skirt was full and it swished and whispered and there was a sash that wrapped around and tied in a big flat bow in the back. When I turned around to view myself in the mirror, I gasped. Me in a wedding dress! So this is why girls want to get married!

I walked out into the salon and stepped onto the pedestal. "Well?" I asked, since nobody said anything. I put my hands on my hips and frowned at them.

"That's Doll Moss right there," Andy said, relieved. "Without the bratty look on your face, I almost didn't recognize you!"

"You dog," I scolded. "So? Anybody else?"

"Stunning," Electra pronounced. And with that blessing, she sat back and looked out the window. Her work there was done.

"Me! I want one!" Ava cried.

"Enchanting, my beauty," Lily said with a nod.

My mom gave me that look that you get on graduation day and college-acceptance-letter day and your first period day and your first school dance day and all those days that a mother is proud to have a daughter. And I felt so lucky to have such a nice mother.

"The bridesmaids' dresses will be in next month, the bridal gown in January," the designer told us. "Is that enough time?"

"We have until March," my mom said, nodding.

We went to lunch at Prego and Andy regaled my mother with hilarious stories of his "dating" exploits that made her cover her mouth and blush and probably be glad that I had never fallen for him. And I couldn't stop thinking that I had a wedding dress. My very own wedding dress. My very own wedding dress that I was going to wear to become somebody's wife! A pretty princess wedding dress just like in all those pictures in those magazines that Karen had forced upon me, that I could look at and smile at when I was old and gray and remember how fun it was to be young.

It was one of the best afternoons of my life.

Chapter 14

I called Roman to tell him about my dress. He said, oh, no, you shouldn't have to call me, it's so expensive. We hung up and he called me back so he could pay for it.

I didn't think he sounded very excited. He rushed me through the whole description, then topped it off by saying that it was so girlie of me to think he'd want to know every detail about something I was wearing.

"What do you mean, that's so girlie of me?" I demanded, kind of offended!

He laughed a little. "It just is."

Okay, he dresses like the poster boy for Calvin Klein. And I wasn't talking about some random garment I'd gotten half price; I was talking about *my fucking wedding dress.* As in the one I was wearing to *our wedding?* And I kind of wanted to tell him that my other boyfriend probably *would* want to know!

"Well...whatever. Anyway, why do you sound so rushed?" I asked him. "Isn't it the middle of the night there? Like, weren't you sleeping?"

"Rushed? I'm not rushed. Sleeping, yes. I was sleeping. I'm

just here in my house here," he replied, talking fast and sounding pretty dumb.

"What does your house look like?" I asked, almost cutting my hand in an attempt to twist off a bottle cap. I'm such a moron. I needed a bottle opener.

"It's a bungalow." He sounded like he was getting out of bed and going into another room.

"What is the exact definition of a bungalow?" In my mind I pictured a straw hut.

"It's like a little square house."

"Oh. Neat. Do you sleep in a hammock?"

He laughed. "You are so adorable, Dalton, but no, I sleep on a mattress."

I heard night noises. "Are you outside?"

"Yes, I came out onto my patio to have a cigarette. So what else?" he yawned.

For a second I thought that he was acting very suspiciously. Almost like he'd had to make himself scarce with me on the phone because there was another woman there. But what other woman? Please. I'm just paranoid because of my own behavior. Just like how when you're a massive shit-talker, you think everyone else is always talking shit about you.

"What else what?" I asked.

"Any other news about our big day?"

"My mom spoke to your mother. She's putting together the east coast guest list to send to my mom in the next couple of weeks."

"Fantastic! Have you picked a wedding date?"

"March 15."

"To make up for my total lack of involvement, I'll take care of the honeymoon. Would you like to go to Martinique? Or I'll take you to Rio and you'll love it!"

"No, I mean, yes, I would like to go to Martinique, or Rio…but won't you have to go right back to work when you come home from Cameroon?"

"Not if I can help it. You probably won't even want to marry me when you see me again, I look so fucking worn-out from this job."

"What are you doing over there, building houses?" I asked.

"No, I'm sending other people out to do that. But occasionally I have to jump in and help."

I thought that conjured up a pretty sexy image. I pictured Roman all shirtless and sweaty with some hard hat and a hammer.

"Well, as long as I'm up I better call the house and make sure everything's going okay for those kids. You take care, baby."

"You, too."

When Roman's away he rents his house out to nerdy seniors at Georgetown because he knows they're there to study and won't trash the place. The house is nice. There are cute pictures of me everywhere. There are lots of books and fine art and it's very clean. It has a front porch with wicker furniture and navy cushions. We sit out there and drink iced tea or wine and talk for hours. Sometimes we hang out with his friends and I feel important and grown-up as they talk about advocacy and policy and politics. His friends all work for organizations or associations like Roman's or they have impressive government titles. Their girlfriends or wives are all lawyers or advocates or congressional aides. Everyone's pretty smart out there. Seems like an okay place.

"You're dreaming," Jeremy told me a while back. "That place sucks. That city has no soul. You will fucking *hate* it."

"What makes you say that?"

"You think people out here are phony? People out there are blank-faced pods. You think entertainment is a dirty business? Better plan on packing a shitload of soap for all the filth of politics. So L.A. people judge you by what you look like? Better plan on reading six newspapers a day in D.C. and even then they'll think you're stupid because you didn't go to William and Mary. And you say your car is a piece of shit, but just wait until you can't drive it anywhere because the traffic out there makes the 405 look like a deserted country road. And in the east, come January, boots don't have high heels, toots. Oh, boy. You are in for a *big* surprise."

Yeah, that kind of scared me.

I put my hands behind my head and stared up at the ceiling. The sun was filtering in through the slats of the blinds and making patterns across the desk and floor. There's another picture of Roman on the desk, but I'm in it instead of a fish. In the picture I am wearing a long-sleeved black shirt and lots of makeup. I think it's a nice picture of me.

I wonder all the time why Roman even wants a wife. He seems to have everything he needs.

Jeremy and I were engaged in a full-scale e-mail war for a week. He had replied to my scathing e-mail in an even more scalding tone that I was a *bitch* and that my juvenile antics were getting tiresome. I wrote back furiously, typing that if I was such a bitch he should just marry Pristina and then he wouldn't have to worry about it anymore. He wrote back that I was the one getting married so I shouldn't be worried about anything that had to do with him. He wrote back that I am *fucked* up and im-ma-tour.

It's at times like that when I understand Roman's reticence about sending e-mails. They can really come through just awful. Those stiff, digital words can seep with venom.

I decided to suck it up and sent him a card with a little blond girl on the front, counting to ten. The inside read, "You can come back now."

His reply was a message saying that he would like to talk to me. He said he would meet me at our favorite Starbucks in Venice. We hadn't been there in a long time, but how symbolic because we used to go there a lot when we first started hanging out. We would walk around wishing it was still the sixties so that we might see Jim Morrison writing poetry on the beach. Then we would go home and get high and watch *The Doors.*

I drove toward the beach wondering what he even saw in Pristina because she was so not like me it wasn't even funny. But once when I asked that he simply told me they had a lot in common. They met in kickboxing class. Jeremy was taking it because he felt fat and Pristina was taking it because she felt hostile. They both lived in the Valley at the time. They liked to go to indie films. They liked to eat seafood. They liked to ride roller coasters. They liked to drink coffee. The clincher? They both loved a good game of golf. Please. I've hardly seen the man move unless it's to grab the remote control.

The day was overcast and chilly. I love Venice. It's a dirty place full of crazy people but it always makes me feel right at home.

"You need to cool it with the attitude," he lectured me as we sat on our bench, slurping Frappuccinos and being serenaded by a man playing a guitar for money. He was pretty good—but neither of us gave him any money.

He ran a hand through his hair. I wanted to tell him it was greasy. I wanted to tell him to quit using Suave and start using Finesse.

"You have to stop ordering me around like you do," he told me.

"What? I do not order you around."

"Yes, you do. I have a girlfriend. I can't just be at your beck and call."

"You're really fucked up, you know that?"

"You're one to talk." He reached for my hand and inspected my engagement ring. "If you and Roman split up, you could sell this."

"I thought you said it looked fake."

"It does…but I know it's not. And what it actually looks like is a little handcuff."

I turned his hand over in my own. He was wearing some

cheap ring on what would be his marriage finger. This ring matched a smaller, more delicate version worn on the marriage finger of Pristina. These two, they were so in love once that they bought these his-and-hers rings from a jewelry stand at a farmer's market. They wanted to boast of their commitment to each other. Apparently, they still do.

I leaned forward, still holding his hand. We were facing each other, our legs folded. I looked into his eyes. "I'm going to kiss you right here and now."

He drew back. "Don't."

I did it anyway. I grabbed him by the shirtfront and just kissed him.

He put his other hand on my knee. I was wearing my favorite jeans. They are worn and thin from years of love and abuse, but being with these old jeans is like being with an old friend. They've been there for me in times of both celebration and distress. These jeans got me through college. Not entirely unlike Andy's homework and Dylan's open-door policy.

He squeezed my knee. "Doll…let's not fight, okay?"

"Okay."

He looked off in the distance. "I just don't want us to fight right now. If we fight too much it feels like we're wasting time."

I knew just what he meant. I nodded.

"So what do you want to do tonight?"

"Ava asked me if I wanted to go out for karaoke with her theater troupe."

"Okay. That's what we'll do, then."

I don't really like hanging out with Ava's theater troupe. They bother me. All the girls are very beautiful and thin. They all sit around comparing their headshots and talking about commercials they've been in or movies they've done. They all talk about getting agents and getting auditions and having their SAG cards. I think they don't like me because once I said that acting classes must be pointless because if Kevin Costner and Keanu Reeves had gotten so far then I wasn't so sure it was talent that the producers were after. I'm not in it for the money, their minds told me. I'm not in it for the fame. I'm an artist. I'm an *actor*. It's my *craft*.

Jeremy cracked me up singing "It's Gonna Be Me" by *NSYNC at the karaoke bar. I couldn't believe he even knew the words! Of course I had to top him by mimicking the vocal stylings of Britney Spears. Afterward, we went back to his place. He lives in West L.A. because he moved after he realized the Valley was unhip. His neighborhood is actually Palms but you can still get away with calling that West L.A.—as long as you don't elaborate. His apartment is a very small studio but I like it because it feels cozy when it's just the two of us, like we lock the world out. Never mind his classic *Star Wars* figurines and hordes of Miami Hurricanes memorabilia and his photographs of Pristina and the contents of his cupboards consisting entirely of Splenda and hot sauce from Taco Bell. These are the things that make him Jeremy.

In the morning we watched *Titanic*. It's kind of a tradition. We've probably spent more mornings aboard that big doomed ship than I could count mornings I've woken up next to Roman. It's funny how a guy who lives for gory B horror can admit to loving such a sappy film. It's endearing all the same. We laughed and tossed out shared favorite quotes as he got ready to go spend the day with Pristina. Some people would probably find it weird how he walked around in his towel, making coffee and quoting a romantic movie with me as I lolled in his bed and waited for him to kick me out so he could go to his girlfriend's house. But somehow it felt quite normal because it's just the way we are. It's just us. Without Pristina and Roman in the respective realms of our lives, we might be just a little different. We might be a little more caring, or a little less. We might make a future together. It's hard to say how it would have unfolded if they hadn't existed when we'd met. I like to think we would have been stellar.

But like this…it's just the way we are.

Chapter 15

"Your sister's coming home and I'm sending her to L.A. when she does," my mom told me when we were on the phone talking wedding a few days later. The yacht was being renovated, the invitations were at the designer's, and the flowers and food were next on the agenda.

"Why?" I asked.

"Because she has a three-day weekend. And she likes visiting her mother," she explained.

I let her comment slide. "What I meant was, why are you sending Maddy to L.A.?"

"Because she needs to talk to you," she replied, undaunted.

"About what?"

"This boy she's dating," my mom said casually. "She's been hinting about the seriousness of it. I sense she needs advice about...things."

"Are you sure you want her getting that from me?" I asked dubiously.

She laughed. "Be a good girl and talk to her. Maddy looks up to you, you know."

"But did she not receive the same valuable 'do and don't' instruction from Grandma Jane and Grandma Mary that I got?"

Grandma Jane said: Don't get pregnant and above all remember that when used properly, sex is a very powerful weapon.

Grandma Mary said: Kissing's okay—but only above the neck. No one's going to want to buy the cow when the milk is free.

"I'm talking about a real conversation about sex and what it means, Dalton. Especially that first time."

Yeah, but first time with who? I don't really want to tell her about my actual first time.

Besides, it's different with every person. The first time I did it with Roman, I wore sexy lingerie and we drank Dom Pérignon. He kissed every inch of me and worshiped me fully, like he was unwrapping a pretty package. The first time I did it with Jeremy, he screwed me hard and fast like a virgin boy with a prostitute. We were so wasted we fell off the bed.

I mulled over how I would put it to Maddy. I decided not to hype it up, so that maybe she'd want to stay a virgin forever. I don't ever want some beastly man to get his grimy paws on her. I want to keep her all pure and perfect always.

I was completely swamped at Charisma. My gala was going to be spectacular. I had reserved one of the ballrooms at the Biltmore in downtown L.A. I had booked the band to play holiday favorites, and a popular DJ for the dancing that would come later in the night. I had already started receiving some impressive donations for silent auction gifts—things like fancy dinners and spa days and even a trip for two to Maui. I sent the cash donations by courier to the charity itself. I was on the phone left and right with the Christmas for the Children assistant. We laughed about having to do all the work for our bosses, but really, we secretly liked it. At least I did.

Karen came in to talk about how nervous she was for her wedding. I didn't really think she was nervous. I think she was just sniffing around to see if I was. You can get along with a ladyboss as long as you make it known that you never think you're in her same league. You have to try to keep up, but you must never get even one step ahead.

She's going to be married by a rabbi in a traditional Hebrew ceremony even though she is not Jewish. I wonder if Jewish people worry about being sinners the way us Christians have to. Probably not. Us Christians have Jesus to contend with. And they say Jesus is just great but how could the guy be so great when they say only those who accept Him are getting into heaven? Doesn't that pretty much wipe out most of the world's population? What about the people in the Amazon who've never even seen the white man? What a crock. Maybe I'll become a Scientologist! Wouldn't Grandma Mary be pleased.

Karen folded her arms and glanced at the calendar, where the stick man had moved to October 31 and had a pumpkin head. "Are you doing anything special for Halloween?"

"Actually, I'm supposed to pick up Electra in twenty minutes," I replied, glancing at the clock. "We have to go shopping for our party. We have one every year."

Electra is, coincidentally, the assistant to Karen's bitch best friend Cynthia. She is a well-known talent agent over at ICM, and is apparently such a rampant nightmare in the workplace that only Electra can handle her. Don't think Electra doesn't feel superior over this fact. And don't think Karen and Cynthia don't think it's just delightful that their assistants also happen to be best friends. Really special is all I have to say.

"Well, that sounds fun," she told me. Then she placed her hand atop my head for a moment, and told me to leave early.

For our party we did our costumes to the theme of *The Wizard of Oz*. Ava was begging and she loves *The Wizard of Oz* so we finally gave in. I agreed to be Dorothy even though I've always thought Dorothy was a whiny dipshit. Of course Electra got to be the Wicked Witch of the West. Ava was actually in a high school production of the play. She also played Sandy in *Grease* when we were in college. Now *that* is what I call an achievement. If I were ever in *Grease* I would want to play Rizzo. If *Grease 2* were a play I would take up drama just to play Stephanie Zinone. I can't believe Michelle Pfeiffer doesn't count that role among her best performances.

The night of the party Jeremy called to say that he and Pristina had a major fight so it turned out he could come. He showed up bombed.

"Want some candy corn?" I asked.

He pushed the basket away. "Forget it. I just want booze."

We put *Halloween* on the TV with the sound muted so that we could play "Thriller" and other monster classics from a special CD I'd compiled. Everyone totally got into it, grooving in the living room.

"Do you think he's all right?" Ava asked, concerned, when Jeremy slumped in the corner and made hostile conversation with a bottle of Jack Daniel's.

I nodded. "He'll be fine. He's just bummed about Pristina."

"Shouldn't you console him?" she asked. She sipped cider and looked adorable in her Glinda the Good Witch costume. She had her platinum hair fixed in swirly curls with silver glitter strands woven in and she was wearing a sparkly white dress and a gauzy cape and carrying a wand with a silver star on the tip.

"Not when he's being so cranky. We'll just end up in a fight." I was wearing a blue jumper and a white shirt and little ruby slippers that Ava decorated for the occasion. She took plain pumps and glued red sequins on them for days. I wore lacy white ankle socks and a brown wig with two braids.

I felt a hand on my shoulder. I turned around to see Jeremy staring at me, eyes all red. "Let's go for a walk."

When we went outside, he took my hand. We walked up to Sunset. The cars were backed up for miles. There were people everywhere in costumes. The weirdos come out in full force on Halloween. I love this night.

"Pristina's really driving the marriage thing home. She's become obsessed about the idea of us getting engaged," he said, sounding glum.

If Pristina were hanging off the edge of a cliff, I would step on her fingers until she had to let go.

"She's driving me batty," he went on. "She just won't shut up about it!"

"Why don't you ask her, then?"

"I just don't think I'm ready," he told me.

"Hmm…you think?"

"Oh, shut up, Doll."

"I was simply making a point."

"No, you weren't. You were being snotty."

"Maybe I was. Maybe I'm sick of your stupid girlfriend."

"Maybe I get sick of your stupid fiancé."

"How could you? He's never here!"

"And that's just perfect for you, isn't it?"

"Go fuck yourself!"

He was very drunk. He let go of my hand and pulled me into his arms. "You talk really nasty, you know that? Didn't your mother ever wash your mouth out with soap?"

"Fuck no. Why would she? Saying *fuck* isn't a crime. It's just a word."

He tipped my chin up and kissed my nose. He started singing "Somewhere Over the Rainbow" at the top of his lungs.

"Stop it!" I screamed, twisting away. "I hate that song!"

He kept right on singing it.

"If you don't shut up I'm never speaking to you again!" I yelled.

He kept at it. Some girls dressed up like hookers walked by and laughed at us. Oh, wait, those *were* hookers.

I started running up the street. I could still hear him singing. He started to chase me. I screamed bloody murder, running along in my Dorothy costume, my little ruby slippers pitter-pattering on the pavement. Jeremy was dressed like Jason Voorhees. He was wearing a black jumpsuit and Doc Martens and a hockey mask. He was also wielding a huge machete.

I imagined that it looked pretty bad. I must have ran for half a mile, shrieking all the way, before a police car pulled over and the cops got out and stopped me.

"What's going on there, little lady? You okay?" they asked. I saw Jeremy duck down a side street. I knew the pussy was running back to the house. He would ask Electra for the money to bail me out of jail. Aw, forget it. He'd just leave me there and suggest that everybody go to IHOP.

"I'm fine," I said, catching my breath. "You're not going to arrest me, are you?"

"Do we really look like cops?" one of them asked.

I glanced at the police cruiser parked at the curb. "Well, yeah. Aren't you?"

They cracked up. "My brother's a policeman," the other one told me. "We rented these costumes and took the car while he was sleeping. Everyone keeps believing us. We even pulled someone over and gave them a ticket. Pretty good, huh?"

I frowned at them. "Are you fucking crazy? That's got to be seriously illegal!"

"Nah, it's Halloween. Anything goes."

I had them drive me back to the house and invited them to stay and drink. Electra pulled me aside and said had I lost it bringing cops to our party with Rose and Lionel's autumn harvest aflame and Suzanne brokering her babes to Luciano-Marciano and all of Ava's Mafioso cousins? I told her they weren't real cops and she relaxed.

Jeremy was outside smoking. When I went out there he laughed at me. He said he'd never seen someone run like that. He said I ran like I was really in a *Friday the 13th* movie. He said it would have been so funny if I'd tripped and fallen down.

"You're a shit," I told him. "You're just a shit. I can't think of anything else to call you."

"Have a smoke with me, Doll."

I lit a cigarette and watched Ava and Dylan through the windows. They were talking in the kitchen, looking very serious. Electra and Pretty Boy were fighting because he was supposed to come as the Tin Man but he didn't. Instead he came as Tarzan. She said that ruined the whole motif. I was starting to think this wasn't a very fun party.

"Do you know how much I love you?" Jeremy asked.

I rolled my eyes. "Don't say that. Don't. You don't love me. You're just drunk. Everyone loves everyone when they're drunk."

He sneered at me for a second. Then he laughed. "You're right. But you wonder deep down inside, don't you? If maybe I really mean it?"

"You're a son of a bitch. You don't love me at all. Like I said, it's the liquor talking."

"Maybe and maybe not. The point is, you'll wonder forever if I was serious tonight. And you'll never know."

Chapter 16

Mr. and Mrs. Arnold Moss
cordially invite you
To attend the marriage of their daughter
Dalton Jane
To
Roman Christopher Duquesne
On this the day of our Lord
Blah blah blah…

The invitations were white with shiny black writing and glittery lilies embossed on the front. The little wedding guide my mom keeps said we should send them out at the end of January.

Maddy brought a bunch of wedding samples I was supposed to choose from. Flowers and cakes and entrée options and shit like that. Electra made sure to remind me that there should be a special choice for her. As if I could forget. I think salmon with spinach or chicken with marsala wine sauce for the barbarians and, of course, cheese-and-portobello ravioli for the well-mannered sort. And a marzipan cake with glistening sugar frosting. And snapdragons and sweet peas and tea roses all over the place.

I took Maddy to Le Petit Four in the Sunset Plaza. We ordered a barbecued chicken pizza and a salad to share. She got an iced tea and I got a cocktail, and we sat outside eating and pretending we were on the Champs-Elysées as we watched the shiny cars go by. In all fairness to this bitch of a city, she does have a certain charm. And I suppose there are millions of people who would love to be able to say they live in L.A.—Hollywood to boot. I suppose also that during a lovely autumn afternoon so close to glamour and glitz, it's easy to have such thoughts.

I wasn't exactly sure how to start, so I just went with, "Mom seems to think you're desperate for a sex talk."

"I wouldn't say I'm *desperate*," she replied. "Honestly. I'm not some total idiot. I get straight A's and I happen to know plenty about sex already."

"So what exactly do you want to talk about?"

"I'll tell you, but I want you to be straight with me," she told me. "No more 'Maddy is too young to be hearing this shit.'"

"Maddy, did you just say *shit?*" I laughed.

"No, that's what you said," she informed me.

"When?"

"When I was twelve and I went to visit you at Chapman. Electra and Ava were talking about blow jobs and you said to them to shut up because 'Maddy is too young to be hearing this shit.'"

"Okay, so you're nineteen now and if you want to talk about blow jobs, we can."

She sat back to gaze at me keenly. My little sister looks a lot like I do, only her blue eyes have some brown in them. "I don't want to talk about blow jobs."

"Good. Neither do I. So what's the deal? I thought you were saving all this for marriage, anyway."

She shrugged. "Did you?"

"Uh, not exactly."

"I didn't think so."

I stirred my drink. "Don't you think Jesus might have a problem with you losing your virginity before marriage, though?"

"Jesus knows the world's a whole lot different now than it was when He walked the earth."

"But Reverend Nelson says that means we have to work that much harder to resist temptation," I reminded her.

She laughed. "Sis, are you putting me on? You never put any stock in what Reverend Nelson says."

"No, but I know you do. And I may tease you about it, Maddy, but I actually think your faith is a very special thing. And I don't want you to make a mistake because you're in love. Love does wacky things to a person's head. I know because I was in love when I lost my virginity. Of course, I was a lot more naive then than you are now."

She raised her eyebrows. "You, naive? Never."

"I'm all talk half the time," I told her. "Anyway. If you love this kid, that's great. But don't go hopping into bed with him just because it suddenly seems like a good idea. You have your beliefs and they are very important. I, unfortunately, never had them."

She frowned. "Why didn't you, though? We were taught all the same things."

I shrugged. "Mom says I'm rebellious. She says when other kids were putting snails in shoe boxes with twigs and leaves, I was pouring salt on them."

Maddy laughed. "That's gross, Doll. But I know what you're getting at. You don't like being told what to do. And Mom and Dad never really told us what to do, but we sure heard it a lot in Sunday school and fellowship. Church is really just a place that teaches life lessons. And the Bible really is just a big book full of stories we're supposed to learn from."

"Right. Some of them are good, though."

"You really think so?"

"Yes."

She looked pleased. And to be honest, I wasn't lying.

She sipped her iced tea. "Tell me about losing your virginity. How old were you, and who did you do it with?"

And so I told her. Her eyes were wide when I finished. She was quiet for a while. I hoped I hadn't tarnished Charlie's image in her eyes, because she adores Charlie.

"What happened to make Charlie get back together with Aurelia right after?" she finally asked. The waitress came by and I ordered a fresh cocktail and another iced tea for Maddy.

"Who knows," I said. I'd heard that Aurelia called Charlie that night and said she would just die if she couldn't have him back, so could he please go to the Sadie Hawkins with her just to try it?

I accepted my fresh cocktail from the waitress.

Maddy stirred a packet of Sweet 'n Low into her new iced tea. "Sis, okay, but are you saying if I sleep with Gabriel he's going to act like some total jerk afterward?"

"That's impossible to predict. I mean, I've slept with plenty of people who were perfectly kind afterward. I'm just saying, why do it? If you love him, and he loves you, then he can wait. Can't he?"

She went a little pink. "If you must know, I'm the one who brought this up between us. Gabriel's a real gentleman. He's soooo nice, Doll. He's premed like me and we both want to go to Tulane for med school. We talk about the future. We talk like we're going to get married—but not until I'm twenty-five. Like you."

I smiled.

"See, but I knew you would know to say exactly what I needed to hear," she said. "That's why I wanted to talk to you. And I know you think you're not a good Christian, but you are. Because you believe in me enough to believe in what I believe in."

I sipped my cocktail. "So you're not going to have sex, then?"

"Maybe so, maybe not. I'll have to put some more thought into it. Besides, you know what I hear? That after you do it with somebody you just start sleeping with anybody and everybody! I believe that. Some of the girls at my school are such who-ores! They do it with guys they don't even know."

I rolled my eyes. "Whores get paid, Maddy. College girls are just experimenting. And women the world over do it with guys they don't even know. Yes, it's true. Once you've been with one person it's not such a big deal to be with another one. And the next, et cetera. That's why you should hold on to your virginity. Sex is special with the right person, and when you've already been with loads of people before you're with that person, you sort of wish you'd saved it just for him."

She took my hand and examined my engagement ring. "But can't it be special with other people besides the right person, too?"

"Sometimes. Sometimes there's more than one right person. Like, of course sex is special with Roman. But it was special with Dan, too. Because at the time, he was the right person."

"Dan," she said. "I saw him yesterday. I told him you were getting married. He said he knew. Then he lit a cigarette and said, 'Maddy, don't you dare tell my wife you saw me do this.' Then he walked off with his shoulders all bunched up."

I touched my necklace as I watched two little girls in pink platform sneakers run up to a very thin blond woman dressed all in black, her arms laden with packages. She signed their little notepads and they ran off.

"Why did you and Dan break up?" Maddy asked.

"Because I was a seventeen-year-old dumb-ass."

"That doesn't tell me very much. What'd he do to you?"

"It was something I did to him, actually." I reached for my cigarettes. "So, is this kid someone I would like?"

"You'll get to see for yourself. I'm bringing him to Thanksgiving."

"How festive."

She looked all goofy and lovestruck. "Can I ask you something?"

"Have at it."

"How many people have you slept with?"

"I am *so* not telling you that."

"Aw, man," she said. She looked disappointed. "More than three?"

I gave her a look. "Come on, Maddy."

"More than *five?*"

"I told you already. I'm not going to go there."

"Please?"

"Forget it."

"Have you slept with Andy?"

"God, no," I said, horrified. "*Hell,* no."

The waitress took our plates away.

"Will you dance with me at your wedding, sis?" she asked. "To our song?"

"Of course." Our song is "Dedicated to the One I Love."

Maddy smiled at me. "I love you, Doll. You're the best big sister ever."

Even though I'm Maddy's only big sister, that was one of the nicest things I'd ever heard her say. I told her I loved her, too.

Ava decided to go for the lead in a play called *The Men in Me.* It's about a woman named Yvette and the obstacles she overcomes as a single mother to two little boys. I thought it was decent. I thought if Ava got the part I would invite Karen and Sal to come and see it because maybe Sal would like her enough to want to represent her after seeing her in action. I helped her go through her lines and crossed my fingers. No big surprise, but drama is really her forte.

When she rehearses she likes to dress up. Right then she was wearing her favorite costume—pink satin pajamas and matching mules with little marabou pom-poms on the toes. It's her way of pretending she is a pinup queen from the days when that's what sexy starlets were called. She rolls her hair in huge rollers and walks around the house in gaudy clothes and clouds of perfume saying darling this and darling that. Having Ava around is like having my own personal living Barbie. She is my childhood fantasy come true.

Electra came home from in-line skating with Troy. Her face was all rosy from working out. She flopped down in Ava's angel armchair. Ava's whole room is done in angels, which is pretty creepy. Of course Electra fears no good or evil.

"I've been thinking about how fun it will be when we both move east," she told me. "New York is just a hop, skip and jump from D.C. We'll be able to see each other a lot."

"So you're definitely going?" Ava asked, looking up from her script.

"When Josh proposes," Electra said confidently, getting up.

"Are you so sure he's going to?" Ava asked, raising one eyebrow.

"Of course. They all do eventually, unless they decide to break up instead. And would he ever be a fool to break up with me? The fuck!"

Ava shook her head as Electra flounced off to take a shower. "She amazes me."

"Me, too. But at least with her what you see is what you get."

"Yes, that's true." Ava let the script fall to the floor. "What am I going to do when you go to Washington and Electra goes to New York?"

I rescued the script and handed it to her. "You're going to stay here and make something of yourself. Then when you're a big star you can come visit whenever you want."

"You think?" she asked, her eyes wide.

I nodded. "I know. You're very talented, Ava."

"I am?"

I rolled my eyes. "Yes, but I shouldn't have to tell you. You've had some decent work. Now, let's run through those lines once more, shall we?"

She smiled at me. Then she kissed my cheek and got back to work.

Chapter 17

Things were kicking along quite nicely, I must say.

Then came that phone call.

"It's Jeremy!" Ava screamed from her bedroom as Electra and I did exfoliating face masks in her bathroom and traded *Glamour* and *Marie Claire* as we dried.

I crawled into Electra's room and picked up the phone. "Hello?"

"We broke up," he told me.

"What?" I asked. *"What?"*

"Pristina. And me. Broke up," he said slowly.

"Are you kidding me?" I asked, feeling a thousand things at once. Delight. Panic. Fear. Elation. Guilt. I felt like I'd waited to hear those words for so long. And now that he'd said them, well... Goddamn it is all I have to say. How fucked-up is life?

"No." He sounded really down. "It was pretty bad. Can I come over?"

"Of course."

Electra eyed me as I scurried back into the bathroom and began washing my face.

"Something major?" she asked.

"Kind of."

She yawned and returned to the glossy pages of *Glamour*. Jeremy looked terrible when he arrived. He was forlorn and downtrodden, and asked immediately and quite pathetically if he could go home with me for my parents' Thanksgiving. In fact he seemed more worried about the idea of not having anywhere to go for Thanksgiving than he did about losing Pristina. Electra has always said he is too needy. She says he can't stand to be alone—that's why he got himself a companion for when Pristina was busy. Boy, she can really make a person feel just great sometimes.

We sat in the living room and got high so he could mellow out. Ava wandered in, all tarted up in black leather like she was a dominatrix.

"What's going on?" she asked, hands on hips.

"Pristina broke up with him," I told her.

"How come?" Ava asked him.

"Because she was ready to get married and I wasn't."

Ava gave him a knowing look. "You just weren't ready to get married to *her*."

"Don't act like you know anything about it. Where's *your* marriage proposal?"

Ava stuck her nose in the air. "I can have any man in this town."

"And do!" he sneered. "Off to 'audition' at the Beverly Hills Hotel?" He was feeling bad and so that meant everyone else should. No one can be happy if Jeremy's not doing much better. But if you're upset and miserable about something, he just tells you to seek help.

"Fuck you. I'm going to pick up dinner from the Sunset Grill. If Dylan gets here before I get back, try not to act too stupid."

"Oh, great," Jeremy said, rolling his eyes as she flounced out of the house.

I gave him a long stare as he pouted. "Try not to be such a cock, okay?"

"What for? I hate that guy. He's obviously got some issues if he's with Deprava. I'd never be interested in someone so nuts. I don't care if she's hot. I seriously wouldn't fuck that lunatic with someone else's dick!"

"Well it's a good thing you have me, then."

He gave me a patronizing look. "Try to have some sympathy, Doll."

"If Roman dumped me you would laugh in my face about it!"

"That's not true."

"Yeah, right!"

He looked frustrated. In a way I felt bad for him, but what was I really supposed to say? I *knew* if the situation were in reverse he'd have little sympathy. He'd just say *I told you so.* Besides...it didn't help me at all for him to be single. Available. Out there. It only opened a door to make things just that much more complicated...if either of us chose to further complicate them.

Roman's the best thing that ever happened to me. He was like an unexpected, undeserved gift that just dropped into my lap. But Jeremy is important in his own way. Sometimes Roman is so over the top with his intellect and his career and the fact that he's from a whole other generation...and Jeremy may come across as an average guy and kind of a shithead, but at least he's someone who's a lot like me when you break it all down. It's like if I had to say which was the better friend, Ava or Electra. I could never say that. I love them both for what they give me.

But the fact is that Roman's the one who gave me the ring. He's always been mine. Jeremy's never been mine. And Roman has never made me play foolish games. I've always known he was The One...or The Right One at least.

I reminded myself that just because they had broken up,

nothing had changed. Jeremy was and always has been company. Roman is a communion of sorts.

I told myself that just because Jeremy can be as entertaining as a day at Disneyland…I sure the fuck wouldn't want to be at Disneyland forever.

I wish Roman were here, and not in Africa. I wish I were with him, away from it all. I should just get on a plane and go. Or make him come here. Or stop keeping Jeremy in my life and justifying it by acting like it's just routine, like he's just some friend of mine like I tell everybody. He's so much more. I can't deny it.

Electra came out of her room. She sat down on the opposite couch in nothing but a pair of skimpy purple lace pajamas. "What's going on?" she asked, lighting a cigarette.

"Jeremy and Pristina broke up," I told her. Jeremy moaned and covered his face with his hands.

She laughed delightedly "Really? How funny!"

"Damn!" he shouted. "Can't I get any fucking comfort over here? I thought you guys were my friends!"

"Uh, yeah," Electra said, rolling her eyes. "That's a good one."

"You're a real bitch, Electra."

"Yeah?" she asked, none too sorry. "Takes one to know one."

"I'm going in your room," he told me, getting up from the couch. "Do you have any good movies in there?"

"Yeah, *The Thing* and *Night of the Creeps*."

"Good." He made a face at Electra as he passed by her. "When you come in, can you bring me a white Russian?"

"Does it say *slave girl* on my forehead?"

He shook his head and sighed as if he had the weight of the world on his shoulders. "Never mind, then."

When he had closed the door, Electra put her hands behind her head and gave me a smug look. "So now what?"

"Now what what?"

"Well, now that he's single…"

I rolled my eyes. "It doesn't change anything on my end."

"That's good, Doll. Just making sure."

I took him his stupid white Russian, anyway. He was lying on my bed all slack and depressed as if he was dying.

I sat down with him. He looked awful.

He put his hand on my thigh, all drugged and subdued. "What would I do without you, Doll?"

"Maybe you'd still have your girlfriend."

He shook his head. "Don't flatter yourself. We didn't break up because of you."

"Well, that's good."

He set his drink on the nightstand and pulled me down with him. "I'm sorry," he said, mumbling it into my hair. "I'm being atrocious."

"But at least you realize it."

He rubbed my back. "Well, I'm kind of in a bad way right now."

I felt his arms go limp as he passed out. And then I moved away and went to the window to look at the cloudy moon. It was morning in Cameroon. Another bright, sunny day was dawning in Roman's world. How I envied him. His ease, his maturity, his dedication to his profession, and most of all, his devotion to me and me alone.

Karen took that whole next week before her wedding off from work. I was slammed. It was nice being in charge. I acted like I was the ladyboss. I ordered the lowly interns around and made them get me Frappuccinos from Starbucks and lunch from City Deli. I held up my hand when I was on the phone and they had someone on hold for me, which left them bouncing outside my door trying to decide how to handle the situation. I said things like, "That's not going to work for me" and "I needed that five minutes ago." I had a fucking blast.

"Dude, I walked in on Deprava puking her guts out in your bathroom earlier," Jeremy told me as we drove to the Beverly Hills Hotel for the wedding. He was driving me in my car. I was wearing the cutest little dress ever. It was lavender and short and it had a gauzy, iridescent little coat thing that went over it. Ava ordered it from the Victoria's Secret catalog a few years back. She had never even worn it. I had on new Via Spiga shoes to match. Via Spiga makes the cutest shoes.

"Your point?" I asked.

"Well, she could be *pregnant,*" he shuddered. "She's pale and she's always throwing up. My sister was like that when she got pregnant."

I rolled my eyes. "Come on. You don't know. She's pale because she doesn't go in the sun and she's always throwing up because she makes herself barf after she eats. You just don't know. Ava would tell me if she were pregnant."

I know this because Ava told me she was pregnant once before. It was right before graduation. I went with her to have the abortion. They made me wait for her in a bright waiting room with lots of good magazines and pamphlets about birth control and STDs. I read everything they had and then went across the street for a doughnut. While I ate it I watched the cars go by and remembered how when Lily and I were little, we always rode our bikes down to KD, the little doughnut house, and got custard-filled doughnuts with chocolate frosting and little cartons of chocolate milk. We would sit at one of the little tables and eat them and pretend we were grown-ups. We would talk about our pretend jobs and our pretend husbands and our pretend kids. We would say things like, "Do you know I had to reschedule my meeting for Tabitha's recital?" and "I was at the mall the other day and I couldn't even find a spot for the Mercedes in that piss-poor parking lot" and "Charlie has really been getting on my nerves. We're talking about divorce!"

When I went back to pick Ava up she said all she remembered was getting an injection and then waking up and feeling like someone had moved things around in there. She said she got juice and a cookie and free counseling about

Amanda Hill

being sexually responsible. The father was Ava's boyfriend, Jims. He was the hottest and most zany guy in school. A real hippie Phish-following Jerry Bear tattoo type. He and Ava dressed alike in tight satin shirts and hip-hugger pants. They looked like a rock star couple. They wrote poetry to each other and pondered their existence and their love through mind-expanding drugs. She wanted to have the baby but he said it wasn't safe because "they" might come and take it away. When we got home he got her high and they watched a documentary about animals in the Arctic. Jims moved to Montana right after we graduated because he was afraid "they" were coming to get him. He left without saying a word to Ava. She spent four days lying on her bed, staring at the ceiling and listening to Pink Floyd. When she snapped out of it she pretended nothing had happened and she never spoke of him again. No one knows where he is now. It is my personal belief that Angelo and Giannini took care of him the family way.

Jeremy almost crashed us and had to quickly swerve around another car. The driver drove right up beside us and gave him a dirty look. That is so lame. I hate it when other drivers do that. You're like, ooh! Scary!

"I still say that chick's way fucked up. And watching her puke her guts out was really sickening. I almost joined her just from having to see it."

I lit a cigarette and turned sideways to look at him. "Listen, puss. If you don't want to see that shit, then turn around and walk out the next time you walk in on it. And quit saying Ava's way fucked up. Give her a break. Her life has not been easy."

"Please. I'd love to be able to say my dad's a mob boss. That is seriously cool. Like, I would totally work it. I would tell *everybody.*"

I rolled my eyes. "That is so dumb. If you went around telling everybody your dad was a mob boss, you'd get his ass thrown in prison. Get it?"

He shrugged. "Hey, it all goes back to what I was saying. She's way fucked up. That chick needs therapy."

"Would you shut up already? Have some respect for other people's problems."

"This from a girl who's only happy when it rains."

"I hate rain."

"I meant like the song?"

I punched him on the shoulder. It got very quiet in the car.

"I'm so deranged," he finally said.

"You don't have to tell me that!"

"Pristina called me, by the way."

"Oh, really?"

"Yeah. But I was pretty cold to her on the phone. I'm not the one who ended it. She is. She can go fuck herself. I never want to see that bitch again."

"Roman called me. He's spending Thanksgiving on Kilimanjaro."

He looked over. "What?"

"He's going to Mount Kilimanjaro. He's taking a vacation to Kenya."

"What a guy."

A Jewish wedding was a lot like any other wedding I'd been to. Jeremy paid close attention to the ceremony. I must admit that Karen looked absolutely breathtaking. There were all kinds of important people there and lots of celebrities. Sal has some completely impressive clients and he knows a lot of celebrities who aren't clients. I'm not starstruck. As a matter of fact I am so over it. But it is pretty neat to be in the same room with people like John Travolta and Kelly Preston. She is gorgeous.

"This is an awesome scene. Thanks for bringing me," Jeremy said in a moment of kindness. The reception had started and we were dancing to a slow song. He hates dancing but I made him. The wedding photographer took our picture.

"You're welcome."

"Karen and Sal are cute. They're going to be a real power couple."

"Yes, they are. But I cringe when I think about that kind of lifestyle."

"You're a *little* snob, you know that?"

"I am not a little snob," I argued. "I'm just saying, different people want different things. I'm happy for Karen. I'm just saying I probably wouldn't want to see myself locked in the same future."

He pulled me very close. "Put things into perspective, Doll. It's not like he's tying her to a rock for sacrifice. Life is what you make of it, no matter where you are. And it appears that even drowning in this wretched pool of fame and fortune, she'll have a great life with him."

I had to laugh. "I suppose."

He sighed. "It's kind of weird being with you…without Pristina."

"You'll have a new girlfriend before I'm married. I'd put money on that."

"How much?"

"Five bucks?"

"Deal." The band was playing "Unforgettable" right on schedule. I knew this because of course I'd written the song chart. Jeremy looked at me for a long moment. "I really appreciate you letting me come for Thanksgiving."

I nodded. "It's no biggie. My mom loves having lots of people there. And you're not the only one—Electra and Ava have been spending Thanksgivings with us for years."

My mom likes to take in all my friends as if they're her own children. She says they are all like little lost souls. I guess there's some truth to that. My mom says she has such wonderful daughters that she feels she should give something back by nurturing other people's forsaken children. My mom is a very sweet lady.

"Your family is really great."

"I know it. I really lucked out."

"Yeah, you did."

Jeremy's parents decided to call it quits while he was in college and they went through a messy separation and divorce. His mother ended up marrying his father's best friend not long after it was final, and then his father got back at her by marrying Jeremy's little sister's cheerleading coach. His little sister ended up running away from home and coming back married and pregnant while she was still a teenager. She lives in Orlando now with a lazy husband and a bratty kid. Jeremy said the whole thing with their parents scarred her for life. He said it didn't affect him at all.

Chapter 18

Thanksgiving at my parents' house is a lavish affair. My mom gets up at 5:00 a.m. to put a gigantic turkey in the oven. She makes twenty pounds of mashed potatoes and gravy. She makes this delicious salad with tangerines and coconut and marshmallows. We have green bean casserole and sweet potato pie and hot rolls fresh from the oven. Her stuffing is the envy of every wife in the neighborhood and she never gives out the recipe no matter how much all the other wives beg.

Electra, Jeremy, Ava and Andy made the drive home with me. Ava played DJ and tortured Jeremy with her musical selections. She played some real classics like "Ice Ice Baby" and "Every Rose Has Its Thorn" and "I Will Survive." I thought by the time we got to Ventura he was going to kill her.

"Want to come in for a drink?" I asked Andy as we got our stuff out of the trunk.

"Nah. I'm supposed to go to Happy Hour with Charlie and Pete and if I start drinking at your house I'll never make it."

I watched him cut across the Sampsons' lawn and unlatch their side gate. Andy can get to his parents' backyard by walking right through the Sampsons' backyard and then climbing over the fence. Apparently this is easier than walking around the corner on the sidewalk, and Mrs. Sampson usually gives him a brownie.

My dad shook Jeremy's hand and whisked him off to talk man stuff and drink beer as soon as we walked in the front door. I knew Jeremy would impress my dad with his knowledge of college football and cars. Roman and my dad smoke cigars while they talk about war and politics. They drink brandy while they trade stories about living in Africa. They play poker and compare visits to Russia and how different it was when my father was there studying during the Cold War and Roman was there sightseeing after the fall of the Iron Curtain. They'll speak in another language to throw us all off but I really know they're just talking about Louis XVI and Czar Nicholas II and George Washington as if they knew them personally.

"Everything okay?" I asked, when I went to check on them.

"Fine, fine," my dad said jovially. Jeremy nodded and waved me along.

It was weird to see Jeremy with my dad. I stood in the doorway and watched them for a few minutes. I had explained bringing Jeremy by saying he was this guy I was friends with in L.A., and he had no family on the west coast. My parents bought that without a blink because that's charity. It's what they don't know that makes me feel like a worm: that my charity wouldn't exist if Roman were in town.

My mother and my friends and I congregated in the kitchen and ate lemon squares and talked wedding. I showed my friends the photographs of the flowers and cake I'd chosen. My mom said Reverend Nelson was looking forward to getting to know Roman better, having only met him cordially a few times before, but I knew Reverend Nelson was secretly disappointed about Roman being Catholic. I guess because Catholics can sin all they want and be absolved through confession just like that. Reverend Nelson baptized me when I was a baby. My mom says I hardly cried when he sprinkled water on my forehead. I asked her if it sizzled. She shook her head and pinched my cheek.

Maddy and Gabriel arrived and were accosted at once by Electra and Ava, who wanted to play with them and fawn over them and seemed to view them more as Wholesome Barbie and Ken than Maddy and Gabriel. Gabriel was nice but nerdy. Way nerdy.

"Isn't your sister's boyfriend adorable?" my mother asked, bringing cups of hot chocolate overflowing with marshmallows into the living room on a tray.

"Uh, yeah," I said, sitting on the arm of a couch. I watched Electra, herself having never known what it's like to have a sibling, giggle at and pet and cuddle Maddy.

"Gabriel's *adorable!*" Ava echoed, making the poor kid blush.

"Uh, how 'bout a movie?" I suggested. The idea was met with winning approval, especially from Maddy and Gabriel.

Jeremy was supposed to sleep on one of the couches in the bonus room, where there is an entertainment system with a big flat-screen TV and a pool table and a foosball table. The pictures in there are all of inanimate objects and sports legends. There is a bar with a neon sign over it that reads Mos Eisley Cantina and a round green clock where the numbers are balls and the hands are pool cues.

Instead, he waited until everyone was asleep and then came into my bedroom. I was lying awake, remembering the day I'd picked out my daisy wallpaper. We had sex in the dark. I felt naughty like I was still a teenager. I spanked him and we giggled about it.

The house was overrun with family the next day. My dad's brother, Uncle Stuart, came with his wife, Aunt Sarah. Their son, Cousin Andrew, came with *his* wife Sarah. They brought their tyrannical youngsters, Andrew Jr., Camden and Jolie, who stole off with pudding cups and took over the TV in my room. Grandpa Dover and Grandpa Tom took over the living room TV, where they watched the fishing channel and reminisced about all their great catches. Grandpa Dover and Grandpa Tom don't interfere in anybody's lives the way their wives do. They just come for the food.

My grandmothers drove my mother crazy trying to help in the kitchen. They were hovering around when I went in there to get beers for my friends from the fridge. My friends had escaped to the bonus room, where they were watching *Terminator 2* and talking about how they were possibly going to eat themselves *to death*.

"What a fine idea to have the wedding reception on Kitty Lovejoy's yacht," Grandma Jane told me, with approval.

"You should have agreed to have the reception in the church rec hall," Grandma Mary scolded me. "Reverend Nelson was very disappointed."

Why did the words *oh fuck that old sleaze* suddenly come to mind? Reverend Nelson was always disappointed! It was part of his job!

"Reverend Nelson ought to mind his own affairs and then maybe that wife of his wouldn't be such a trollop" was Grandma Jane's comment. "You know Shirley Kemper saw her at the Bombay with that new math teacher over at St. Bonaventure?"

"For the love of God, Jane. What things to imply about our good pastor and Libby Nelson!"

I couldn't help it. A giggle escaped my lips.

Grandma Jane winked at me. Grandma Mary sighed wearily.

I opened the beers and gave my mother a special look. She gave one back that said, please be patient with her, she's old and she's going to die soon. My mom says you have to respect your elders because they don't live as long as you think they will. She's been telling me that about Grandma Mary since I was five. Okay, twenty years later!

"How 'bout one of those brews for your old grand-mamma?" Grandma Jane asked as she opened a bag of shredded cheese for the green bean casserole. For Thanksgiving she had gone all out in a sassy black pantsuit and a zebra scarf. Grandma Mary was wearing sea-green polyester pants and a matching angora sweater. Grandma Jane wore diamonds. Grandma Mary wore pearls.

I handed her the beer and escaped.

The next day my dad and Jeremy watched football all day and us girls went shopping at the Paseo Nuevo in Santa Barbara. My mom bought me so many cute things that I could barely fit them all in the trunk when we went home. Because she had hostessed such a nice Thanksgiving for us all, I bought her a new Coach bag while she was paying for three new pairs of shoes for me at Nordstrom. She was so touched that she almost cried right there in the store.

Saturday night we went to a bonfire on the beach. Charlie brought Daisy and when she saw me she jumped into my arms so we both fell down in the sand, cracking up. When I saw her I remembered all the good memories we shared and how much fun it had always been to be her friend. She had the most killer parties and we were always getting let off because her father was the mayor. She looked like she'd just walked off the set of *Blue Crush*. She smelled like her same old mixture of sea and sunshine and some incense like sandalwood. When we were little we always had joint birthday parties because our birthdays are only two days apart in June. And at her house in the Ventura Keys, the Kiplingers have their own boat dock where we liked to sit out at night and watch seals and the sunset while feasting on In-N-Out.

We yelled at each other for not talking more and caught up a little bit. She told me she'd had to come home from Panama because her girlfriend had run off with all her money. She's been bisexual since we were kids.

She had some great weed that we smoked with Jeremy and Charlie. When we moved away to talk by ourselves I knew they were going to talk about me.

"So let me get this straight. Charlie's band is playing your wedding reception?" she said to me.

I nodded. "Well, they really go off. We heard them last night at Kieran Kemper's warehouse. Huge crowd. Charlie says they have a big following."

"Yeah, I've got one of their CDs somewhere," she said. She lit a cigarette and so did I. The night was salty and cold. "Fully rocks. Only, with Charlie headlining your wedding reception, why do I picture you grabbing the microphone for a little serenade and him not stopping you?"

I laughed. I know this will happen. I will sing "Take Me Home" just like Sophie Ellis-Bextor.

"I got my dress, by the way. Lily brought it over to my parents' house."

"Are you home for good now?" I asked.

She shrugged. "Maybe. Life on the run isn't all it's cracked up to be."

I kissed her cheek. Some things never change, and you wouldn't want them to.

"So who's this guy you have with you?" she asked, looking over my shoulder at Jeremy.

"A friend," I replied.

"Do you do him?"

"Sometimes."

She didn't seem concerned. "Oh. Well, too bad your main man isn't here. I'd like to meet him."

"Oh, you will. He'll be back in a few months."

"I had a great weekend," Jeremy told me as we drove home on Sunday afternoon. "Really a good time."

I looked at the back seat in the rearview mirror, where Ava, Andy and Electra were sacked out and curled up together like kittens. "I'm glad you did."

"I really like your friends. Especially Charlie. His music is fierce. He's cool."

"Yeah…he's all right. What did you guys talk about?"

"You, mostly."

I rolled my eyes. "How predictable."

He lit a cigarette and passed it to me. "Ventura's a nice place. How come you didn't move back after college?"

"Same reason you told me you left Miami. I couldn't move forward there. You understand. You wanted to get away, too."

He lit a cigarette for himself. "Yeah, true. I did. But you know something? I'm learning that you shouldn't always try to get away. Sometimes you should just stop and realize that you're fine just where you are."

"That's some good advice."

He changed the CD from No Doubt to Evanescence. "That's some sarcasm."

"Yeah, it is," I said. "And it actually brings to mind a question I've been wanting to ask you."

"Please do."

"Did you ever feel guilty when you were away from Pristina, being with me?"

"Yeah, sometimes."

"How did you deal with it?"

"I told myself fidelity has a loose definition," he replied, examining his unshaven face in the vanity mirror. "You feeling guilty over there, toots?"

"Maybe."

"Why?"

"I don't know," I said. "Maybe because fidelity, to my knowledge, has a fixed definition."

"Either way, I see it as a personal choice—not a fucking law. Just what is your 'fixed' definition of *fidelity,* anyway? And where was it last week?"

"I guess when two people decide they'll only be with each other." I didn't answer the second part of his question.

"Or when a man gives a woman an expensive piece of jewelry and she then feels obligated to feel guilty for being with another man, right?"

He didn't wait for me to answer. "Do me a favor, Doll. Drop me off at my apartment when we get to L.A. Then don't call me anymore."

"You're not serious."

"Like hell I'm not. I made it clear to you time and again that you and Pristina had nothing to do with each other, and that was the God's honest truth. So don't go putting your Roman doubts on *me*."

"That's right, bow out."

He turned up the music and we didn't speak the rest of the way. When I screeched to a halt in front of his apartment complex, he got out and slammed the door.

"What's his problem?" Electra asked, coming to.

"He's mad because I told him I felt guilty," I replied, peeling out onto the street.

"He'd be fighting mad if he knew he was going to miss out on dinner at El Compadre. Can I call and tell him?"

"Oh, are we going to El Compadre?" Andy asked, instantly alert. "Fabulous!"

When we got home there was a package waiting for me from Roman. After everybody had gone to bed I went out onto the front porch and opened it. Inside was a letter and a beautiful necklace. Roman said he was dreaming of our wedding and the day we would be together again every moment that he was asleep. He said he lived to sleep because these were the sweetest dreams he had ever imagined. The necklace was silver with a charm on it that I couldn't figure out.

I looked up into the hills and watched the lights glitter and wink at me like we shared a secret. And I fingered the dagger on the chain around my neck and thought that it was sad that my own fiancé didn't even know me well enough to notice that I always wore the same necklace and hadn't taken it off the whole time we'd known each other. And even sadder was the fact that he'd never even asked me about it.

I put my face in my hand and cried. I guess I never realized a person could have just about everything and still feel like they have to search for more. Just like I never realized it was possible to fill your life with people and still be so lonely sometimes.

Chapter 19

"I think it's nice that you keep sending me presents," I told Roman, via cell phone. I was having my acrylics filled and getting a pedicure at Very Pretty Lady a few days after the Thanksgiving weekend. "But it makes me wonder, Roman."

"How?"

"I feel like you're just sending them to make up for your absence."

"You didn't like the necklace?"

"No, Roman, I liked the necklace," I replied. "But what I'm saying is, the meaning isn't there. Haven't you ever noticed I always wear one necklace, the same necklace? I've never taken it off, not even in the shower."

"You mean the knife necklace?"

"Yes, that's it," I said, relieved. So he *had* noticed.

"Okay, Dalton. I'll tell you a story. Bill and I played hooky a couple of weeks ago and got totally wasted. We're sitting in this bar and he starts telling me about how Angela's been bitching right and left about him being gone for so long on this project. So this guy sitting at the next table breaks in and tells Bill he should send Angela some jewelry. Turns out he's a traveling jewelry salesman. Opens up a big case of stuff right there. Bill picks out this necklace for Angela and tells me I should get one for you, too."

I pointed to a bottle of bloodred polish when asked to pick a color for my toes. Bill is Roman's best friend. Angela is Bill's wife.

"I said, no, not necessary, Dalton always wears her *athame*. And Bill says, what the fuck's an *athame?* I explained then that it's the magic knife a witch carries, a symbol for the element of air. The jewelry salesman asked who Dalton was and I told him you were my fiancée. He goes, you're marrying a *witch?* So Bill starts singing 'Witchy Woman' until we're dying laughing. Long story short, I got to thinking about Angela being on the warpath. I thought, what if she calls Dalton to brag about Bill sending her this necklace and then I get a call from Dalton wondering why I'm not sending her jewelry? Like I said, we were totally wasted."

"I'm impressed that you know what an *athame* is," I said. "Even though that is one seriously ridiculous story."

"You're telling me. So listen, I don't care if you don't wear the necklace. I sent it to you as a means of you being part of my shenanigans here—so one day the four of us can sit down and laugh about me and Bill getting drunk in Cameroon and being accosted by some traveling jewelry salesman. I *like* your knife necklace."

"It was a present from Dan," I told him. "But that's not why I wear it."

"I think you wear it because it's a symbol of your desire to cut through the bullshit. And if you *were* wearing it because it was a present from Dan, I wouldn't think that was weird. I wouldn't even think it was weird if you told me you really were a witch. I'll be Darren Stevens to your Samantha any day."

I moved my hand as Sunni nearly cut a finger off with one of her manicure tools. "You're so corny, Roman."

He laughed. "I know. But hey—at least I can admit it."

"I'm glad you're getting out instead of just slaving away all the time," I told him.

"Me, too. I don't recommend going to Mount Kilimanjaro in November, though. It rained the whole time we were there. I'll make sure the weather's on before you and I climb it."

"We're going to climb Mount Kilimanjaro?"

"Hell, yeah, we are. Then we're going to take a picture up top and send it to your parents, and make them put it on the wall right beside the one they took up there in the seventies. Oops—Landon's on the other line. Better grab that. I love you."

"I love you, too."

I slid my phone back into my purse. "I'm going to climb a mountain," I told Sunni.

She shook her head. "Why you worry so much? Life difficult enough."

Jeremy waited a grand total of thirteen days before coming back to me. He showed up at The Well on the ruse that he was making an appearance for Ava's birthday party. He even brought a present—an arrangement of pasta bundles to match the vegetables on their labels.

"You're not as bad as you want to be, *fessacchione*," she told him, kissing his neck. Never mind that her endearment translated to *fucking idiot*. In Ava's breathy voice, all Italian sounds like *amore*.

"Let's exchange words," he suggested to me, after fighting his way through a mass of streamers and balloons.

"Want me to provide escort?" Dylan asked, looming between us. He'd shaved his head completely and resembled Mr. Clean in a rugby shirt.

"Not necessary," I replied. I took Jeremy's arm. "Come on. Let's smoke."

We went outside. He pulled out two cigarettes and handed one to me.

"I respect that you're putting some thought into your marriage," he said, shifting from one foot to the other. It was cold outside, California December.

I nodded thoughtfully.

He ran a hand over his hair. "I think we have a lot of fun together, though…that we have something special. In the universe that's ours and ours alone. However, it does lack a certain quality when we're not speaking."

"I feel the same way," I admitted.

He pulled me into his arms.

We went back into the bar. The party was raging. Everyone was having fun. Roman was having fun in Cameroon, too. He was getting drunk with *his* friends, sharing confidences with the people who were right there. It didn't mean he wasn't thinking about me.

"You think about Josh on nights like this?" I asked Electra later.

"Sugar, I think about Josh every night," she told me. Then she waltzed off with Pretty Boy and I had to laugh.

Having Jeremy around so much was nice. He was practically living with us. We would take long drives along PCH or up and down the Sunset Strip, listening to good soundtracks. We would go to Book Soup and browse the shelves for hours, and then walk over to Red Rock to sit on the patio and drink pints. We went to Malibu some nights and shared our thoughts with each other and the ocean. We appreciated each other and L.A.

I thought maybe we shouldn't be making so many good memories. I might start wanting to make them all the time.

And I knew he was driving Electra crazy. Like when we bought *Halloween III* on DVD and watched it three times in one weekend.

"This is getting ridiculous!" Electra shouted when she and Troy returned from hiking and found us lounging in the living room, stoned and zoned out in front of the TV.

"This movie is so stupid. It doesn't even have anything to do with the other *Halloween*s. Michael Myers isn't even in it. And don't you losers ever do anything else but get loaded and watch dumb movies? You're like Mr. and Mrs. Unfuckingproductive!"

It was just how I pictured our life together. Entertaining and without purpose.

"You gotta love Tom Atkins," Jeremy said. He pushed Play to start the movie again. "Sit down and watch. Oh—but make us some popcorn first, huh?"

"What I'm about to do is direct my own version of *The Slumber Party Massacre* with you as the first victim," she replied. "Are you ever planning on going back to your apartment?"

"Yeah, maybe."

He said no fucking way was he going to some chick play, though, so I lost him on the opening night of *The Men in Me*. Ava was great. When it was over she got a standing ovation. Her face glowed and glittered and she looked incredibly beautiful. I felt inexplicably sad watching her up there. I really hoped that one day she'd make it. I'd like to see everybody's dreams come true and not just mine.

"She's good," Sal said when I met up with him and Karen after the play. "Have her send over some headshots and a résumé."

My work there was done. I took off then even though everyone else was going to go party. I didn't feel like seeing anybody but Andy so I asked if he would come over. He did and we talked about life and our friends and everything we had ever done and all the things we didn't know or understand. It was like what we used to do in high school and college, and other girls would get jealous of me and wish that they could have that part of Andy's life, too.

Ava came into my room the next morning as I was panicking over the balance of my checking account. At least the good payday comes toward the end of the month. It's the good payday because it's the one where I don't have to pay rent from it. Our rent is twenty-two hundred a month. Split three ways that is still seven hundred and thirty-three dollars. Electra chips in the extra dollar out of the goodness of her heart.

"I got you a Diet Pepsi," she said, handing it to me.

"Thanks," I said. "What's up?"

She sat down on the bed. She looked like she'd been crying.

"What's up?" I repeated.

"I'm just really strung out on Dylan." She bit her lip, then continued, "Electra was right. It's just not the same now. He pulls away and I want him closer. That makes him not want to be close, so he pulls further away. I feel like I'm not his star anymore. He didn't even come to my opening night! I just don't understand how someone who's the most important thing in your life sometimes views you as one of the least important things in theirs."

I nodded. Yeah, I could understand that.

She huffed out a breath that made her bangs flutter over her forehead, like butterfly wings. "I know it's going to sound so fucking pathetic, what I'm about to say...but I'm still going to say it. I love him, Doll. I love him so much. I love him more than anything!"

"More than your lavender suede Arturo Chiang mules?"

She laughed a little. "I don't want to lose him, Doll."

"He's still hanging around," I pointed out. "He organized your birthday party."

"Yeah, but we argue. I tell him these things about loving him the way I do, and he laughs at me! *Bastardo*. He says I'm full of shit and that he knows I just used him to get over Tim," she sighed. "And in a way...I did. But it changed after that. I realized that Dylan, he's been there the whole time. He's always come around and made sure I was okay, whether it was after a guy or something with the family or, I don't know, losing a part I really wanted. I just realized, Dylan has never said, 'Oh, *bella,* you're so fucked up, I can't deal.' He's always just said, 'Oh, *bella,* I love you. I love you no matter what.' And that is so important."

"It really is," I had to agree.

She went on. "If I lose Dylan, I know it'll be just like when Jims left. I know I won't live through that a second time."

"You said Jims," I said, shocked.

She shrugged. "I can say Jims. Just like I can say other things. I just choose not to."

"I have always suspected this." I thought about what to say to her because this was Ava being serious and I wanted to be serious, too. "Look, Ava. Dylan's no prince. But if you think he's the man for you, I don't think it's pathetic that you're sitting there saying you love him and don't want to lose him. As a matter of fact, I think he loves you, too. I *know* he loves you, too. He just doesn't know how to deal with it."

"You think?"

"I've known Dylan as long as you have," I reminded her. "His fuck-all act is exactly that. He's seriously lame if he thinks we aren't onto his methods."

"Don't you be calling him *lame,*" she warned. "Because you and he, you're actually a lot alike."

What a compliment.

She got up and went into the bathroom. I heard her sniffling and griping.

While she was gone I did a Christmas budget. As a holiday I think Christmas is too commercialized and I know for a fact that the dates are all wrong when you try to celebrate it in a religious sense, anyway. I learned that in a religion class in college. I would rather believe scholars than zealots.

All the same, I love spending money on people at Christmastime. I love to see their faces when they open up something they've really been wanting. I was going to get Roman this globe he'd been eyeing for months before he left. It lights up on the inside and the mountain ranges are ridges so when you touch it you can feel them.

Ava came back into the room and resumed her position on my bed. "So what should I do?"

I set my Christmas budget aside. "Well, what can you do, really? If you've told him you love him, and he's laughing about it, I think you can keep right on telling him and he'll keep right on laughing. I know. What Dylan really needs is for someone to set him straight about you. Maybe you should have one of your cousins whack him."

"Oh, enough with *The Sopranos* jokes," she said, glaring at me with dark, sparkling eyes. "I'm being fully serious. I know. *You* set him straight about me. He listens to you. He respects your opinion."

"Aw, forget it."

"Why not? Don't you want me to be happy?"

"More than anything, Ava, but come on. You want me to go to Dylan and say he needs to go legit? I'll just open myself up to a whole round of criticism if I do that."

"Please." She got off the bed and walked toward the door. Before walking out she paused and turned around. "That's fine, then. You just sit there and be a bitch to me when my whole life's happiness is hanging in the balance. I really appreciate it."

"Come now."

"You don't even care! Now my love, my one and only love may leave me and I may never be famous and I may never have anything but what I have right now, which feels like nothing most of the time. I may never find *it*. And I am stuck here until I find it, unlike you, who has already found it and still wants more! It drives me fucking crazy!" she shrieked. "You!" she shrieked again. "You have the nicest, most *normal* family I've ever met. You're spoiled fucking rotten. You have a kind, wonderful fiancé who's going to marry you and save you from everything that you think people end up hating about their lives. And to top it all off, you have a man around to keep you company while he's gone! And you don't have a conscience so it's not like you even have to feel guilty!"

I glared at her. "I do, too, have a conscience! And just 'cause I don't talk about how guilty I feel all the time doesn't mean that I never do. But the fact is that I was hanging out with Jeremy long before Roman decided to propose and make it something serious. And besides…Roman's not here and Jeremy is. What am I supposed to do, tell him to get lost? It's not that simple. He's a friend of mine, in case you don't remember that."

She shook her head. "I don't care," she said stubbornly. Then she ran out of the room and a few seconds later I heard the front door slam.

Electra came in, looking all refreshed and healthy. Pretty Boy came right in with her, looking the same. Mr. and Mrs. We Love Our Beautiful Bodies had been out on an invigorating morning bike ride.

"Ava just ran down the street cursing your existence in Italian, Doll. What did you do to her?" she asked accusingly.

"Yeah, Doll, she looked all strung out," Pretty Boy observed.

"I did nothing," I said. "She just went off on me."

"Well, since Ava only goes off when she really has something to say, did you at least learn anything?" Electra asked. She folded her arms in wait and her pretty boy did the same.

"Sure," I said, cowering under the pressure. "Sure I learned something."

"Well, what was it?" Pretty Boy demanded.

It was that I really don't have it that bad. But I've never really thought that I do. I just get confused sometimes because nobody knows how it's supposed to be…including those of us who maybe have it made. Should you be happy with what you've got? Should you hope for more? What would make you happy? What is making you sad? Should you accept your fate? What is your fate? Do you even have a fate? Everybody has these thoughts…don't they?

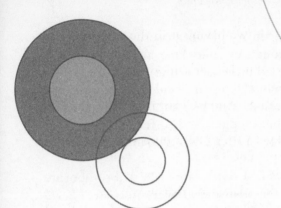

Chapter 20

"Hey, Roman?"

"Yeah, baby?"

"Do you think I'm like, totally selfish and inconsiderate and won't help people?"

"Uh, no, Dalton. Not at all. What's wrong?"

"I had a fight with Ava. Seems Beauty and the Bastard are having some problems."

"And what, you're supposed to transform the Bastard into a prince?"

"Something like that."

"Well, good luck to you. I'd like to see Ava with a man who knows her worth. I think Dylan could be that man."

"Yes, but therein lies the problem."

It was late at night and we were talking on the phone. It was daytime in Cameroon. He said he had one of the pictures I had sent him in a frame right on his desk.

"How's our wedding coming along?" he asked.

"Great. I am planning the most beautiful wedding ever."

"It sounds like it. Are we having it in the daytime or at night?"

"The ceremony is in the late afternoon. Then the reception goes right into sunset."

"Beautiful! I'm sending you a Christmas package, so be on the lookout for it."

"I will. You won't get your present until you get back."

"That's right. My present is you."

"You're sweet."

"You're the sugar that makes me that way."

When we hung up I went out of my room and got a bowl of canned peaches from the kitchen. Ava was sitting in the living room, mowing down a huge bowl of spaghetti and furiously glaring at the TV.

"Okay," I told her. "I'll say something."

She jumped up and threw her arms around me. "You're the best!"

Jeremy came over and brought *Dawn of the Dead* and we watched it in my room with candles burning. He told me about a book he had read that he thought I would like. Something about witches. I did not absorb one word he said.

He told me he was still angry with Pristina for breaking up with him. He said one of his friends had seen her and she told him to tell him that she thought he was a dickless bore. Wow! I had to respect that tyrannical bitch just a little for spouting such a slanderous comment.

"Do you think I'm a dickless bore?" he asked worriedly. Every now and then Jeremy gets very insecure. He lets me see that side of himself for about twenty minutes and then turns into that strangely appealing porcupine once more. I don't know which part I like more. Maybe what I like is knowing that underneath that prickly creature, there is something soft.

"No," I replied.

"Is Roman a bore?"

"Roman? No. Roman's challenging and exciting and

smart and worldly. He's impulsive and spontaneous. He's definitely not a bore."

"When did you know you wanted to marry him?"

"Well, I never really sat around wanting to get married," I told him. "So I wasn't just like, oh, I totally want to marry this guy. But I knew he was special from the beginning. I knew I wanted to stay with him, get to know him. He was funny. He was upbeat. He didn't make a huge deal over every little thing—but he did remember the important things. He treated me like an adult. I liked how he didn't notice my flaws. Or didn't seem bothered by them. Something like that."

"Maybe what you considered your flaws were actually assets to him," he told me. "Sometimes it works out like that even though you'd never suspect it."

"My…are you feeling deep."

He looked at me with inquisitive eyes. "Does Roman see a different side of you than I do?"

I nodded. "Kind of. He sees this one…but not the way you see it. It's not like I put on some false face for him, or for you. It's just…different. It's hard to explain. You wouldn't like my Roman side, anyway."

"And why is that?"

"Because you've gotten too used to this one. If I started acting with you the way I do with him, you'd think I was being fake. Phony. Weird. I don't know. I can't settle on the word. You just know the real me, Jeremy. But so does he," I said thoughtfully. Man, I really am twisted. I don't even make any fucking sense to myself!

"I get what you're saying," he told me. "I was different with Pristina."

"Right. Exactly. I know you were. Because that was you being *her* Jeremy. Like when I'm with Roman, I'm being *his* Doll. I'm not even Doll to him actually. I'm Dalton. Of course you get what I'm saying."

"I always do. But you love him."

"Yes. I do."

"Then why be with me?"

"Because there's just something about you I can't seem to find anywhere else," I said with defeated clarity that surprised even myself. "But even so…we are just friends, aren't we?"

"I wouldn't say we're *just* friends, Doll."

I laughed lightly. "Oh, of course. Now that you're single. Because now you have a lot of room, don't you? And I think you wish I would leave Roman because you feel all alone without a respective partner. So I leave Roman. And a few months from now you meet someone new and you say, sorry, toots, but I'm in love. Get lost. We were always just friends, anyway."

"That's not true. And that's not what this is all about," he informed me. "That's not why I initiated this conversation."

"Then what's it all about?" I demanded. "You tell me. Because in my knowledge of things, you and I were just doing what we were doing for a very long time because it was pretty goddamn convenient, wasn't it? It was a *nice arrangement*. Only now…now…well, you know what I'm saying! You never fucking cared about me the whole time I was dating Roman before we got engaged. You never seemed to want me so badly as you have lately when you probably could have had me before if you'd only asked! And it makes me angry that you keep trying to pull me in your direction *now* when for more than two years you just used me to fill up the spaces because you thought you had something better somewhere else. And it makes me angry that you act like I have no feelings when in truth, you're the one who's never shown me shit for emotion until just recently! You were never interested in anything about me until I got this fucking ring put on my finger!"

"That's right. Get it out," he told me, all totally patient like he was a therapist.

I pointed my cigarette at him. "Don't patronize me. What do you want?"

He took the cigarette from my fingers. "I don't know, exactly. All I can tell you is that it's different now. You're right—it's been different since you got engaged. And the fucked up thing about that is, now that it's different you *are* engaged. I don't want to lose you. And it makes me angry that you sit there and say I thought I had something better somewhere else, when in truth you're the one who's always flaunting how you have something better!"

I snatched the cigarette back. "I don't flaunt that! And it's not like you bother to live up, anyway!"

"Live up?" he demanded. "Oh, toots—you don't even want to go there. Roman, yeah, he's Mr. Perfect according to all the magazines, isn't he? Carrie Bradshaw and Company would have surely given their approval. But who listens to your confessions, holds you when you're crying in the night? That's right—me. It doesn't matter, though. The way you talk, Roman has it all and I have nothing, so why would I ever bother to compete with him?"

"You forget one pertinent detail that was there when we met," I reminded him. "You had *Pristina*. The sober, non-smoking, career-oriented Pristina, who was practically a saint from the way you described her. And made it sound from the get-go like *that* was what you really wanted. You made it obvious from day fucking one that I was just to be an amusement away from what you considered the real thing. So what's your defense?"

"I walked into a random lobby one day—when I wasn't even supposed to be the one making that delivery, by the way—and met a girl I thought was really something," he said. "And yes I did have a girlfriend, but I was willing to take a chance. Keep in mind that I didn't even mention Pristina until you told me *you* had a boyfriend! What were you doing, going out with me, if you had a boyfriend?"

"What were you doing asking me out if you had a girlfriend?"

"Like I said, I took a chance."

"And you think I didn't? You think I still don't?" I asked incredulously.

"Yeah, but what does it matter?" He grabbed my hand. He held it up to my face. "When you're wearing *this?*"

I snatched my hand away. "All right then, let's talk about that. Do you want to get married? Trade in this ring I'm wearing for the one you're going to give me? Start saying 'I love you' when we get off the phone? *Start carrying my purse?*"

He glared at me. "You are so out of line, toots…you don't even know."

"And you are so out of line with your depth here that you can't even answer my fucking questions when *you're* the one who forced me to ask them."

He propped himself up on his elbow and looked at me. His eyes were serious and his voice was low. "All right. Fine. No. I don't want to do any of those things. But that doesn't mean that I never would."

"So am I just supposed to throw Roman out the window because someday you *might* start feeling amorous enough to want me for good?" I demanded.

"If you think it's worth it," he replied. "I mean…how do you care about me?"

"How do you think?"

"I'm never sure."

"I care about you *a lot*. But I can't nurture that and nurture the other thing, too," I said.

"The other thing being Roman?"

"Very good." I studied my nails. I needed a fill.

He sat up to face me. "Well, why can't you fucking nurture how you feel about me? If you could fucking manage *that*, then maybe we could get somewhere! Maybe I could see myself really wanting to do all the things you were just talking about…if I thought it was worth it!"

"I don't have the energy to nurture both things!" I replied. I put my forehead in my hand. "We didn't start off together.

But Roman and I did. Just as you and Pristina did. You and I were just…"

"A little something extra."

"A little something extra," I repeated.

"And now I'm throwing down the gauntlet on you and you can't handle it."

"As usual, you're turning things around to suit the way you see things. And that is just *dumb*," I said. "You just don't see things the way a normal person would. You really don't!"

"You want to know how I really see things, toots?"

"Yes. I do. Since you seem to think you know me so well."

"I do know you so well. I know you better than most people, don't I?" He looked very serious and his pupils were dilated.

"I'm waiting," I informed him.

He shook his head at me. "It's pretty pathetic, really. Poor baby. It must be hard to feel like you have to keep yourself in a deep dark world where you are always the bad girl, you are always the sinner, you are always in the wrong. I do know the real you, Doll. And I'd have to say, you like that place because you think it makes you more interesting."

I was quiet.

He flopped onto his back. "Anyway, I guess that's what I see."

I frowned at him. "Yeah? Well, you know what I see?"

"What?"

"The door. Get out. Just fucking get out."

He got up, shaking his head. "Yeah, I figured it was about that time."

I lay on my bed when he was gone and felt like a big dumb asshole. I could just let him go, never call him again, not take his calls if he deigned to call me, dedicate myself to Roman the way Roman deserves. Stop being so wishy-washy. Stop with these breakup and make-up scenarios with a man I shouldn't be breaking up, making up with.

Jeremy, though. He was just trying to be deep with me. He wasn't trying to offend me. And nothing he said was really that offensive. I mean it wasn't offensive that we were sitting there getting at the truth. And didn't I invite him into my home and heart and bed because he *did* know me better than most people? Wasn't that one of the very reasons I liked having him around? I dialed his number when I was sure he was home. He picked up on the third ring.

"I'm sorry," I said.

"You're my friend, Doll, and I'll always love you...but this shit has got to stop."

"What shit, exactly?"

He made his frustrated noise over the line. "This shit where we go back and forth over something you're obviously never going to give either me, or yourself, an honest answer about. And this shit where you try to be so abrasive! Give it up already. Give it up with *me,* at least. If I care enough to ask, then you shouldn't throw me out. This Queen of Misery crap is getting really old, really fast. Someday I won't come back."

"I'm *sorry.*"

He sighed. "I need a week. Call me then, okay?"

He hung up the phone. And I rubbed my temples. I could kiss it off right here and now and still have everything I've ever wanted. But I want Jeremy, too.

I called back and got his answering service. I left a message that if he wanted to, he could pick me up the following Saturday night for the City of Angels Christmas for the Children Gala. It was a black-tie affair and I had to be there by five to make sure it was all set up. I'd already reserved his ticket. All he had to do was bring a toy.

The doorbell rang on Saturday at four. I opened it and Jeremy was standing there. He was wearing a tuxedo and holding an enormous bouquet of dark red roses.

"Don't get any sappy ideas," he said quickly. "I know this is your big event."

I took them, giving him a level gaze. "Are we made up, then?"

"We're definitely at a ceasefire," he agreed. He kissed my cheek and came in, disappearing quickly down the hall when he noticed Dylan lurking about, smirking.

I put the roses in some water while Electra stood by and tsk-tsked.

"My cold heart is melting," she said sarcastically.

"Electra…"

She smiled. "Come on, Doll. You've known me for a long time. Would I ever let something like that go without a bitchy comment?"

"I suppose not. I'm just nervous."

"I know you are. But don't be. This thing will go off fabulously and you look fucking great." I was wearing a long, slinky black velvet dress.

"So do you." She was wearing a short, slinky red sequined dress.

She fussed with a diamond earring in the mirror. "Now where is Ava? I swear that girl would disappear if we weren't always looking out for her." She went off down the hall, calling sugar, sugar and making kiss noises.

"Hey, perfect timing," Dylan said, waltzing out of the kitchen with a beer in hand. He winked at me and whistled. "Looking hot, Dollface."

I pretend-stuck my finger down my throat and he laughed. I elbowed him, not gently.

"Owee! Why so hostile?" he asked, dragging on his ever-present cigarette.

I appraised his look. Apparently for Dylan, *black tie* really meant *no* tie. I decided now was as good a time as ever to say my piece.

"I'd just appreciate it if you'd stop being so shady and just decide about her once and for all. You've made her crazier than she is already with your antics," I said. "She loves you, Dylan. You're all she wants."

"Uh-uh. She wants fame, too."

"And that's another thing. Why didn't you come to see her in *The Men in Me?*"

"Aw, forget it," he groaned. "I said *bella,* there's no way I'm goin' to some chick play. I said besides, I need to save myself for when I see ya in a movie with my man Johnny Depp. That'll be solid. Besides, I had a poker tournament."

"I'll tell everyone we know that you know all the words to 'Please Don't Go Girl' if you aren't there when she actually is in a movie with your man Johnny Depp."

He looked slightly panicked, but it passed quickly. Heh. Heh. Heh. "Aww, sinkin' to blackmail…what a good friend you are! Hey, you want to roll my lucky dice on it?" He pulled them out of his pocket and shook them around in his hand, raising his eyebrows repeatedly.

"The fuck *no.*"

He looked smug. "So if I do as *you* imply I should be doing…what's in it for me on your end? I'll scratch your back if you'll scratch mine."

I narrowed one eye. "You're going to get more than your back scratched if you don't shape the fuck up."

He winked again. "Promise?" Heh. Heh. Heh.

Karen had arranged for a limousine to take us over to the Biltmore, so we piled in and fixed drinks and pressed our noses to the windows to behold the city skyline in all its clean winter glory. Downtown was all done up in red and green and glittering gold garland. In the night sky it looked like an enormous forest of Christmas trees.

The ballroom was empty when we arrived at the hotel. The band was setting up and the tables were set with pristine white cloths and red-and-green napkins, and all the little sparkly silver sleigh centerpieces I'd ordered. I went around with the charity people and checked things off on my clipboard as my friends hit the bar.

Except for one setback in which it turned out the potatoes would be au gratin instead of red rose and rosemary,
dinner went off fabulously. By the time the toy exchange was
over and the silent auction had gotten under way, I was in a
great mood. I was looking forward to dancing the night
away and having a blast.

"Oh, Doll, come here for a second," Karen called as I
passed her table.

"Doll's my prodigy," she told the people seated beside her.
"She set this whole thing up all on her own without even a
lick of my help. Honestly."

"It's lovely," Karen's bitch best friend, Cynthia, said genuinely. I took in her clinging Valentino gown, her straight-
out-of-*Vogue* Chanel pumps, and her incredible resemblance
to Grace Kelly. No wonder she's such a ball-buster. What a
classy broad.

I glowed. "Do you think it's good, Karen?" I asked.

"Good? It's stunning, Doll. I knew I was right on when I
put this one in your hands." She stood up and gave me a hug.
"If you weren't moving, I'd say you deserved a promotion.
Ah, hell, maybe I'll give you one, anyway."

I beamed. I was glad she'd pushed me to be my very best.
She wasn't such an ass *all* the time.

Jeremy came over. "What's going on?" he asked, over the
music. The DJ was getting ready to go on.

I linked my arm through his. "You remember my boss,
Karen?"

Karen furrowed her eyebrows at me.

Cynthia looked Jeremy up and down. "Oh, I forgot you
were getting married soon, Doll. So when's the big date for
the two of you?"

"Oh, *we're* not getting married," I laughed. And laughed.
"He's just my escort."

Jeremy noticed Pretty Boy beckoning to him with a sig-
nal to go outside and blaze it. He gave me a kiss on the cheek
before disappearing.

Karen pulled me away from the table. "That's that other clown again!" she said accusingly. "You aren't fucking him, are you?" she demanded.

"Karen!"

She tilted her head and looked off in Jeremy's direction. "Well?"

"He's a good friend of mine," I said, feigning shock. "What are you implying?"

"Nothing, I hope." She glared at me and I hurried away.

To be honest, I would have liked to have had Roman with me on this night, so he could see one of my accomplishments come to life. But he was too busy with his own career. So busy that he hadn't even called to wish me luck. I thought with the time difference, he was probably just being polite.

I made Jeremy dance. "Are you having a good time?" I asked.

"Yeah. You did a good job on this, Doll."

"Thanks."

"Seriously. I'm sure it took a lot of work on your part."

"It did. But I enjoyed it."

He spun me around under rainbows and stars and psychedelic curlicues. And I reminded myself that just a mere continent and an ocean away, a man who had always been mine was waiting to marry me.

Chapter 21

Jeremy came by my office the day he was going home to Miami for Christmas. I was leaving work early to take him to the airport. The stick man had moved to December 25 and was wearing a Santa hat.

"What's Roman doing for Christmas?" Jeremy asked, looking at the calendar.

"He's going to Paris with his family," I replied.

"He can go to Paris to meet his family but he can't come to L.A. to see you?" he asked doubtfully. "Color me a moron if I'm wrong here, but isn't France like as far from Cameroon as California?"

I shrugged. Yeah, it's annoying. We had a little bit of a row over it, actually.

"Paris?" I'd asked, when he told me.

"It was my mother's idea," he'd explained. "She told me they were going to Paris for Christmas and that it might be nice if I met them there. Guilted me, is what she did."

"I could handle Paris," I'd said thoughtfully. "Why don't

I fly to New York and meet them and then we can all fly to Paris to meet you?"

"Uh, not a good idea," he'd said quickly.

"What's the problem, Roman? You don't want to spend Christmas with me?"

"That's not it at all, Dalton. I just think after spending all day getting to New York and then all night getting to Paris, to see me for maybe two days, doesn't really sound like something you would enjoy. And it's not like we'd have any time to ourselves. My whole family is going to be there— my sisters and my brother and all their spouses and all my nieces and nephews…it's just, well, I don't really think you would have a good time."

"You think you know what's best for me?" I'd demanded. "I've started noticing you're always telling me what I would and wouldn't like. How do you know? Maybe I would just like to see you. Have you considered that?"

"I would like to see you, too, baby. Wouldn't you rather it was a romantic occasion, the one we've been waiting for, than have to spend it with my entire family?"

"I guess."

"But you're not sure."

"Well, no. I'm not sure about a lot things, actually. I'm not sure you really know what goes on in my life when you're out of it. I'm not sure you would even want to know."

"Dalton, I'm sorry I had to leave. I'm sorry I finally got the opportunity I've been working toward in my career and it coincided with our engagement. I knew this would be difficult for you."

"But it's not difficult for you?"

"If only you knew."

"But I *don't* know. How come we don't talk the way we used to? How come every time we do, it feels like you're there, but you're not? Something's up with us."

"Nothing is up with us, Dalton. I'm just incredibly stressed out over here. Like I said, if only you knew. I will be home in six weeks. That's all. Should I just quit now, or can you wait?"

And that was pretty much that.

"Aw, forget it," Electra said when I told her I thought Roman was being totally weird. "Why would you want to go to Paris for Christmas, anyway? It's freezing there this time of year. If he were going to Barbados, then I would protest. But not over stupid Paris!"

Jeremy and I went to the mall for lunch and ate Baja Fresh in the Marketplace courtyard as we watched people go by in a frenzied rush of holiday gift-buying.

He took my chips. "Will you miss me, Doll?"

"Of course. I wish you were coming to Las Vegas with us for New Year's."

"I know. That would be pretty awesome."

I didn't point out that the reason he wasn't was due to the fact that before his and Pristina's breakup, the lovebirds had planned to spend New Year's in the Bahamas. I guess she'd mailed him her ticket with a little body drawn on it, *X*'s for the eyes and a very obviously sawed-off wee-wee with red magic marker drops of pretend blood dripping from it. Wow.

"Where are you guys staying again?" he asked.

"The Venetian. Apparently Josh got some high-roller suite." I rolled my eyes.

He laughed appreciatively.

We lit cigarettes. The people next to us hurriedly moved their table away, coughing and gagging. They were acting like we had just released a chemical weapon. They were acting like they needed gas masks. I wanted to throw my cigarette at them. I wanted to light a cigar.

I leaned back in my chair. I looked him over. Just then I had never seen anything as wonderful as he was in all the universe. I know I will remember him until the day I die, even if I am ninety, and I haven't seen him in sixty-five years. I know I will remember his seascape eyes and his vampire teeth and his goofy smile and his frustrated sighs. Just like I know

I will remember how much he bothered me and how much I longed for him to disappear.

When we got to LAX, I pulled up at the curb.

"Get out, will you?" he asked.

I got out. I went around and waited for him to get his bag.

He hugged me long and hard. "I'll miss you."

"Then I'll miss you, too."

He looked at me for a long time after we'd spoken. Then he grabbed me up in a long kiss. I thought that whoever was watching probably thought we were some serious lovers, crazy upset about having to be apart for the holidays.

He let go. "You have a good Christmas," he told me. He tousled my hair. Then he was gone.

I watched him walk away. He was inside the terminal before I ran after him, leaving my car idling at the curb.

"Jeremy!" I screamed, just as he was about to get on the escalator leading up to the gates.

He turned around.

I ran into his arms. "Have a safe flight."

He smiled at me. Then he rubbed my back and was gone.

I took some time off and went home for Christmas. Maddy and I laid around watching movies and eating snacks and talking about her classes and Gabriel and my work and, of course, the wedding. It was cozy and relaxing.

"So what's going on with Gabriel?" I asked. "You never call me anymore."

"I'm sorry, sis, I've just been soooo busy with school," she told me. We were sitting out on the back patio, drinking café au lait and watching the morning fog roll in over the Pacific. "It's going great with Gabriel. And I am still a virgin. I kind of like making him wait," she giggled.

"I think you kind of like putting on the devil's skirt, Maddy," I told her.

"Hey, you're not the only one who's allowed," she informed me. "And wearing the devil's skirt is *okay* as long as you're just borrowing it for a while, right?"

"Right. Make him wait."

"Who's waiting for what?" our father asked, coming outside.

"Omelets, Daddy," Maddy told him. "We're waiting for your avocado omelets."

"Well, why do you think I came out here?" he asked. "To pick the avocados!"

My father makes me laugh. He's so jolly. I guess he really has nothing to complain about, so he doesn't. He's just happy. I like that.

"Didn't you have your own version of the Pink Ladies when you were in elementary school?" Maddy asked later, while we watched *Grease* in the bonus room.

"Uh-huh. Fifth grade. We called ourselves the Sparkles, though."

"Funny," she laughed.

"Yeah, it was pretty cute."

I zoned out to "Summer Nights" while I remembered. We'd worn little red satin jackets with silver glitter letters on the back that my mother had ironed on for us. We'd walked around school like we were the shit and reigned on the playground.

But then came that day when the new girl came to school and my life would be forever altered by her presence. Of course I hated her on sight because she was intriguing and pretty and everyone whispered about her in awe. Everybody looked to me and I wouldn't let anybody talk to her. There would be no competition in *my* schoolyard.

One day we went up to her and asked if she had what it took to be a Sparkle, just to be bitches. She laughed and said, no thanks, that was stupid. I did not like being defied on my turf. So I hit as low as possible and told her we didn't need any white trash in our group, anyway. I didn't know what white trash was at the time, really, but

I thought it sounded good. And she had to be white trash because she lived right next door to Chastity Brewster, and everybody knew that Chastity's parents were in a motorcycle gang and were the biggest loadies in town. Kitty Lovejoy called *them* white trash. What I'd said made her cry.

The next day she came to school with a blue satin jacket that said *Sparks* on the back in gold glitter. She asked Liz Major and Katie Gold and Lainey Thompson to be Sparks with her. We all got into a huge fight at lunch and I ended up slapping that bitch. It felt good to feel my hand crack against her cheek, like electricity. I ended up getting suspended for two days and was the only girl in the history of my elementary school ever to receive that honor.

That bitch never forgot me. She made my life hell for all the years to come. And when I see her around town now I can almost still see my red handprint across her face as it was the day we waited outside of the principal's office in fifth grade. That face that belongs to none other than Aurelia Sparks.

"Girls, turn the movie off and get ready for dinner!" our mom called up the stairs, bringing me out of my reverie. "We're going to Yolanda's!"

Maddy and I cheered. I threw on my favorite jeans and a black sweater and some chunky red shoes and hurriedly brushed my hair. In the car on the way there the four of us sang Christmas carols and laughed about how corny we were as a family.

I could have died when we got to the restaurant, because right off we ran into the Michaelsons and Dan was with them. My mother invited them to join us and I had a sneaking suspicion that the Michaelsons and my parents had actually planned to meet there. Dan and I sat at opposite ends of the table and didn't speak. Our mothers and fathers talked like they didn't know how uncomfortable the situation was. I *hate* it when they do that and they *always* do it.

"Where are you going, Doll?" my mother asked, when I got up from the table.

"Uh…the bathroom," I replied. Instead I hightailed it outside and lit a cigarette. The air was cold and smelled earthy and wet like trees and the ocean. I remembered all these things. My first diamond ring that Dan bought me after saving all his pizza delivery money for months. The time we accidentally put a huge dent in a really sweet Mazda RX-7 right here in this parking lot and had driven away without leaving a note, only to get to school the next day and hear Liz Major screaming that some asshole had dented her brand-new car at Yolanda's last night. How after we'd broken up he'd sent me a tape of Bon Jovi singing "You Give Love a Bad Name" and I'd retaliated by playing Ugly Kid Joe's "Everything About You" on the answering machine to his teen line.

He came outside with his hands stuffed into his jeans pockets. Dan has dark hair and dark eyes. He looks like the prototypical guy who may have played a popular high school jock in an eighties teen movie.

He swung his leg out and kind of kicked at the ground. He looked up and I nearly stopped breathing. I guess some people just do that to you all your life. I guess with some people it never ends. So why does it? I guess because we do stupid things to each other and then we don't struggle to resolve them.

"Hi," he finally said.

"Hi."

He cleared his throat. "You know I was just sitting in there thinking…our parents have been doing this to us for years. And they're going to keep doing it. So I don't think we should have a problem with each other anymore."

I sighed. "To be honest, Dan…it's not really you I have a problem with. It's just the whole situation. Your wife… mainly."

"Well, I guess I can understand that."

"It's just all too weird," I told him. "Where is she tonight, anyway?"

"Home. She's got a thing about leaving the kids." He shrugged. "Sometimes I have a hard time getting out myself. She has a hard time with it...I mean."

"Don't be making marriage sound so binding," I told him. "I'm about to enter into the state of matrimony myself."

"Yeah...I heard." He took a deep breath. "Congratulations."

"Thanks."

He laughed. "You still wear that necklace," he noticed, reaching out to touch it.

"You still drink Shirley Temples at dinner!"

He blushed and looked down. "Yeah..."

I wanted to collapse in a pile of tears right there in the parking lot. Instead I just went with it. "I hope you're happy, Dan."

"I hope you're happy, too."

"I hope you won't take it personally if your parents are invited to the wedding but not you and the missus."

"I won't." He looked around with a smile. "Remember the time we hit Liz Major's car?"

I smiled back. "Of course."

"I never told anyone, did you?"

I shook my head.

He looked wistful. "Well...anyway..."

"Yeah. Anyway."

He touched my shoulder and turned to go back into the restaurant.

Who knew when Dan and I would be alone again, like this, for how long. He was married. I was about to get married. The best Mexican food in California would be delivered to our table at any moment. Maddy would be sent to come looking for us, with Dan's little brother, Elias.

"Dan."

He whirled around.

Apologies and explanations would be trite at this point.

"Wait up," I said. I stepped on my cigarette and scurried in through the door as he held it for me.

Later that night Maddy came into the bonus room after my parents had gone to bed. I was watching *Silent Night, Deadly Night* and drinking a bottle of wine.

"Do you hate seeing Dan?" she asked, sitting down on the couch with me.

"Man, you ask a lot of questions."

"I know—I'm nosy. So do you?"

"Yes."

She reached for the remote control to mute the movie. "He still looks at you a lot. He was looking at you all through dinner."

"I know."

"So how come—"

"I slept with his best friend."

"Why did you do that?"

"He was hot," I replied. "And I didn't think Dan would ever find out. He did, though. And he wasn't too pleased about it."

"I can imagine." She looked thoughtful. "Is that why he married Aurelia? To get back at you?"

"No, I think he married Aurelia because she was here."

"Oh. Well...thanks for telling me why you two broke up. I've always wanted to know." She got up from the couch and kissed me good-night. "Mike Radcliffe *is* hot, by the way."

I went into my room. The glow of the green lava lamp shone on a young James Spader on the *Tuff Turf* poster. Bits of silver paper and red ribbon from my earlier attempts at wrapping presents glinted like confetti upon the yellow carpet. I sat down in my papasan chair and lit a candle and a cigarette.

When I heard that Aurelia was marrying Dan I couldn't *believe* it. I wanted to call her and tell her okay, she'd *won*, she'd proved her point and she'd done enough...but did she really have to marry my Dan? My Dan who listened to my girlie music like the Go-Go's and Voice of the Beehive without complaint and even learned the words to sing along? My Dan who'd written me a love letter every day that we were together. I'd buried them at sea right at the moment they took their vows. That bitch. Having the nerve to fix it so that even if I wanted it to be so again, Dan could never again be my Dan.

Just like she fixed it when she told Dan about the night his best friend came on to me and I didn't resist. Lily's house was the venue. A party raged while Kitty and Al were thousands of miles away, in Atlantic City. Dan was at home with the flu. Everclear and Coke was the cocktail of choice. Eddie Jr.'s bedroom was the scene of the crime.

For a long time I looked back on that period in my life as the point where everything took a turn for the worse. I burned with an unholy hate for all of them. They represented everything I hated about myself.

Now I know that other people can't be held responsible for the way we feel about ourselves. And that if my life took a turn for the worse because I couldn't resist temptation, that was *my* fault. Now I could own up. Say yes, fucking my boyfriend's best friend was what ruined our relationship—not Aurelia's big mouth.

The candle flickered when I got up to open the window. I turned on the radio at low volume. Radiohead was signing "Creep" on KROQ.

My thoughts turned to Roman. I wondered why I didn't feel like a scarlet woman for having my Jeremy affair, the way I'd felt like a scarlet woman at school that Monday when Dan called me a whore outside of my precalculus class.

Maybe because I'd known Dan was the real thing.

Sometimes it was hard to think of Roman as the real thing because he was hardly ever close to me, except in my mind. His presence, for the most part, was based on his absence. I felt guilty for cheating on Dan, after I did it. But I don't always feel guilty for cheating on Roman, because Roman's not just at home with the flu. He's at home in another life. Like he's not really a part of my life a lot of the time.

I held my engagement diamond up against the flame and watched it sparkle.

Childhood years hold an importance that adult years never can. By adulthood, we're too experienced, too jaded.

I've made some mistakes. I'm still making mistakes. But I refuse to choke on those bitter pills.

When it comes to Dan…I'll say it was what it was, and it is what it is, and our lives will always intersect at the memories, and that's the only place they ever should.

When it comes to Roman…I'll say it's forever when it feels like forever.

The next day was Christmas Eve and Lily and I dropped food donations off at a homeless shelter and then took a bunch of clothes and toys to a battered women's home. We looked at the women and all those kids and were thankful that we had been so blessed. We spent that evening in her living room at the beach house, having drinks and desserts with our friends. Daisy and I got out an old photo album and laughed and reminisced.

"Remember this one?" Daisy asked, pointing to a picture of us on the carousel in the Ventura Harbor Village. She slung an arm around me and I felt her breath on the back of my neck. "I'm so stoked that we're still such good friends, even if we only talk like once a year. We always had such good times, didn't we?"

"The best," I agreed, slinging my arm around her, too. Her hair tickled my arm. Daisy has long hair almost to her waist, just like I do. We kind of look alike.

It's funny like that. Sometimes you don't talk to someone for a long time and you just pick up right where you left off.

I like that about certain people. I like knowing that you just lost touch. Not that you'd gotten in some horrendous fight that made you stop speaking.

"I think Daisy still has a crush on you," Charlie told me when we were in the kitchen.

I rolled my eyes. "Oh, please."

"She always did, Peaches. I'll bet she'd still do you." He poured us each a glass of wine. I was already fuzzy. "I'd still do you, you know."

I raised my eyebrows. "Really."

He shrugged. "Yeah, sure. I've always wanted to. I mean, it's always been a fantasy of mine. I wanted to see if it was different later."

"You mean because I'm not a virgin? Because I've had experience, or what?"

He smiled and put his arm around me. "Maybe that. I don't know."

"Hmm."

"So you want to?"

"Want to what?"

He laughed. "You want to have sex again?"

I thought about it. "Not really."

"Why not?"

"Does it not cross your mind that your gig in March is my *wedding*." I waved my hand at him and he took hold of it. "Besides, I'd rather remember it as it was."

He shrugged and released my hand. "I guess I understand that. No, I do. You've got a point." He kissed my cheek and went back out into the living room.

When I got home my mom was stuffing our stockings. "Oh, honey!" she exclaimed disappointedly. "I can't believe you caught me."

"Don't worry, Mom. I've always known there's no Santa Claus."

She laughed and pulled me against her. "Did you have fun at Lily's?"

I nodded.

"We're having them over tomorrow for dinner. The Porters, too."

I nodded again. "Sounds fun."

"Good night, honey."

"'Night, Mom."

I lay in bed looking at the funny shapes of my things in the darkness of my bedroom. It felt good to turn Charlie down, to leave that right where it was. It felt good to do the right thing.

Chapter 22

We were on the plane to Las Vegas for New Year's and I was sitting next to Dylan and Ava. Ava had pink highlights. Dylan had six mini liquor bottles on his tray even though it's only like a forty-five-minute flight.

"Why do you have to sit between the two of us?" I griped to Dylan.

Dylan leaned back in his seat and put his hands behind his head. "So's I can feel like a first-class pimp. On my way to Vegas with not one but two fine-ass ladies."

"You *are* a first-class pimp," Ava assured him.

"Yeah, but more pimp than first-class!" Electra said, from behind us.

I rolled my eyes. Karen had asked if I was free to help her with a New Year's Eve charity ball she was putting to-gether at the last minute. I told her I was going to Las Vegas but I could skip it if she needed me to. She said no, that she'd better start getting used to not having me around. Then she ran out of my office sobbing. I think she's pregnant.

The phone rang on New Year's Eve day while I was alone in the suite. "Hello?" I said into the receiver.

"It's me," Jeremy said.

I raised my eyebrows. "Why does it sound like you're in a casino?"

"Because I *am* in a casino. I'm downstairs."

"Are you serious?" I asked, my heart pounding. I was thrilled. What a thing to do! And I thought Roman was spontaneous!

"Uh-huh. I changed my flight to come through Las Vegas and now I'm here."

"I thought you were staying in Miami through New Year's?"

"It was boring. All my friends back home are losers now. I wanted to see you."

"You did?"

"Yes. Can I come up?"

"Sure." I turned off the TV and paced around until he knocked on the door. He put his suitcases down and hugged me. Then he perused the suite and whistled. He took my hand and we walked to the window together. Dusk was falling down on the Strip. Lights were flashing and celebration was in the air.

"I can't believe you really came," I laughed.

"Are you glad I did?"

"Well, of course," I told him. "I think it's wonderful that you did."

We went downstairs and walked around. A band was playing in one of the lounges so we had a few white Russians and talked about Miami and Ventura. It was so good to have him there. I felt complete and whole again. It's times like this when I can't exactly remember which of the men in my life is the jerk, and which is the gem. Even with this gem on my finger.

"You'll never believe it!" Electra shouted, when we returned to the suite. "Josh proposed! Can you even believe it?"

"I sure can," I told her. She was wearing an engagement

ring twice the size of my own. She told me Josh had taken her to pick it out that afternoon and she was supposed to wait until midnight but she'd convinced him to let her have it right away.

Electra was so excited about her ring that she didn't even make any snotty comments about Jeremy showing up. Josh poured Cristal for everyone and we toasted to their happiness. It sort of reminded me of the night we drank champagne to celebrate my engagement to Roman. I didn't know where he was right then, exactly. We hadn't spoken since Christmas Day.

That night we eschewed the crowds on the Strip and went to the party in the Damiano penthouse at Caesar's Palace. Anna, decked out in a backless sequined shirt, paraded around with Luciano-Marciano on her arm. At one point I could have sworn I saw Angelo and Giannini almost get trigger-happy when someone popped a champagne cork. Jeremy was so in awe that he had to go around talking to everybody. He is very charismatic. I wonder if after everybody gets to know him, they think he can be as irritating as I sometimes do?

As usual, I ended up with Dylan.

"Look at that spread," he told me, as we looked out at the blazing, magnificent hotels and the glittering view of the city beyond. "I tell you, when Ava and I do it right, this is where we're gonna spend our days."

"I knew you couldn't resist my strong arm," I said, flexing my biceps.

"Your strong arm had nothing to do with it, bitch," he informed me. "I been down with Ava this whole time. It just took me a while to figure it all out. Yeah, I'd be driving around and hear a song that reminded me of her, and I'd start thinking about her. Knew it was for real like that. Takes a special woman who can love a special man like this one, don't you know?"

I pictured him cruising in his low-riding Nissan Altima,

tinted windows rolled down halfway, baseball cap on backward, sunglasses on, bumping along to "Hypnotize" or something like that. I love that. I love it when white guys think they got game. I'm cracking myself up.

"What kind of song?" I asked.

"Something like 'Daughter' or 'L.A. Woman.' One of Ava's favorite songs." He sipped champagne with a shrug. "She's the only one for me and I'll admit it. She's my girl."

I put my arm around him. "I'm so glad."

He glanced down at me. "You want her to have everything, huh?"

I nodded as I looked up at him.

He put his finger under my chin. "We been friends for a long time, Dollface. I feel like I've watched you grow up."

"I don't know if I really have," I admitted.

He put his arm around me. He pulled me tightly against him. "Growing up has nothing to do with having a successful relationship, honey. It has nothing to do with making a lot of money, or working the perfect job, or thinking you know where you belong and why. It's just a place where you try to make good decisions for yourself and the people you love and be happy with them. It's something internal. It's all right here." He patted his heart.

"You know…you can be pretty charming when you're not acting like such a fuckhead," I told him.

"And *you* can be pretty charming when you're not acting like such a *bitch*," he returned. Then he kissed the top of my head and wandered off to refill his glass.

When midnight came everybody went crazy kissing and hugging and throwing shit in the air. Jeremy squeezed my hand and kissed me.

"I love this," he told me. "I love being here with you tonight!"

"I love being here with you tonight, too. You do know that, don't you?"

He nodded earnestly. "Yeah, I really do!"

"Happy New Year, Jeremy."

"Oh, yeah, same to you, Doll."

I wondered how Roman had spent his New Year's Eve. This was the year that we would stand up in front of everyone we knew and declare our promise to love and cherish each other for the rest of our lives. And here we were starting the year totally apart. In separate countries, on separate continents, and in two completely separate worlds.

Chapter 23

A letter showed up in my Charisma mailbox in the midst of the hideous rainy January. It was postmarked from Cameroon and was addressed in Roman's handwriting. Since I had never gotten one of his letters at work, I knew it was bad news.

It was a long, apologetic note explaining how his schedule got delayed and he wouldn't be coming home until May. *May.* May, May, May. He was supposed to be back in D.C. by the middle of February. I was so glad I hadn't sent out those invitations, like I'd planned. I was so glad nobody had to worry about changing their travel reservations. I was so glad my head could just explode.

"The fuck! Roman's not coming back until May?" Electra demanded later as we had dinner at Kate Mantalini after work. *"May?"*

"Yeah, that's what I said."

"That'll be almost a year that he's been gone."

"I *know!*"

"What a bummer," she told me, making a face. She admired her engagement ring immodestly. "I feel bad for you, Doll. But it's not the end of the world, is it?"

"No, it's not. Just a minor setback." So minor I wanted to *kill* him, as a matter of fact! "Everything's still the same. I'll just have to push everything back a bit." Yeah, no big deal. No problem!

"Yeah. Hey, you know something funny? I'm actually starting to look forward to New York with this rock on my finger. It's not like I have to see Preston just because we both live on the same island. Manhattan is a pretty big fucking island. And I *love* Josh's apartment. And I *love* the nightlife there. And I can quit working and go to NYU for my master's. And *then* I can work at the UN! I guess it won't be as bad as I originally thought. Funny, hmm?"

"Hilarious."

"I'm putting things into perspective," she told me.

"I guess that's what we all have to do."

At home I chain-smoked and drank cocktails and thought about where my life was going. I decided to call my fucking fiancé. I didn't care that it was early morning in Africa and he was probably getting sick of me waking him up.

He yawned. "You got my letter?"

"Yeah, I got your fucking letter," I told him. "And I have to say I am *pissed* that you are in Africa for another four months. Four fucking months, Roman!"

"I knew you would be upset, Dalton. But this is my job. Better you understand that now than after we're married, right?"

"But I've been making plans. My mother has put down deposits that are nonrefundable. Karen has already started looking for someone to replace me at work. I mean... What were you thinking?"

"It sounds like you're upset."

"No shit."

"My baby doesn't like being inconvenienced, does she?"

"Stop talking to me like that! Stop patronizing me."

"I wasn't."

"Then stop calling me your baby. Because I am so not up to being your baby at the moment. And can I just tell you that I feel like a fucking idiot having a fiancé that I haven't seen since July. July, Roman! It is *January!*"

"Dalton...you've been very patient. You've been so good about everything. You have. Just be patient for a few more months and we'll be married and everything will fall into place, okay?"

Fall into place? I wanted to tell him everything was just as likely to fall apart. "So I'm just supposed to bide my time until then? Just do everything half-assed because it doesn't really matter, anyway? What about my life? Should I just put everything on hold for you? What if you never come back? What if you decide you need to stay there another year? I can't wait any longer! This is too ridiculous! I want a boyfriend, a real one. And not just one who seems to exist most of the time only in my imagination!"

"I'm right here, Dalton. It's not your imagination."

"You're not right here," I reminded him. "You're in Africa. What am I supposed to do for entertainment? Lock myself in my room and read the Bible?"

He didn't say anything for a few seconds. "I never said you shouldn't go out and do things. I never said you had to lock yourself in your room and read the Bible, Dalton."

"Yes, but don't you see what I'm getting at?"

"Yes. I do."

I hated the things I was saying to him. I hated having to act like that kind of girl.

"Please just understand that this is the last time you'll have to deal with this," he finally said.

"Is that a promise?"

"Did I or did I not ask you to marry me?"

"What the hell is that for an answer, Roman? You don't even know me."

"Yes, I do. I know you're just upset right now and it

will pass. What is it, really? Are your friends giving you a hard time?"

"No…it's not that."

"Tell you what. I'll try to come home a few weeks early and I'll come straight to L.A. without even going to D.C."

"No…don't bother. In fact, why don't you just call me when you book your return flight and I'll quickly throw together a wedding like it doesn't take *months*. See you there, whenever!"

"Did I detect a little sarcasm just now?"

"Get *screwed*."

"Oh, no…now you're really cross."

"You're doing it again. You're mocking me! Are you *mad* at me?" I asked incredulously. "Because it sure seems like you are. You're being a total fucker and I don't know why when it's *me* who has the right to be seriously furious here. In fact, I'm about to throw this stupid ring down the garbage disposal. Because it's bullshit. You said you were afraid to lose me and put this ring on my finger so you wouldn't. But I want more than just some diamond. So what gives?"

Silence.

"Dalton, let's not do this now. I have to go, okay?"

I glanced at the clock. "Why do you have to go? Isn't it like three in the morning over there?"

"Yes…and that's why I have to go. I need to sleep."

"Oh, have some *fucking* sweet dreams, then!"

He was quiet for a moment. "I'll talk to you soon," he said. Then he hung up.

I lay back on my bed with my hand over my eyes, picturing Roman, wondering what the hell was going on. I looked at my Madonna poster and wondered what lucky star she was born under.

But then I remembered how her mother died when she was little and she never got over it. That must have been hard.

And she starved on beer and popcorn and had to eat out

of Dumpsters sometimes when she was first trying to make it as a dancer in New York City.

And she's gotten a lot of shit over the years for just being who she is. A lot of controversy. A lot of criticism. I guess being Madonna hasn't always been easy.

I grabbed Charlie's old, tattered Stussy sweatshirt out of my dresser drawer and put it on. I went into the breakfast nook to sit at the table and composed a long letter to Roman in the darkness, tender light shining in from the street lamps. I lit candles and the house started to smell like cinnamon and vanilla and hyacinth. In the letter I told him that I was very angry with him for staying in fucking Africa for so long. I told him that I was spending all my time with a guy named Jeremy. I told him we'd been having a really intense thing that had started as a harmless, hopeless fling but was really more like a very serious affair now. I told him that I thought I might be severely in love with Jeremy, but it didn't matter because Jeremy kind of hated me and only hung out with me because he was into self-torture. I told him that this was all ruining my self-esteem. I said I was so lonely and felt so alone most of the time that being engaged felt like a farce. I said people may call me Doll but that's not what I am and he can't just put me in a box when he's not around and expect me not to move until he has time to play with me again. I said I couldn't believe I was marrying someone who didn't even know the things that were going on in my head, or know anything about me, really.

The letter was over fifteen pages long. It was past midnight when I finished it. I tore it up into a thousand pieces and burned the evidence.

Jeremy decided a night out would cheer me up. Normally a night out would have consisted of pints at this dive he likes called The Irish Times. Instead he took me to Gladstone's for dinner in Malibu and we ate lots of shrimp and drank lots of beer and afterward went walking on the beach with a blanket and a bottle of wine. We set up shop near some rocks and talked while we boozed, nature the only witness to this unnatural affection.

"I think Roman sucks," he told me.

"You think?"

He nodded. "Maybe you should tell him to forget it, Doll."

"Oh, don't start that! I'm not going to tell him to forget it just because he's late coming home."

"Well, it's crummy, him doing whatever he wants with no thought about how it affects your life. Don't you think?"

"He has a career that he's very devoted to," I said.

He raised his eyebrows. "So devoted that he's letting you slip right through his fingers?"

"He's not letting me slip through his fingers," I told him, my voice icy.

There were stars out across the ocean, on the horizon, over Hawaii or some other faraway place. They were white and shining like little lies in the sky.

He moved quickly. I was pinned down on the blanket in seconds. His eyes were the only bright spots in the dark, dark night. They glowed like an animal's when you come up on them with headlights.

"This is the last time I'm going to bring this up," he told me, nose to nose. "I'm here now. I'm here. But you can't count on me staying unless you say you want me to because I have to get on with my life if you're not interested."

I turned my head to the side. "If there's one thing I've noticed about you, it's that you're not that easy to get rid of. You've had as many chances to walk away from this as I have."

He spoke softly into my ear. "I could still meet someone else. What do you think about that?"

I turned my gaze back to his. My heart was pounding. "I'm the one who told you that you'd have a new girlfriend in no time."

"True. But how would you feel if I did?"

I thought about it. "Pissed."

"That's right, you would have a fit about it. But I'm serious now. I'm getting damn sick of this crap and if you don't move soon I will. I like you a lot and I think we could work. I didn't when I was with Pristina but that was because I had a girlfriend."

"And I still have a fiancé, by the way."

"And even though he's being totally crummy, you refuse to take a chance that I may be the better choice?" he demanded.

"I'm going with my instinct on this one. You know how I feel about you and I can't even begin to imagine my life without you in it…even though I've been telling myself every day since July that time is running out and at some point I'm going to have to say goodbye. And I hate that thought. But I still say that as soon as I throw Roman over, you'll lose all interest in me. And I can't take that risk."

He looked thoughtful. "So that's your answer?"

I sighed. "Jeremy…as much as I care about you, I do love him, too. I can't turn my back on that just because you think I'm great now that you have nothing else to nurture."

"All right then. I guess at this point it's anyone's game."

I rolled my eyes. "Come on."

"Come on nothing, Doll. You're a real pain in the ass, you know that?"

I tried to twist away but he held tightly to my wrists. "One of these days you're going to drive me insane," I told him.

"No…the other way around."

"Then let's just get the fuck out of here."

He looked at me for a long time. Then he lowered his head and kissed my lips. I shivered in the coldness of the damp beach air. And I felt like it was the first time I'd ever kissed anybody. I refused to feel guilty for enjoying him. Fuck Roman for leaving me here and not coming home for so

long. Fuck him for not asking me to go to Cameroon because he was so "busy." Fuck him for not caring that *I* have
needs, too.

Chapter 24

Roman sent me two new sweaters, as a peace offering, I think. One was pink and one was black. It was a nice gesture, but really. As if a couple of sweaters were going to make up for his absentee lifestyle. The labels were French. Maybe he bought them in Paris over Christmas and saved them for a rainy day. He must have sent them almost immediately after sending his "I'm not coming home until May" letter because I got them just before the Golden Globes. I was taking Ava because I almost always take Ava when I go to these things, and also because I didn't want Karen getting on my case about Jeremy again.

And boy, was he pissed about not going.

"You know I'd kill to go to something like that!" he shouted angrily. "I may never get this chance again!"

"Ha! That's a good one! If you'll recall, I asked you to go last year, remember? But you couldn't because you were with Pristina," I hissed.

"Yeah, but I'm not with Pristina now."

"Well, that's not my fault."

"You're a real bitch."

"So are you!" I yelled before hanging up on him. It was careless of me and I knew I wouldn't hear from him for weeks, but the foul mood I was in, I didn't really care.

I was pretty bitchy to Roman, too. In fact I didn't even call to thank him for the sweaters until Valentine's Day. I decided to do it while I was getting ready to go out to dinner. My parents were coming down with my grandparents to take me out and I'd made reservations at Il Cielo.

"I got the sweaters," I told him, as I brushed some of Ava's glittery pink blush onto my cheeks in front of the bathroom mirror.

"I was starting to wonder if you had."

"Yeah…a few weeks back. So thanks."

"You're welcome." He sounded a little testy. "I knew the black would work but I wasn't so sure about the pink."

"I'm wearing the pink one right now."

He laughed. "A special touch for your family?"

"Sure it is. I don't want to give off the impression that I'm in mourning."

"And why would you be? In mourning, that is."

"Because I'm just so sick of it," I told him. "Sorry to be so juvenile, but it's the truth. I spend all this time with other people and claim this fabulous divine love with my fiancé, and then don't even know half of what's going on in your life." Not to mention what he didn't know about my life.

"Dalton…"

"I know, I know. Things will really get started for us when we get married," I recited. The more I said it, the less I believed it.

He was quiet for a moment. "If it means anything to you, I miss you. I miss you a lot."

"So what are you going to do about it?"

"I'm going to marry you when I get back."

So not the response I was looking for. "Hey, that's great.

Anyway, I think I just heard my parents pull in. Happy Valentine's Day, lover."

He countered my sarcasm with, "You keep forgetting the time difference. It's already the fifteenth over here," and then I slammed down the phone.

Being engaged is great.

When we were settled at a table in Il Cielo's courtyard, Grandma Jane made a toast and we all raised our wineglasses. She said something about me making them all proud for growing up to become a beautiful young lady. I thought that was nice. While I feasted on Ravioli di Amore, my grandparents Moss told me they were giving me their silver, and my grandparents Dalton told me I was getting their crystal. How fun to get wedding presents. And how fun to eat from forks and drink from goblets that have been in my family for generations. Like royalty!

"Ship it all to the house in D.C.," I told them with only a shade of hesitation. "That's the address I put on the registry. I don't want to have to worry about packing more than I have to already."

There was a message from Roman when I got home. He said he was sorry. I called back and left him a message, saying that I was sorry, too.

I thought there was something going on with Jeremy beyond our fight over the Golden Globes. We'd had fallings-out before but none had ever felt so cold and distant. It was like we were strangers. I even had to go so far as to initiate a phone call.

"Oh. Hi," he said when he heard my voice.

"Hi. Listen, this is stupid. I'm sorry about the Golden Globes, okay? It's just that Ava looks forward to that shit like you don't even know, and even though I knew you would totally love to go...are you even listening to me?"

"Huh?" he asked distractedly.

"What are you doing?"

"Nothing. I'm sort of busy. Did you need something?"

I frowned at myself in my mirror. "What do you mean by that?"

"Nothing. I'm just…I told you. I'm busy right now."

"Oh. Okay."

"I'll call you later, okay?"

He hung up and I stared at the phone. What the fuck was that all about? He was so hot and cold. I fucking hated him!

Karen started cutting back my workload at Charisma. She even took me off of Jack Nicholson's Oscar night party. It left me with a lot of free time. Jeremy was *really* giving me the cold shoulder. The last time I'd asked him to come over he was flighty and fidgety and said he didn't feel like it. I'd screamed at him that I was getting sick of it. He'd screamed back that he was getting sick of me.

"What's going on with Jeremy?" I asked Andy one night as he came by to pick me up for a cooking class he'd conned me into taking with him. That's right. Cooking. Gets the girls, apparently.

"Huh?" He was looking through my closet for his favorite sweater. I'd borrowed it a while back and he was panicked that I might accidentally take it to D.C. with me if he didn't rescue it.

"Jeremy. He's been very aloof."

"I think he's distancing himself."

"Oh," I said thoughtfully. If he was I sure didn't like it.

"He's taking this class, too," Andy told me as we drove to Santa Monica College for our first session.

"And you had to tell me?"

He shrugged. "I guess he forgot."

Maybe he had. But I thought I had it all figured out when I got there. His cooking partner was this young girl named Breeze and he seemed to know her already. She was tiny like a little baby girl with tiny hands and a tiny, pointy face. She had skin like she was still drinking milk at every meal and taking Flintstones vitamins in the morning with her Pop-Tarts. She had a dyed blond pageboy haircut and huge boobs and she laughed outrageously loud in this squeaky little cackle. All the guys in the class thought she was the cutest little thing on the planet. The two of them had a good time making ginger chicken and sesame noodles while Andy and I burned ours to a crisp.

"What the fuck was that?" I demanded like a psycho as we were leaving.

"What?" Jeremy asked innocently.

"You and that girl."

"Who, Breeze?"

"That's the one."

"Nothing. She's so pretty, don't you think?"

"She's all right. But how old is she, twelve?"

"She's twenty." He sounded testy.

"Twenty! Isn't that a little *young* for you?"

"Isn't thirty-five a little *old* for you?" he sneered in return.

"At least Roman was born before *Nightmare on Elm Street* was released!" I screamed. "And what about *Star Wars?* Have you considered that her generation has their own trilogy? That these are simply a few movies starring Natalie Portman?" I put my hands on my hips and tapped one foot.

He leaned up against my car. "I told you you would have a fit about it, toots."

I eyed him suspiciously as Andy made himself scarce. "You didn't meet that girl tonight, did you?"

"Don't call her *that girl,* and no. I met her a couple of weeks ago."

It occurred to me then that I'd never really seen him with another woman. I'd always known about Pristina, but he'd never flaunted her in front of me. And it incensed me that he'd flaunted that tiny toddler.

"Are you dating that girl?" I demanded.

"We've been hanging out," he said, shrugging.

"Are you hanging out with her because you threatened to find someone new and I didn't take the bait?" I asked.

"Oh, please. Don't flatter yourself. I've been hanging out with her because she's cool and I like her."

"So that's where you've been," I accused.

"Yeah, so what? And by the way, why are you so worried about it? You're fucking engaged!"

"Yeah, that's right. I fucking am!"

The thought of Jeremy hanging out with that child was too much for me. True, I'd been warned. True, I was engaged. True, I should have been glad about it. But still.

So when Andy had a champagne party I called Jeremy to see if he wanted to go with me. He said he was already invited and that he would see me there. I was pissed at him for being so independent of me.

And as I'd suspected he would, he showed up with Breeze.

"What the fuck?" I screamed, drunk. I had been there all day drinking champagne before the party even started. Andy had begged me to slow down but I hadn't listened.

Breeze gave me a patronizing look. "Is this the one you were telling me about?" she whispered, clutching Jeremy's sleeve with one of those tiny hands of hers.

"What the hell is that supposed to mean?" I sneered at her. She didn't even cower. Instead she raised her eyebrows and looked smug. She had tiny eyebrows. She reminded me of Aurelia Sparks.

"I want to talk to you," I said to Jeremy. I took him by the arm and led him away from the hideous intruder.

"I like her," he informed me, in the kitchen.

"What the fuck?" I repeated.

"I really like her. She's great. She's fun. She makes my stomach sick with butterflies. She's my girlfriend now."

"What about me?" I demanded, splaying a hand across my chest. "Do I mean nothing to you at all?"

He let out a patronizing laugh. "Please! You're engaged! You've never been able to mean anything to me."

"Weren't you just telling me a few weeks ago that you thought we could work? Didn't you fly all the way to Las Vegas from Miami just because you wanted to be with me on New Year's Eve? Haven't you been hinting at me to get out of my engagement for months now?" I screamed.

He folded his arms. "I guess. But just because I kicked around the idea of us doesn't mean I was totally serious. And yeah, I did want to be with you on New Year's Eve, but that's because I knew I would have more fun with you than anyone else. You're my friend, Doll…but all that other stuff— it was just a fling. It was just something to do."

"Are you serious?"

He nodded. "Look. I'm really into Breeze. And I think you're great sometimes but that's where it ends with you and me."

I felt like he'd just punched me in the stomach. "Are you kidding me?" I demanded.

He shook his head. "No. You really are delusional, Doll. You need to get over me, seriously. Your infatuation with me has always been unhealthy. I have to put an end to it right now. It can't go on any longer."

"Isn't that the pot calling the kettle black!"

He shook his head again. "No. It's always been you hanging on to me like some sick obsessive lunatic. Get over it and get over it now. Please."

I started throwing things at him. I threw the jars from Andy's spice rack. I threw a baguette and a few slabs of Gouda. I wanted to kill him.

He kept shaking his head like I was a lost cause and turned to walk out of the kitchen. He bumped into a guy who was standing in the doorway. "Sorry about that, man," he said apologetically, touching the guy's shoulder the way he'd do to any stranger he'd accidentally run into.

Turns out, though, that guy wasn't a stranger.

It was Roman. He'd been standing there the whole time.

"Why didn't you tell me he was coming?" I demanded of Andy a few minutes later.

Jeremy and Breeze had left immediately, and Roman had followed without saying a word to anyone. Maybe they all rode down together in the elevator. The whole scene had sent me right to the bathroom, where I'd thrown up straight champagne into the toilet. It burned the back of my throat and made my eyes water and my nose sting. Andy came in to rub my back and hold my hair.

"He said not to tell you. He's the reason I had this party in the first place."

"Next time, think, Andy, think! Why would you have invited Jeremy if you were having this party for Roman?"

"Uh, well…because Jeremy told me you and he weren't, uh…being more than friends anymore. I assumed you knew." He put his thumbnail between his teeth. "So you uh…you didn't know?"

"Brilliant."

"I'm really sorry, Doll."

"Where'd he even meet that girl?" I asked, my heart beating irregularly.

"He met her at Bar Marmont on Valentine's Day, while you were out with your folks. They've been dating ever since. Maybe I should have said something, huh?"

"That might have helped."

He sat back against the bathroom wall and looked thoughtful. "So what now?"

I crawled over to him and put my head on his knee. "Fuck. Fuck!"

He stroked my hair. "Why don't you try calling Roman?"

"He doesn't have a cell phone."

"What?" Andy asked, shocked. "How does he get through life?"

"Andy…"

"He didn't say where he was staying, either," he mused. "Oh, duh! I guess he was planning to stay with you."

I started crying. And I thought I would never, ever stop.

Chapter 25

All of my friends had dresses in their closets that they were supposed to be wearing to my wedding, rescheduled for the first of June.

My mother had a whole stack of reprinted invitations to send out in a few weeks.

Roman saw me trifling with another man. I wondered where he had gone. He had looked at me, kind of confused, just before walking out. I hadn't seen him in more than seven months. We were supposed to be on our honeymoon.

And Jeremy...in love with someone else.

How had I gotten myself into this mess?

I wanted to crawl into a hole and die. I wanted to lock myself in my room and listen to The Cranberries and Coldplay and Sarah McLachlan. Instead I got into my car and it drove me up to the beach house.

Lily listened to the whole story and then sent me to the grocery store for some therapy. My cart was loaded with fixings for a Boboli pizza and ice cream when I rounded the corner and ran right into Aurelia Sparks. Literally coming at me so I couldn't make an escape without her noticing.

When it rains it really does fucking pour.

I was pleased as always to see that age hadn't done her any favors. She looked beyond exhausted. She wore absolutely no makeup. Her ringlets had been chopped right off and now her hair was cut like a boy's. She had the new baby in a Snugli on her chest and a toddler in her cart.

We stopped next to the dairy case. Our carts faced each other like we were bulls going head to head.

"Hey, Doll," she said.

"Hey," I replied. I was wearing black hip-hugger pants and a long-sleeved black shirt. I had on dark black Chanel sunglasses. I knew I looked hip. I felt hip. I had a Kate Spade bag. I had Charles David shoes. She was wearing a denim smock. Probably from Ross Dress for Less. She looked homespun and comfortable. That bitch.

She was just standing there staring at me. It's almost like she's waiting for me to initiate a conversation. It's like she wants to go beyond "Hi" or "Hey" but never does. Never has. Never will, maybe, unless I take control of the moment.

I decided to do just that. Why the fuck not.

I pulled my shades up onto my head. "So what's new, Aurelia?"

She looked slightly taken aback, then hid it in a shrug. "Nothing, really, except for this little one. Crosby."

I nodded, like I approved.

She rubbed the back of her baby's dark head. "And you? I heard you were living in Hollywood and engaged to some guy in Africa and working as a wedding planner."

"I don't plan weddings," I said. And who knows if I'm engaged anymore. I took my sunglasses off and fiddled with them. Suddenly I wanted to cry again. Right then and there. To Aurelia Sparks of all people. My God. I really was losing my mind. Fuck *that*. "I'm an event planner. All the rest is true."

"Must be exciting. I never get out of this place." She gave me a knowing look. "Funny, huh? When I was younger I used to think I was going to become a Dallas Cowboys cheerleader and marry Troy Aikmen."

"That *is* funny," I told her. "Of course, I used to think I was going to live in Hollywood and have a glamorous job and end up with someone really worldly."

Her face flushed and she narrowed her eyes. "You have always been the most heinous bitch. I hope you know that."

"Thanks, Aurelia. With you I've always worked extra hard at it."

It was cold next to the dairy case. I wanted to eat all the pudding in the store. I wanted everything to be the way it was before. No, I wanted everything to be different.

"Everything's really not that great, if you want to know the truth," I told her, feeling myself collapse a little. "Which I'm sure gives you some kind of cunty pleasure or something."

She raised her eyebrows.

I went on. "My fiancé, the one who lives in Africa? He showed up last night, unexpected, and happened to overhear me screaming at my lover over the fact that *he* just fell in love with Kindergarten Barbie and decided to drop me on my ass. Now he's gone and I don't even know where he went."

"Wait, you lost me," she said. "Your lover?"

I nodded. "Jeremy. Roman's my fiancé."

"I see."

"It's complicated," I added. "Roman's this great guy, right...only he was never here. So I got involved with Jeremy, who's actually kind of a jerk. But see...I loved them both. And then the great guy proposed and ran off to Africa and left me with the jerk...and I started thinking I loved the jerk more than the great guy, and after a while the great guy seemed like a jerk and the jerk seemed great...and I was confused...and lonely...but not really lonely, just alone or something...and afraid of the what-ifs."

She looked slightly concerned. Confused. Concerned. Interested. I don't know.

"I don't know why I'm telling you all this," I said, fiddling some more with my sunglasses. "I just thought that maybe you, Aurelia, could explain it to me. Why *you* are standing there with two babies and Dan at home and *I* am standing here falling apart next to a bunch of dated goddamn milk cartons."

She was quiet for a few moments. Then she started laughing.

"What the fuck is that?" I demanded. "God, talk about being the most heinous bitch."

She stopped laughing. "Sorry, really. Okay, not really. But it's just like, you have to be so *bad-ass* all the time. I mean, don't you think it's kind of a cop-out?"

The toddler, Daniel Jr., grinned at me through a mouthful of animal crackers. He had a little toy truck in his hands. That was supposed to be *my* baby.

"Let me ask you something, Doll."

"Ask away."

"Which one do you want?"

"Roman," I replied. The name flew out of my mouth with no hesitation, no force.

"Then what are you doing here?" she asked.

"I thought Lily…"

"You thought Lily what?" she said, before I could finish. "Would tell you to tell everyone else to get fucked and recommend that you prance off like you rock?"

I didn't reply. That was exactly the kind of thing Lily would say.

Aurelia pulled a juice box from the stash in her cart and punctured it with the attached straw. She handed it to Daniel Jr.

"I have a better idea," she said to me. "Why don't you swallow your stupid pride for once? So your fiancé knows you had an affair. What's done is done, obviously. And this may sound like a novel concept to you, but why don't you explain yourself? Tell him what you just told me. Maybe throw in an apology while you're at it. Or, you can hang out at the beach house all night eating pizza and ice cream and moaning about how you're always fucking everything up."

"That was a pretty grand assumption, that last part." Even though that was exactly what was going to happen.

She let out a spurt of disbelieving laughter. "Come on, Doll. It's *me* standing here. Consider how much we've been through together. The things we've shared. A fine fucking line exists between love and hate." She glanced at Daniel. He was oblivious. "Just don't be so goddamn self-important. Humble yourself for once. Don't ask me why I'm standing here with two babies and Dan at home, either. You could have swallowed your stupid pride back when you messed around on Dan and it would be you standing here right now, in my place. But no. Instead you said fuck it, I don't belong here, anyway, and ran off. And now here you are again." She laughed a bitter laugh.

I folded my arms. "Wow, someone's a little sensitive about her position in life."

"Oh, you make me *sick*." She spat out the words. "Always having to pretend you're so much better than everyone else. As if you were chosen for some superior existence. Only, you were pretty insecure about that, weren't you? Hiding all your uncertainty behind all your fancy things—all the things you thought would make it okay that you were different—because you *were* different, that you could never just be happy with everything you had!"

I took a step back. "If I didn't know you any better, I'd say you were jealous of me."

"Bravo. You had *everything* and you didn't even appreciate it. You didn't even want it. You were always sure there was something else, something better out there that only *you* deserved while the rest of us should have to take whatever we could get! It was nauseating. It's still nauseating."

"Excuse me," a man said, ducking in between our carts to grab a few containers of yogurt off the shelf. He gave us a slightly annoyed look. "Carry on."

I felt my cheeks color. "Look, we can't just stand here all day insulting each other, Aurelia."

"Hey, you're the one who started telling me your woes," she snapped, sounding not entirely unlike a Chihuahua. "Just like you're the one who started this whole thing back when you had all the opportunity to make it easy for me, but made it *so fucking hard* instead. I'll never forget the way you treated me…and what you said about me. Ever."

"I really didn't even know what white trash was at the time," I confessed. "It was just something I'd heard Kitty Lovejoy say about your neighbors."

She shrugged. "Yeah, well…that has followed me through life, Doll."

"Oh, just get over it," I told her. "Because you have totally hogged out on your just deserts."

"Not really, Doll."

"Consider the outcome."

She rubbed her baby's back. "You consider the outcome, Doll. You would have never lasted like this, had you gone into it when you were given the chance. I have to. Because it's all I know."

When I looked at her in her unsophisticated ensemble and her cart full of wholesome groceries, standing there with two tiny kids and everlasting existence in our hometown, I thought about something.

I wouldn't want Aurelia's life.

Even though she had Dan, and Dan's name and Dan's children. She's still here; but I got out. Now I can go back whenever I choose. Now I can go back and enjoy myself, without feeling trapped. Remembering doesn't mean I'm stuck. I know what the world is like elsewhere. I know what it's like to live another life. I've gone away to college and lived in a big city and had crazy times. I've had adventures. I still love home. I just didn't want to stay there forever. I didn't want to wake up one day and wonder why I'd never gone beyond the county line.

It occurred to me that I'd spent way too long thinking of Roman as my absolution. That I'd spent way too long thinking there was something wrong with me that he was supposed to make right. That I'd put too much into assuming that by running away with him, I was going to be normal, and happy always, and never again make mistakes.

And amazingly enough, as it all dissolved and broke down in the presence of that bitch Aurelia Sparks, I realized I really loved Roman beyond all of that. And I knew I really wanted the life we were somehow meant to have together. The life I've always wanted. The life I've been waiting for. Not because I think he's going to take me away. Because I want to be with him, wherever. Africa. America. Washington. Los Angeles. Ventura. Heaven. Hell. Everywhere. Anywhere.

"Hello, are you there?" Aurelia snapped at me. "Because I'm not done."

I had to get out of there. I had to find Roman. Right away. I had to see Roman, talk to him. Tell him everything. An older woman snuck a longing glance at the cottage cheese as she wheeled her shopping cart past.

Aurelia went on, face crimson, eyes ablaze. "I've been waiting years for this confrontation, so don't think you can just walk away without letting me speak. Okay, so I probably should have minded my own business instead of telling Dan about Mike. But I was seventeen and I hated your guts. I hated you for what you did with my Charlie."

I folded my arms. "What I did with your Charlie? Your Charlie came to me, if I recall. He was lured by the fact that one summer I lost a ton of weight and grew some enormous boobs and got damn foxy. And from my end, you had *nothing* to do with Charlie and me. I'd known Charlie since we were babies in a playpen—long before you *ever* came in to play."

Her eyes were scrunched up into little slits. "Yeah, but he was my first love. He was my first everything—and I was supposed to be his. Now, just imagine my surprise to find out I got him back in used condition! You took his virginity. He was ruined," she added hatefully.

"Get over yourself, Aurelia. I hardly think that was reason to tell Dan about Mike. I didn't take Charlie's virginity to wreck you."

She shrugged as the baby conked out against her chest. "Well, you taking Charlie's virginity *did* wreck me. So when the opportunity presented itself I decided *I* would wreck *you.* That's why I told Dan about Mike. I knew you'd be too proud to ever fix that."

"God, you really are *evil,*" I told her.

"Yeah, but that's okay," she said innocently. "Because Jesus has my back."

"Never have been able to trust that guy," I mused. "And if He's on your side, I'll *gladly* go with Satan."

She laughed a little.

I shifted my weight from one foot to the other. I was getting impatient. I had something to do and I wanted to do it.

"Look, Aurelia, I think we've said all we needed to say."

She cocked her head. "So, do you think we're even now?"

"I suppose. I mean, I will always have Charlie's virginity."

She smiled smugly. "True. Just like I'll always have Dan's babies."

That bitch.

"So what are you going to do?" she asked.

"About *what?*"

She rolled her eyes. "Your current situation?"

"Oh. I have to find Roman. Tell him everything."

"For once, it sounds like you might actually be doing the right thing." She looked down at her baby. Its mouth was moving in its sleep. "I have to get going," she told me. "I need to get the boys home, and besides that, I'm cooking dinner

for Dan's parents tonight. Anyway…it was a real pleasure seeing you."

"Oh…you, too."

I watched her push her cart down the aisle and disappear.
Aurelia Sparks. Mrs. Dan Michaelson.

My nemesis. My archenemy. My number-one rival.

My savior.

Chapter 26

I raced north on the 101 freeway. The last flight leaving Los Angeles for Cameroon was taking off at ten p.m. A last-minute flight from L.A. to Cameroon costs more than three thousand dollars. I charged it to myself instead of my mother this time. If I was going to be an adult and deal with my adult mishaps, I was going to have to take responsibility for myself like a true adult would.

I dialed numbers with fervor. Andy was stuck at work. My roommates weren't answering. Finally, I got Dylan. The Mighty Ducks were playing the Kings at the Staples Center.

"Go to my house and pack a bag for me," I commanded, over the crowd cheering in the background. "Roman went back to Africa this morning and I'm going there tonight. My passport's in my top desk drawer. The key's in the flower pot on the back patio."

"You got it!"

No questions asked, no complaints. Now that's a friend. I squealed into the driveway as Dylan ran out of the house, my Louis Vuitton duffel bag thrown over one shoulder. The console clock read 8:15.

"Get out!" he ordered me.

I ran around to the passenger side and let him take the wheel of my car. He reversed and stepped on the gas.

"Shouldn't you call your boss?" he asked, careening down La Brea.

I dialed Karen at home. "I can't come back to work for a few days, maybe longer. I have to go to Africa," I told her, as Dylan sped into the 10 heading west. "I had an affair and my fiancé found out."

"I knew it, goddamn you!" she yelled at me. "Good idea, go to Africa! Tell him you were taking medication. Tell him you were brainwashed by a cult. Tell him whatever you have to!"

"I'm not going to lie."

"I don't really care how you do it, Doll. Just don't let him go. I don't plan a wedding without expecting to go to it, understand me? Oh, did I tell you I'm pregnant? Sal and I are painting the nursery right now!"

The console clock read 8:45 when we hit a traffic jam on the 405.

"I'm not going to make it," I said frantically.

"You'll make it," Dylan promised, swerving in and out between cars. He lit two cigarettes at the same time and handed one my way. We puffed in unison.

My cell phone rang a message. I dialed my voice mail. It was Jeremy.

"Look. We should probably talk. Call me."

I disconnected and turned my cell phone off. You don't walk away from someone you've known for almost three years without saying anything. Jeremy and I had things to say. They were going to have to wait, though. Talking to Roman was more important. Talking to Roman was *most* important.

Traffic thinned out and Dylan whizzed toward the airport

at lightning speed. He pulled up in front of the terminal at
five after nine.

"Thanks, Dylan," I said, hugging him. "I owe you one."

"You don't owe me shit. You just go do what you gotta
do," he said, rubbing my back. He kissed the top of my head.
"Good luck, Dollface!"

"Thanks!" I called over my shoulder, as I ran into the
airport.

The Air France flight from Los Angeles to Cincinnati to
Paris to Douala to Yaoundé was boarding when I made it to
the gate. My heart was still accelerating when I slid into my
assigned seat and closed my eyes.

It takes almost two days to get to Cameroon when you
figure in the different time zones. When I straggled off the
last of numerous airplanes, it was around two p.m. on Tues-
day afternoon and I was pretty sure I was half-dead. It was
very hot there, like New Orleans in the summertime. I had
to ask for a taxi in French. I've always put *fluent* on my résumé but I know what I said came out like: *Need I taxi a
take find for boyfriend me.* The taxi driver laughed and asked
where I came from in America. When I said Hollywood
he shouted, "Ah, Tom Cruise!" He was very jolly.

Normally I prefer to go into such situations looking the
hottest. Only right then I was wearing the same outfit I'd
thrown on before driving up to the beach house on Sunday.
I hadn't showered since Saturday. I had spilled cranberry
juice all over myself on the plane. Beautiful.

The taxi driver drove fast and crazy through the tree-
lined streets of Yaoundé and when he dropped me off he
seemed disappointed by my tip. I remembered Roman
telling me once that a good tip in Cameroon is an American souvenir so I gave him a box of matches from a dreary
lounge called Daddy's and a pen from Universal Studios that
I found in my purse. He got all excited and told me the
rains fall on good days too. I had no fucking idea what that
was supposed to mean. I was pretty sure he was crazy.

The ICRA offices were on the eighth floor of a tall building. They were clean with white walls and air-conditioning. There were framed art prints. People were sprawled out at desks all over the place, looking happy and earnest. They looked all fresh and earthy like Gap ads. I'd never seen so much chambray.

"Dalton? Is that you?"

I jumped. It was Bill Mayfair, Roman's best friend...and best man. He had just gotten off the elevator. Nobody else had noticed me come in. The reception desk was empty.

"Hi, Bill."

He looked perplexed. "Is Roman...expecting you?"

"Not really. Is he around?" As if I were just stopping by. I kind of liked that. Like I was a frivolous jet-setter. Yeah.

"Wait here, okay? You can have a seat." He smiled.

My eyes followed his path and came to a stop when I saw Roman through the windows of one of the individual offices. He was talking on the phone and wearing his glasses. Bill stood in his doorway and talked to him as he leaned back in his chair and put one hand behind his head. He looked through the windows and saw me. I was surprised to notice that he looked pleased. He wrapped up his conversation and got up from his seat. He was dressed in khaki pants and a striped shirt with the sleeves rolled up. No tie.

I was sitting in a chair. My legs were pressed together. I clutched my bag as I stood up. I was glad Dylan hadn't loaded me up with a huge suitcase because I had to change planes in Paris and that is just too confusing. They don't move your luggage for you. You have to get it from one plane and put it on the next. No convenience in Europe. None at all. Only I suppose I could go for the three-hour lunch breaks. And the six weeks of vacation in the summertime. And all that wine and cheese. Yeah...maybe.

Roman gave me a tight hug before I could even say hi.

"Pretty shocking," he told me. He stood in front of me with one arm of his glasses shoved between his teeth.

"I know."

"I've been trying to call you," he told me.

"I've been on a plane. Several of them, in fact."

He laughed a little. "I'm glad you're here. I think things are better in person, don't you?"

I nodded. "That's kind of a point I've been trying to drive home for a while now."

He looked off in the distance. "It's really bad timing, I know, but I have to go to Douala this afternoon."

"You've got to be kidding me. For how long?"

He was quiet for a moment. "I won't be back for two days."

"Why do you have to go?" I asked, panicked. Was he leaving me alone in this completely foreign place for two days?

"Because I always go to Douala today. Every week that I'm here."

"Oh." It was a simple reply. And only the crest of a wave in a sea of things I didn't know about him. I realized this then. And I felt young and stupid.

He looked thoughtful. "I'll take you over to the Hilton and you can stay there until I get back."

"There's a Hilton here?" I exclaimed.

He couldn't help laughing. "Man's made some amazing advances, huh?"

"A yes or a no generally gets it done with me."

He stopped laughing. "All right. Yes, there is a Hilton. It's a very, very nice hotel and you'll be comfortable and safe. I have a ton of work to finish here before I leave for Douala, so I have to take you over there right now, okay?"

I shrugged. "Hey, I can walk if it's that much trouble for you."

He shook his head. "No, no, can't have that. This isn't Beverly Hills and you're not to go walking around unless you have an escort. All right, Dalton? All right?"

I nodded. I could feel him looking at the stain from the

cranberry juice. I felt like a stain right then. I didn't feel like a frivolous jet-setter anymore. Just like a frivolous I don't know what.

I sulked in the car on the way to the hotel, not speaking. When we went inside Roman seemed to know the concierge and they chatted easily for a few moments. I could tell Roman was explaining about who I was and the concierge looked amused. When they had finished speaking and my room had been taken care of, Roman took me by the elbow and we rode up in the elevator.

"Don't you even want to know why I'm here?" I asked, jerking my arm away.

"I know why you're here," he said, offering nothing more. I had no choice but to follow him off the elevator and down the hall to my room.

"You can call Bill if you need anything. I'll give you his card and I'll put his home number on it." He looked at me. "Are you going to be okay here?"

"Well…I wish you would cancel your trip. I mean…I did take time off from work and I've traveled a long distance just to see you. It's not easy getting here, you know."

He looked at me again. "Then I'd say we're about even now, aren't we?"

I felt my cheeks go hot. "Oh."

He sighed. "This is a civilized city, but it's no place for a girl like you to be out and about by yourself. You are never to leave this hotel unless you're accompanied by someone I trust. Don't even leave this room, actually."

"Okay."

"I'm serious, Dalton. When I get back from Douala you'd better be right here where I left you."

"Okay."

He sighed again. "If you cannot locate Bill, the concierge downstairs can help you. Also, the American embassy is right nearby. I'll put their number on Bill's card."

"Got it."

He pulled out his wallet and extracted the card. He went over to the little table in the corner and hunched over to write down the numbers. I studied his profile as he paused with the pen poised. He looked like he was trying to remember something. He finished writing and came back to me. He handed me the card.

"What about your number in Douala?" I asked, my heart pounding.

"You don't need that. I'll be back in two days. Charge whatever you want to the room...food or drinks or whatever. Just stay here and wait for me." He held my shoulders and kissed my cheek before he left.

And then he was gone. And I was alone in Africa.

Chapter 27

I really didn't have time to be pissed or sad or confused because I was so damn tired that I keeled right over and slept the day away after he'd gone. When I woke up it was nighttime and the room was dark. I turned on the lights. I took a shower and towel-dried my hair. I put on loose linen pants, blue ones. I put on a clean tank top.

I walked around the room, barefooted, smoking a cigarette. I felt like a hostage.

I guess it could have been worse. I was in a five-star hotel with room service. My windows overlooked the jeweled waters of a swimming pool below and the glittering lights of a new city beyond. How strange to be in a foreign place. I'll never understand the feeling of it…even though I like that feeling immensely.

What if Roman never came back from Douala? Then I would just have to stay in this hotel forever and nobody would ever know where I was.

Or what if he did come back and said it's over, and he

wanted the ring back, and sent me back home without even talking about anything?

What would I return to, really?

Even imagining that Jeremy wasn't at home just then with Breeze…it was still Roman that I wanted. I'd chased him all the way to Africa, when I could have just run a few miles to Jeremy's apartment in Palms. I would admit to being crazy about Jeremy, but without Roman, he would have seemed like a consolation prize at best.

I wanted Roman for good, the way I've always wanted him and not just imagined like I had with Jeremy. And they were two very different things, once I was forced to think about it.

I didn't like being alone and having to think about my life and myself. I felt suffocated by all my thoughts.

I *really* didn't like being alone. I was never alone. Even at home, when I was alone, I had people around. I had Ava and Electra just outside my bedroom door. I had Dylan cackling about, Andy just down the street, Lily just up the coast. But in Cameroon I was alone. Alone, alone, alone.

I had room service send me breakfast the next morning. I stood by my windows and looked out at the lush green hills surrounding Yaoundé, the infinite blue sky. I lay on the bed reading the first book of *Imajica* by Clive Barker. Interesting concepts in there.

By dusk I was goddamn sick of that hotel room. I put on a face of makeup and headed upstairs to the bar. I sat at a table by myself, drinking weird beer with a weird name, and looked out at the city.

The hotel was having a convention and there were lots of men in the bar. I noticed some of them were extremely savory but I didn't do anything about it. I didn't feel like doing anything about it. I just wanted to be with Roman so we could talk and figure shit out. If we even could.

And then Roman walked in.

"Hi," he said. He sat down in the chair across from me. "I thought I told you to stay in your room."

"I thought you weren't coming back until tomorrow?" I asked.

He looked tired. Like he'd been through some kind of serious shit in Douala. "I decided this couldn't wait."

"And what's that?" I asked, picking at the label on my beer bottle.

"You know. Me and you."

"Oh." I rested the side of my face in one hand and gazed at him.

He held up his hand. I placed my other one against it. Palm to palm.

"I'm ready to talk now," he told me seriously. "I could have canceled my trip to Douala, but it seemed necessary yesterday because I wasn't ready to talk then. You really shocked the hell out of me by coming here. I never expected it. I mean, I was literally stupefied." He ran his free hand over his hair.

"Yeah, well, then I'd say we're about even now."

He laced our fingers together. "Yeah...we are."

The waiter came around and asked if Roman wanted a drink. Roman ordered himself one of those weird beers and one more for me. He let go of my hand to take out his cigarettes and lit one for each of us.

"So what do you think of Yaoundé?" he asked.

I looked out the window. "It's nice. Of course, from this perspective, it could be Las Vegas out there. Or Seattle. Or Kansas City. You just can't tell."

He laughed. "Point taken. I'll get you out of this hotel soon. Cameroon is one of my favorite countries. We call it 'Africa in miniature,' because as a country it's like a miniature version of the whole continent. A little bit of everything."

The beers arrived. I noticed a little facial hair I hadn't seen before on Roman as he took a swig of his. I must have been really out of it yesterday. Was that a goatee? Wow...sexy.

"This project has basically sucked, hasn't it?" he asked.

I nodded.

Roman went on. "I almost called you the day after I got here and asked you to come. Then I decided it would be awfully selfish of me."

"Selfish?"

"Yeah, because I wanted you here for selfish reasons. So you could be with me."

"We really need to work on our lines of communication," I told him. "I would have considered it a good thing that you wanted me to be with you."

"I realize that now. I shouldn't have left you in L.A." The city lights twinkled behind him. A jazz band was playing. I sipped my beer.

Sometimes, when Roman got talking, he could really talk. I had a feeling he was on the verge of some long, philosophical monologue about love and marriage. I decided to take the lead of the conversation. Put it all out there.

"I didn't take a lover because you left me in L.A.," I told him. It occurred to me that I was now referring to Jeremy as my lover and not my friend. I was finally telling the truth.

Roman raised his eyebrows.

"I met him shortly after I met you," I went on. "It didn't seem like that big of a deal, having him, because you and I were so far apart, who knew if we were ever going to get serious? I guess what I mean by that is, I didn't take us very seriously. I knew I loved you and that I hoped it would last. Jeremy was my companion all the same."

"How come I never heard about him?" he asked. His chest was rising and falling to an even rhythm, like he was forcing composure.

"It just didn't seem worth mentioning. He never had anything to do with you...until recently."

"You were hiding him from me," he accused.

I took a drag and fidgeted. I didn't like having this conversation. But I had to have it. So I forged ahead.

"He was just in a different part of my life," I told him. "A part you didn't know about because I never thought you needed to know about it. A part I thought I could easily dispose of when we did get serious. But being as you were gone and I was still in that other part…he was still there, too. And it just got…complicated."

"Are you blaming *me* for anything you may have done?" he demanded. "Is it *my* fault that you may have had trouble in handling a long-distance relationship? And if so…would it maybe have been possible for you to say so back in the beginning…before it went this far?"

I shook my head. "I am not blaming you for Jeremy. That's not what I'm saying at all. Jeremy was my thing. All mine. And what was between us—well, it's done. It's over. Truthfully, it was over from the very beginning."

Roman narrowed his eyes. "How was it over from the very beginning if it went on for so long? That makes absolutely no sense, Dalton."

"He was just this goofy guy who invited me out for sushi one night, Roman. I'd seen you a total of three times. You weren't even in Washington when I met him—you were in Nairobi. Anyway, it wasn't like Jeremy and I were going to ever get serious about each other. We were really more like…playmates. He had a girlfriend, this nurse who was always working. I had a boyfriend, this humanities professor who was always off saving the world."

"Did the nurse know about you?"

"No."

He sat back in his chair. "Then it would seem you and Jeremy both explored the possibility that you may get serious about each other at some point."

"That's really not how it was," I insisted.

"Hmm. So after we got engaged, you decided you were just going to keep right on fucking him up until our wedding day, or what?"

"Maybe I thought you were never really serious about for-ever," I said, draining my beer bottle. Roman immediately flagged the waiter to order another round. "It sure didn't seem like it when you asked me to marry you, then took off for six months."

"You've never heard the expression that a diamond is for-ever, Dalton?"

"That's right. Wear this diamond forever. But hey—six months in Cameroon is now nine months in Cameroon. You don't mind, do you? And hey—Landon's set me up for an-other fantastic opportunity somewhere else, oh, I don't know, for a year or so, but it's my job, baby. So how's our wedding coming along?"

The beers were set down on the table. Roman grabbed his and took a long drink. He was agitated. I could tell I'd hit a nerve.

"Nobody ever gets it," he said, wiping his mouth with the back of his hand.

"Roman, I fucking get it, all right?" I said. "I get it. I've always thought the idealist in you was the very best part. I have *never* thought that was a flaw, Roman. Never. It's just that this last time...I got sick of you being gone. I got sick of only getting the parts of you that didn't already belong to what you do. And a lot of you belongs to what you do. A lot. So much that you've been away for almost a whole year. When I'm twenty-five and I'm supposed to be living some of the best years of my life. Doing what? Sitting in my room writing letters?"

He frowned.

"So I guess I just kept living my life the way I'd always been living it," I told him. "And yes—my life included Jer-emy. And I wasn't so sure that this—you and me—was ever really going to happen. You haven't given any input on our wedding. You weren't even there to help me pick out the items on our registry—Andy had to do it. A marriage is more than a wedding, sure. But you try planning a wedding with the thought in mind that the person you're supposed to stand next to at the altar will only show up if they can make it."

He nodded thoughtfully, as though absorbing what I'd said.

"A proposal is a promise, and I know that. I also know promises *can* be broken. They don't have substance without action—the same way a diamond doesn't always symbolize forever. I mean, don't get me wrong about us. We're great together...when we're together. But I need more than a weekend here and there. I need companionship. I need to be able to nurture something—and I can't nurture something that isn't really there. I guess I'm needier than I thought. I like to pretend that I'm never upset, that I'm so independent I can handle anything without breaking down. But I'm not that strong all the time. It's pathetic."

"You're not needy because you wanted me there. I guess like I wasn't selfish for wanting you here. And it's not pathetic, breaking down. People break down because they're human and there's no shame in that. And I think it's pretty damn independent to drop everything and fly to Africa when you don't even know what awaits you. Seriously. I'm impressed, Dalton."

I shrugged. "Well...I knew it was time to face the issue. To face you. Especially in the wake of that whole ugly scene at Andy's."

"I know...I thought it was time to face you, too. That's why I came to L.A."

"What do you mean, face me?" I asked. "I'm the one who totally screwed up. You were just coming to see me."

His face grew serious. "Well...I was coming to see you, you're right. Only there were...other reasons. In-person reasons."

Panic seized my stomach. I almost threw up. I lit another cigarette. I was going to be sorry in the morning.

"What kind of 'in-person' reasons?" I asked. "Was there... something else?"

"Actually, yes." He gave me a very serious look.

And then he told me about Emmaline.

Chapter 28

Emmaline was Roman's ex-girlfriend. The one he'd always been so blasé about. I've seen her in pictures in all of his early photo albums. He makes two or three albums from every project. At his house in Georgetown, there is a tall bookshelf full of them. One time when I was visiting I sat in this big leather chair in his library while he was at work and looked at those albums for hours and hours. It was like looking at travel books because Roman's been everywhere. Whenever I hear the name Emmaline I think of Brooke Shields's character in *The Blue Lagoon*. But Emmaline doesn't look anything like Brooke Shields. She looks like one of those women skiers in lip balm commercials. All athletic and natural.

"You know how I told you Em and I broke up a long time before you and I met?"

"Uh-huh."

He looked uncomfortable. "Well...I kind of lied."

"How do you *kind* of lie?" I asked.

"You kind of lie when you first meet a girl and you really like her and you don't want her to get spooked by all your bullshit and baggage so you just kind of…pare it down a little."

"I see." Those fuckers.

He sighed and looked reminiscent. "We actually kind of broke up right about the time that I was in L.A. for that benefit and happened to set my eyes upon a very pretty girl by the name of Dalton Moss."

"Oh, please." Flattery wasn't going to get him out of this. "Go on. So you were still with Emmaline when you and I met?"

He heaved a great sigh. "No, not really. We had ended it just before. She pretty much threw me out."

"So what'd you do, take up with me to get over it?"

"That's not how it was, Dalton."

"Then why don't you tell me how it was, Roman."

He smiled. "I saw a sexy woman in a black dress, following Karen around the ballroom of the Century Plaza Hotel with a clipboard. Karen was shouting, frazzled, but not you. You were so confident, so self-assured—but not snooty. You were laughing a lot, having a good time. I overheard you telling the bartender to give you a rum and Coke, easy on the Coke. I thought that was great. I saw you outside smoking with one of our celebrity guests, but you were just having a conversation with the guy like he was a normal person, instead of trying to make a connection or get a date. I thought, now there's a woman I'd like to talk to. And I wanted to come talk to you all night, but I kept having to schmooze it up and work the room because fucking Landon wouldn't get off my back." He wrinkled up his nose.

"That's all very nice, but it still doesn't tell me much."

He stroked his goatee. "Women in Washington are too driven—they've only ever been interested in me as a means of having another impressive credential to add to their résumés. You were something *different*. You were interested in *me*. I could talk to you about life. You remembered all the names of all my family members after I only told you one time—meaning you were really *listening*. Your eyes never glazed over. Your stories cracked me up. You talked about the people in your life with so much love. And I got to thinking, my God. So this is what it's like. I look forward to seeing her. She makes me feel good, and not just because of what I've done with my life. She doesn't say things as a means of convincing me that we're on the same track. Fuck that. Washington women are so conventional!"

"L.A. women are conventional, too. The goals are the same even if the game is played a little differently."

"Maybe so. What I'm saying, though, is that I felt we connected beyond the usual expectations. We looked at the people, not the personas. We saw individuals, not ideals. It was great."

"This is all very nice to hear, but what does it have to do with Emmaline?"

He took a deep breath. "You remember that time I told you I was out on my patio having a cigarette?"

Reality was really setting in. I could feel it pounding in my chest. "Yes?"

"Well…I was out on my patio because Emmaline was in my bedroom."

I looked down. No matter all the horrible things you've done, or the awful thoughts you've had, or the way you've lived knowingly with betrayal…it still hurts when somebody betrays *you*.

"I understand," I told him, starting to get up. "You don't have to say any more."

He put his hand up to stop me. "Please sit down. Please listen."

I slid back into my chair. "I'm listening."

"When I got back to D.C., Landon called a project meeting before we all left. Imagine my surprise when Emmaline walked in. When I asked what she was doing there, she told me she'd just lost her directorship in Guatemala due to budget cuts and Landon was able to bring her on board with my team, as my counterpart in Douala."

"Would that be the same Douala you were in such a hurry to get to when I got here yesterday?" I demanded.

He nodded. "Look, Emmaline and I work together and there's nothing to it. We see each other every day unless we're both out on projects. Separate projects. But here, for some reason, well…after a while…well, we started talking…and spending a lot of time together…and she told me she wanted to get back together. She'd been missing me for a long time and when I told her you and I were getting married, she just couldn't handle it."

"Oh, boo-hoo," I said carelessly. I tapped the mouth of my beer bottle to my lips.

"Well, she was very upset," he said, sounding almost offended by my comment. Then he told me how hard it was and how torn he felt and how everything was so confusing. I guess I could relate.

I twisted my ring. "I didn't realize you'd been so taken with this woman. The way you've always talked about her…you acted like you were so glad it didn't last. End of story."

"Well, I wasn't going to tell you the extent of my feelings for my past love. Did you really want to hear about how much I loved my ex-girlfriend? You can't tell somebody that when you first start dating. It just paves a rocky road."

"I guess." Like maybe you shouldn't tell a guy, after you've just spent a totally incredible night together, that you have a boyfriend. Even if it turns out he also has a girlfriend. Had I never said that, who knows? Maybe Jeremy would have gone back to Pristina and said he met someone who got it. Maybe he then would have wooed me and loved me from the start, and we would have been stellar. I'll never know. There must have been a reason I told Jeremy about Roman right away. Like there was a reason I never told Roman about Jeremy.

He sighed frustratedly and stretched his hands out on the

table, like a cat. "I'm just saying…I was uncertain. Not because of you, but because of Emmaline. Surely you can understand that."

In all fairness to what he was saying, I thought about that for a moment. There's something so mystifying about the past. And the idea of returning to something you lost or left is always an intriguing idea. Like going back in time. Like that saying, "If you knew then what you know now…"

Like Charlie saying, let's have sex again.

And me saying, no, let's not. Because you can't really go back in time.

"Are you still uncertain?" I asked.

"Well…" He looked sad. "I asked for an extension of my assignment so I could stay here and figure things out."

"How convenient for you."

He took my hand across the table and I let him. He bit his lip. "She was putting pressure on me to end it with you…and so I…went to L.A. To talk to you face-to-face. But when I got there I knew I couldn't do it because I wanted you, and I remembered that as soon as I saw you, and then I saw you with that other guy at Andy's, and I thought maybe you didn't want me anymore and I knew I deserved it because I'd been such an ass over Emmaline and had been gone for so long…like whatever you may have done was karma to me because of what I had been doing…and I don't know. I freaked out and I left."

I narrowed my eyes. "Wait a minute. You came to L.A. to end it with me?"

He hung his head and nodded into his chest. He released my hand.

"What the fuck?" I demanded.

He looked up. "But I changed my mind. Because right when I saw you, I knew how stupid I had been. It was just that being here, and having Emmaline here…well…I was living in the past. I realize I have to live in the now and the future. And you're my future."

"If I'm your future, then maybe you could have left out the part about how you came to L.A. to end it with me."

"I didn't want to lie."

"Well, you could have *kind of* lied!"

All these months and months and months and I'm totally paranoid that Roman's an illusion half the time... maybe just a trick of the mind...and it turns out he really is? My biggest fear...that it was all too good to be true. Confirmed!

"I must have a very good sense of intuition," I told him. "Because ever since you left I've wondered just exactly what was going on with us. I know I have all my little bullshit and I'm no fucking angel, I'll admit that. But none of that, none of it, Roman, has ever made me want to pick up the phone to tell you it's over between us because I chose something else. Sure, I've thought about it. I'll admit that I am human and that at times I was more interested in a warm body than a voice over an international telephone line. But I've never taken actions to end it, even when I knew I had the opportunity. I sure the fuck never would've gotten on a plane to fly halfway around the world and do it!"

"But you were still living it!"

I nodded. "Okay, fine. I guess I'm pretty goddamn immature. But so are you, Roman!"

"Dalton! I was wrong, okay? This thing with Emmaline...was just me chasing a ghost. I got waylaid because she was here. And that's when I realized what the problem has been all this time. You and I...we need to be *together*. Like you've been saying."

"Oh, yeah, sure, you say that now. It all makes sense when I'm sitting right here. When for the past seven months I've been preparing to give everything up to do what *you* want to do, planning our wedding, pushing someone away who probably would have wanted me if I'd given in to him... when for the past seven months, for you it's been all about Emmaline!"

"Well, from the sounds of things it was all about Jeremy for you," he countered.

"All the same, Jeremy's so not my *past love*," I said.

He held up a hand. "Look...I went to Douala yesterday to tell Emmaline that she can't just walk back into my life whenever she pleases and throw things all out of balance for me. I went to tell her that she and I would never be together ever again. And I came back early because I wanted to settle this and smooth things out between us. Between you and me. I mean, for Christ's sake, Dalton, the second I saw you come in yesterday I e-mailed her and—"

"You *e-mailed* her?" I screamed.

"We have to e-mail each other," he replied patiently. "For work."

"So you could e-mail Emmaline and that was all fine and dandy...but I had to wait weeks for handwritten letters?" I demanded.

"Yeah, but were you really waiting? It sure seems like you had plenty going on to bide your time!"

"Damn it!" I shouted. "I can't believe this!"

"Neither can I. I just told you that you were my choice and this is the thanks I get?"

"Why should I thank you?" I asked him. I held up my left hand. "I thought I was your choice when you put this ring on my finger!"

"That ring was simply a means to an end!" he yelled.

"A means to an end?" I gasped. "The end of what? Your tortured existence of pining away for Emmaline?"

"That's not fair, Dalton."

I folded my arms. "Was she with you when you went to Paris? Is that why you didn't want me to go?"

He narrowed his eyes. "Yes."

"You spent *Christmas* with her! With your *family?*" I shrieked.

"Bill was there, too. It wasn't just the two of us."

"Yeah? Well I took Jeremy to *my* parents' house for *Thanksgiving!*"

"*Thanksgiving!*" he cried, shocked. "With your family? How could you?"

People were staring at us. It was the kind of scene I have always imagined taking part in. A big screaming scene like the kind that only happens in movies. But it wasn't fun or funny like when you're watching a movie. It was terrible. We were spinning out of control. We were crashing.

I shook my head.

"What, exactly, are you so angry about?" he asked me, after a few moments of heavy silence. "I fucked up. So did you. We're both at fault. If we can be mature adults about this, we can work it out. I'm saying that you're the one I want. The only one. I realize that now."

"Yes…*now*. Now that I'm sitting right in front of you!"

He pointed an accusing finger at me. "Yes, and what about you? Didn't it take *me* in the flesh for you to remember I was the one you wanted? How is that any different?"

"Being tempted by your *past love* is so not the same!"

"Will you stop saying that!"

"What?"

"*Past love*," he said, mimicking the low, breathy voice I used to say it.

"Hey, *you* coined the phrase," I informed him.

He gave me a steely gaze. "Can we get past this whole Emmaline and Jeremy thing and realize what has really happened here? We have both been idiots. But the simple, remaining fact here is that we tested our love and our love prevailed. Right? I mean, that's why we're here right now."

I shook my head. I held a finger out to him. "No. You're trying to manipulate your way out of this. Because you know that since I did you wrong, your own cheating shouldn't seem so offensive. But you really wouldn't be quite so understanding about Jeremy if you'd been over here doing absolutely nothing, would you?"

He looked defensive. "Maybe."

"Maybe not," I told him. "Because if we were just testing our love, then we would have been satisfied enough by the answers that we'd found on our own without having to hurt each other. It's out there now. We've obviously hurt each other because we were unfaithful and that hurts. I know you're hurt, just like I know I am. But that's not what this is about. This is about you using me to save you."

He cocked his head.

It was all making sense now. "I think you're lying about not knowing Emmaline was coming here with you. I think you knew that the night you proposed. I think the reason you proposed, Roman, was because you were afraid of what would happen if you and Emmaline were alone here to-gether—and you thought if you got engaged it would save you from the *danger* of her. Like marrying me saves you. It saves you from having to ponder the what-ifs because you can just shrug and say you're married and there's no turning back. It's an out. I am simply your escape from what obvi-ously haunts you so."

He looked at me for a long time before replying. "Well…by marrying me, isn't that your escape? Your excuse? *Your* out? Doesn't it save *you?*"

"I think at this point, that notion is beyond possibility."

I got up from the table and walked out of the bar.

I lay down on the bed in my hotel room. I didn't want to be there but it was the only place I could go. I didn't want to think about Emmaline or Jeremy or Roman and me hav-ing a wicked fight over all the things we'd hidden. I didn't want to think about us both being afraid of shattering the image we'd created for each other.

But as strange as it sounds…it did give me some sense of peace and relief that he wasn't perfect. Maybe because I am so self-absorbed that I thought him having sins and secrets and a strange dark side I'd never seen made mine okay. Normal. Because if Roman of all people could have a strange dark side then the fact that I had one seemed almost ordinary.

Maybe I just hadn't wanted to know about his imperfections. So I simply hadn't seen them. Or maybe I'd seen them and hadn't found them to be imperfections.

Just like maybe he had looked past mine—or hadn't even noticed them.

Maybe because we respected each other, and we were so interested in finding out all the good things about each other, we cleaned up before we presented ourselves. We swept the dirt under the carpet.

I liked knowing that he wasn't perfect. It made Roman less of a deity and more of a man.

And I knew that even with Emmaline clouding his judgment, it didn't mean he didn't love me, too. I loved him the whole time I was off doing what I was doing with Jeremy. I loved him even though I loved Jeremy. It was just different.

I held up my hand and looked at the ring. It was more than just some diamond.

I had come so far. To turn back now…well, isn't that what I've been complaining about this whole time? The time had come to move forward. And I wanted to move forward with Roman.

It was time for me to be the bigger person. It was time for me to quit shrugging my shoulders and saying *que sera, sera*. That's not always the case. Sometimes you have to take responsibility for that shit.

I rolled over onto my stomach. Then I picked up the phone. Roman answered after three rings.

"I'm sorry," I said.

"So am I."

"I can't talk anymore tonight."

He was quiet for a minute. "I'm glad you said 'tonight.' I have an idea for tomorrow."

"What's that?"

"You want to see Africa, don't you?"

We made plans to meet the next morning, and before we hung up Roman asked if I still had Bill's business card.

"Yes. I do."

"Have you even looked at it?"

"No."

"Look at it when you're off the phone, okay?"

I shrugged. "Okay."

"See you tomorrow, Dalton."

I got off the bed and went over to get my purse off the chair. I took out my wallet. I'd shoved the card in there without a moment's thought.

The front was imprinted with Bill's information.

But on the back, in Roman's handwriting, it said, Love YOU!

Chapter 29

"You know, when you said 'see Africa' I assumed we were going to hang out in Yaoundé, go shopping or something," I told Roman the next afternoon, as we were driving along a rough road on the way to Waza.

"You're in Africa now, Dalton. And in Africa, you go on safari."

"Shit. I'm marrying Indiana Jones."

Roman laughed, but didn't even flinch at my "marrying" comment.

We hadn't talked about what was going on during the whole journey to the north. When he'd picked me up at the hotel, he'd told me he'd prefer that we not "get into it" right away. He suggested we relax and enjoy ourselves. I was in complete agreement. We both seemed to be in a giving mood. We both seemed to want to work it out.

Our accommodations in Waza were not of the Hilton variety. Campement de Waza was a safari lodge built into the slopes of the Waza rocks. I found it absolutely charming. Our room was a private straw hut. We stashed our things and then went to the restaurant, where we sat with a group of British backpackers and ate omelets and French fries. Then Roman suggested we hike up to the top of the rocks to watch the sunset.

"This is pretty incredible," I said, awed. The Cameroonian savannah stretched out in all directions, wild and raw, beneath a pink sky.

"Tomorrow morning, we're going into the park for a game sighting," he told me. "Waza's actually the best game reserve on the continent, and this is a primo time for you to be here, despite the heat. The elephants will be everywhere. You'll probably miss the lions, though. They don't usually show up until April."

I snuck a peek at Roman. He'd shaved, but left the goatee. He was wearing a white T-shirt that stretched over the lean muscles of his upper body. His skin was tanned to a healthy glow. He'd slapped on cologne before we ate. That made me feel good. He always puts on cologne when he wants to be all sexy and desirable for me. It's like when I put on some yummy cherry-flavored lip gloss for him so that when we kiss, he gets a sweet surprise.

"So we had our little tantrum," Roman commented.

"Tantrum sounds so childish, don't you think?"

"I hate to disappoint you, Dalton, but sometimes you are childish."

"So what? You're pompous."

"You're superficial."

I was shocked. "I'm not!"

He nodded emphatically. "You are!"

I lit a cigarette and focused on the golden horizon.

"I'm sorry for just running out like that. At Andy's, I mean. It was just all collapsing on me. I suddenly felt like my life was an abused utopia."

I knew just what he was saying.

"I'll admit I did expect a bit much in just leaving and thinking you would deal. I guess I was naive to think that you'd be fine doing what you were doing and that we'd eventually just fall into place."

"Not naive," I allowed. "Just a little too hopeful, I think."

He nodded thoughtfully. "Maybe. Anyway, what I'm saying, Dalton, is that I realize why you did what you did. I'm not saying it was right or that I think it's great. I'm just saying that I understand what may have been going on."

I sighed. "That's very gracious of you."

He rolled his eyes and dropped his hand into his lap dejectedly. "I know. I totally blew it."

"You think you blew it?" I asked. "What about me? I blew it."

He squinted as he looked at me. "I don't know whose crime is more punishable. Do you?"

"Maybe we're criminals of the same kind."

"Maybe."

I shrugged. "Grandma Mary says two wrongs don't make a right, but…"

"Grandma Mary says?" he asked, surprised.

I smiled. "I was going to add that Grandma Jane says if you've both trespassed against each other, then it's easier to forgive the other person. Like it cancels the wrongdoing out of it…or something."

"That's an interesting theory. And probably quite true."

I laughed. "Yes…since we both know we're a couple of fuckers."

He laughed back. "So true."

"I fucked up. I'm admitting it. I'm sorry. If you can live with that, then I can live with what you've done." I took his hand.

He squeezed my hand. "I'll always care about Emmaline. I think I'll care about her forever. But it's different than the love I feel for you. I can't explain it…but it is. Can you live with that?"

I thought about that. I know that no matter what happens, I'll love Jeremy forever. Just like I'll love Dan forever.

Somewhere inside, where the fifteen-year-old in me still lives, I'll even love Charlie forever.

"Yes. I can. As long as there are no more secrets between us."

"That means no more of *your* secrets, either, Dalton."

"No more secrets," I agreed somberly.

"What else?" he asked.

I thought about it. "No more leaving me behind."

"No more," he promised. "Now, what about Jeremy? Is that really over?"

"Without a doubt. Jeremy was…" I trailed off with a shrug. "Important. I'll admit it. But even so, I was always serious about you. Maybe in a wayward way…but still serious. Can you live with that?"

"I can live with whatever I have to, if it means I can live with you."

"Same here."

"I'm nervous," he said. "I feel like we're on a first date. Except there's so much at stake."

"Well, I guess we are just getting to know each other. In a way." I told him that there were things I wanted to share with him and he listened without saying a word. I told him how I'd met Jeremy and that we had an understanding about each other that was immediate and weird. I told him that we'd been two lonely people who took comfort in whatever it was that we were able to give each other. Two people who were too much alike and enjoyed it in a perverse way.

I told him all the things I used to tell Jeremy. I told him about me.

"I like this," he said. "I could get used to this."

"What?" I asked. I crossed my legs and released his hand to light another cigarette. I handed it to him before lighting one for myself. Dusky twilight was taking over the southern hemisphere.

"I don't know. Talking. Hearing about your life, without you holding back."

"I could get used to it, too. It feels good."

He smiled. I looked into his brown eyes. I wondered if our children would have brown eyes or blue eyes. Brown's a nice color. It makes me think of chocolate and coffee and Guinness and walnuts and my dad's beard.

"How come you never told me about any of that before, Dalton?" he asked.

"I never really knew where to begin…or why I even should."

"It's *your* life. It's you," he reminded me. "That's why."

"Well, now you know."

"I'm glad."

I was quiet and thoughtful. "Roman, besides me not being an overzealous Washington woman, why do you even want me?" I asked. "I have all these flaws. I'm fat and sarcastic and I can be seriously mean. I like doing bad things. I'm a horrible Christian. I'm spoiled rotten and awful."

"Well…I'll admit that I *have* always thought you were spoiled rotten. It scares me a little, actually. I just don't know how I'm going to ever measure up to Arnold and Miss Mary Margaret."

I laughed. My dad calls my mom Miss Mary Margaret. He does it because Grandma Mary calls her that when she's really angry with her, as if she's still scolding a naughty teenager. She gasps and says, "Why Miss Mary Margaret! Shame on you!" I guess my dad thinks that is so funny he likes to tease my mom about it.

"You know, for such a confident girl, you are way too hard on yourself, Dalton. *All* women think they're fat. And if you were fat, how would you fit into Ava's clothes—ever think about that? She is tiny, Dalton. You've got a nice soft curvy body. It's sexy. You're sexy. Believe me."

"And the other stuff?"

He shrugged. "I'm not the world's most devout Catholic. I haven't gone to mass in years. Just what makes you a horrible Christian, anyway? Not believing everything you've been told? It's not like you worship the devil, do you?"

"Not exactly. But I have often thought he worships me."

He laughed. "And so the things you think are bad that you do, what are they?"

"I've spent most of my adult life in a bar," I told him. "Or drunk in my living room."

"Who hasn't?" he said. "People who are no fun, that's who."

"I've spent the majority of my earnings on clothes and shoes," I added. "I like to get dressed up and feel superior to chicks who don't look as good as I do."

"So? You're a woman. Nature, Dalton. You can't change it."

"But sometimes I don't. Look good, that is. Sometimes I slob out."

"This I have seen. And I don't *care*," he declared. "To me, you are perfect just the way you are, however you are, however you will be. That's what love is, Dalton. Although nobody's perfect, really. As we've learned, I myself am far from it."

We smiled at each other knowingly.

He put his face into his hand to gaze at me. "So. How do you feel about getting married? Do you still want to do it?"

I thought about it. "Yes. Do you?"

"Very much."

"And then what?"

He shrugged. "And then, whatever we want. I'll take some time off, spend some time in Washington. I've had a long-standing offer to resume teaching at the university. Maybe do that for a year."

"Really? You'd stay in D.C., even without the promise of getting to go away on projects? I always thought that was just where you liked to hang out until you were off again."

"You know something I'm starting to realize? The world will always be there. I happen to love Washington…and to be honest, I've kind of been missing it. Feels like home sometimes. And what's so bad about home?"

"Absolutely nothing," I told him.

"We'll just have to see. You may actually hate Washington. I know for a fact you'll hate winter. Where I come from it seems mild, yes, because we're practically indigenous snow-people in Syracuse. But from your perspective…"

"I'm not some total pussy," I informed him.

He chuckled. "I'm not implying you are, Dalton. I'm simply telling you that it's a whole different kind of place, and that if you don't like it, I won't make you stay."

"Where will we go?"

"Wherever we want. You went to college. I have a Ph.D. We could find work anywhere. Plus, I'm a great fucking cook. Maybe I'll just chuck it all and open my own bistro!"

"You're a pretty interesting man, you know," I told him.

"That's nice of you to say, baby. I usually feel like a jackass."

"Well, I could never tell."

I climbed into his lap. I put my arms around his neck and he put his head on my chest. "We've got a long way to go, Dalton. But the important thing is…we're on the right track now," he said. He closed his eyes. "I'm glad we crashed, as strange as that may sound. I'm actually really relieved about it, though. I think if none of this had happened…well, who knows."

"I feel the same way."

He pulled his head back to look at me. He searched my eyes with his own. "I don't think there is such a thing as forgiving and forgetting, Dalton. I think you forgive and that's it. You never really forget anything, anyway, do you?"

"I forgot almost everything I learned in geometry."

"That's not the same thing," he laughed. Then he gave me a kiss. He tightened his arms around me and smiled as he looked into my eyes once more. "This has been a really good evening, Dalton. The best talk."

"But?"

He gave me another kiss. "But right now…I just want to take you back to that straw hut and get you naked."

"Now you're talking, Roman. Now you really are."

Do I really know anything? No. But I do know this. I will marry this strange roving dreamer, even if that's exactly what he is. And even though I know he was tempted, I know I was tempted, too. We are both human. And that means we can both make mistakes.

I suppose there are no guarantees that things will always be just right. And that's okay. I don't want guarantees.

Feels like forever, though. Finally.

Chapter 30

When my plane landed at LAX, I was glad to be back. I wasn't desperate or horrified. L.A. would always be there. Dirty and fast and sleek and mean. I would leave her but she would never leave me. I've realized I don't mind having her in me. I don't mind having her in my blood. She'll be a part of my life always, just like everything else that's ever happened. And it's no big deal. It's just life. It's my life. It's who I am, who I was. The me I am now, the me I was then, the me I have always been, and am not ashamed of. And don't have to be ashamed of, because I am who I am. This city, she's special. She took me in when I needed a place to go. She introduced me to Roman. She gave me Jeremy. She's my friend. In all her manipulative behavior, her nonsensical tradition, her mystery and disappointment, at least she's always there. She needs people the way they need her. And I don't think I'd want her any other way. I think I love her like that.

Electra and Ava came to get me at the airport. Electra hugged me and Ava threw herself into my arms and bawled like a baby.

"Doll, you are just the craziest person I have ever known!" Electra told me, as I threw my bag in the back of her SUV. "Just flying off to Africa like that? I really thought Dylan was kidding until you didn't come home for days."

"She was just worried about you," Ava told me.

Electra rolled her eyes. "Worried? The fuck!"

I could tell Electra really cared. Her insults are like love bites.

"So how was it?" Electra asked. "What the hell happened?"

I fastened my seat belt as she zoomed out of the airport. "Lots."

"Were there cannibals in Africa?" Ava asked from the back seat. "Were there tribespeople in loincloths and war paint? And lions and hippos and giraffes and great big monkeys?"

"Not really. I did see some elephants, though."

"Wow!"

"Are you still getting married?" Electra asked.

I nodded. "We certainly are."

"I got married while you were gone, Doll," Ava said proudly. She bounced up and down in the back seat.

I turned around to gape at her. "You did?"

"Uh-huh," she giggled. She held out her hand. She was wearing a big glittering diamond ring.

"Ava and Dylan ran off to Vegas and tied the knot like drunken fools," Electra moaned. "Which they think is just hilarious. They were sitting around on Friday night with nothing to do and decided that meant they should be gambling. So boy, did they gamble, all right. Got so fucking wasted they pledged their love and said we do in front of Elvis!"

"Did you tell your father?" I asked.

"Who? My father? No way. You know the family would kill me if they found out I was married by Elvis instead of Father De Marco. It's going to be hard on my papa as it is… Dylan's not even Catholic."

"Did he tell his parents?"

"Who? His? No…are you crazy? He'd have gotten kicked out of the house!"

Electra and I exchanged sidelong glances. Then we laughed. I started singing "That's Amore" and Electra joined in. Ava leaned between the front seats. She kissed both of us on the cheek and then fell back, laughing giddily.

"So when's Roman coming home?" Electra asked.

"Still in May."

"And that's okay now?"

"It's okay."

We talked about Cameroon and Roman and how weird it all is when you have a good relationship. We got Baja Fresh and took it home to eat it on the patio. Fret came by and Electra threw her aluminum foil burrito wrapper at him. He didn't get the hint. She threw a beer can. He jammed.

Electra narrowed her eyes and stabbed at her burrito. "Man…if he hadn't seen you with Jeremy, Doll, and he'd told you about that Emmaline shit…you could have had him on his knees for the rest of his life."

"Yeah, but I don't want him on his knees."

She gave me a strange look. "Why not? What good are men if they're not on their knees begging?"

"I like them better lying down." I stuck my tongue out at her. "Or standing up for themselves."

Jeremy met me in Venice and we sat on our bench drinking Frappuccinos.

He was wearing a special new ring on his marriage finger. The pattern was different but the idea was the same. Ha, I wonder if he'd bothered to tell Breeze that the idea had been recycled. No way. He'd probably really made her sigh and croon over how thoughtful and romantic he was. How symbolic and deep he could be. I wondered if he'd been doing that since he was a teenager—and thought yes, probably. Just like he had probably hurled Pristina's ring into the ocean. More than two years with Pristina and it was as if she'd never even existed. Poof.

"I'm glad you got over me," he said, slurping up some whipped cream through his straw.

"You're so full of yourself, Jeremy."

"I'm right though, aren't I?"

"Right on, as a matter of fact."

He ran a hand over his hair. I'll never forget the color. Like sable. Dark sable like the kind on a calf-length Park Avenue coat when the city sidewalk is icy.

"So, how's it going with Breeze?" I sat back on my hands and looked around at the freaks. The filthy promenade. The polluted beach.

"I'm in love, Doll. She's so wonderful. I've never felt this way before."

"Good for you." I clapped my hands. "You owe me five bucks."

"I do, don't I?"

"Uh-huh."

He pulled a five out of his wallet and handed it to me. I pocketed it for cigarettes.

"I came here today to tell you we won't be seeing each other anymore, Jeremy."

"I came to tell you the same thing, Doll. Breeze says she doesn't want me being friends with other girls. Especially not you."

I raised my eyebrows.

He took the lid off of his cup and downed the rest of his Frappuccino. "I *have* to do what she says. She told me I'd better if I plan on staying with her. So if she says you and I can't be friends, then we can't. It shouldn't be that hard to understand, toots."

I shook my head at him. "That entirely pathetic, seriously disturbed and overall wimpy litany just reminded me of why it's a *good* thing we broke up."

"We didn't break up, though, toots. We were always just friends."

"Whatever helps you sleep at night."

He lit a cigarette and took my hand. "We did have some good times, huh?"

"Sure we did." I lit a cigarette, too.

"You were…" he told me, still holding my hand.

"So were you." I touched Breeze's ring. He touched Roman's.

I thought it was fate because we both knew the ins and outs of every horror movie ever made. I thought it was fate because we both liked Baja Fresh. I thought it was fate how one day he just walked into a random lobby when I happened to be sitting there. But then wasn't it fate when Roman ended up at a Charisma event? Maybe everything is fate, in a way. Maybe we're given a lot of opportunities to see what we do with them, and then we have to take responsibility for our own lives.

He took a drag and looked at me with his penetrating gaze. Those eyes like oceans. "If we'd met under different circumstances, it might have happened."

"It didn't, though."

"I know."

I'll never love Roman the way I loved Jeremy. Jeremy was under my skin. He was infuriating. He was mystically irritating. He was fucking great.

But it would have never worked. I knew that, all along. Still, I think I'll remember everything about him. I'll remember his warm embrace and his cold words. I'll remember his profile in the blue glow of a movie, his voice fading with a goodnight. I'll remember his many misgivings. His fractured charm. His earnest expression. His hateful e-mails. And the way he would say "Hey" all soft over the telephone after hearing my hello. And how he was there. And how much I liked having him there. And how much I liked us. Even when I hated us. Even when I hated him…and when he hated me.

We hugged goodbye on that bench. "Good luck with Breeze, then," I told him.

"Good luck with Roman."

"For what it was worth…Jeremy…"

He hugged me tightly one last time. "Yeah…for what it was worth."

I watched him walk away in his pair of our matching Vans. He didn't turn around once. I watched until he disappeared into the crowd. Then I got up off our bench, threw my cup away and headed for the future with no regrets.

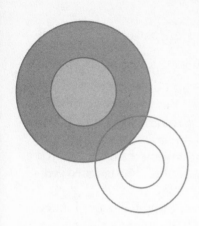

Epilogue

There's something refreshing about knowing I'm marrying Roman. Roman will be a good husband. A good father. He'll teach his sons how to act like men. He'll teach his daughters how to take it when boys are being stupid, and how to give it right back to them. He'll take care of me and fill my life with love. So what if he almost fucked it up. I'm an understanding gal. Because I know that even with his flaws and his insecurities and all the things I discovered when I really took a good look at him, he's a good man. And I deserve a good man. Even a bad woman deserves a good man. And I'm not even really a very bad woman. I guess no one's as fucking immaculate as they think they are or would like to be. And those who think they are need some serious help.

"Of course you deserve a good man," Lily told me as we drove around town on our old cruising route. We were smoking cigarettes and listening to Blondie. Our bellies were full of Yolanda's cheese enchiladas. Our hair was streaming out behind us as the wind blew into the car. "You're not the

devil even though you think you are. If anyone in this car is
the devil it's me!"

"You! Why you?" I demanded. I wanted to be the devil.

"Because I'm a fucking bitch and I don't even care!" she
cried gaily. Then she got serious. "I'm very proud of you,
my honey, for facing up to your wrongs and having a confrontation when you knew it could have finished you. You
did the right thing. And you know something...I *told* you
he was getting it off with somebody else!" She laughed glee-
fully.

"Do you think I let him off too easily for that?" I asked.

She shook her head. "Nope. He'll remember it the next
time he wants some."

The streets of Ventura were sleepy. The sun was going
down over the ocean. I laughed. "But I'll still give it to him."

"Yeah...but only because you love it...you dirty little
slut." She stopped at a light and winked over at me.

It was Saturday night and Kitty and Al were in Mexico.
I'd driven home with Andy for Lily's birthday party at their
house. I knew all of our old friends would be there. We
would be like when we were kids again. It was okay to pretend sometimes.

"So Ava's married to Dylan, and Electra's moving to New
York," Lily assessed. "Good thing you're going with Roman.
What would you do without those two, otherwise?"

"I don't know. It's going to be weird. I've lived with them
for so long."

"Well, people move on. But if you're supposed to stay together, you just do. Like you and me." Impulsively she leaned
over and gave me a kiss on the cheek.

I kissed her back.

"Are Ava and Dylan moving in together?"

"Yes, but not until they figure out how to tell their parents they got married."

"Weird marriage, man! I can't wait for *your* wedding. I
can't wait for the reception. I hope nobody falls overboard,

'cause everybody's gonna be lit. Your mom had my mom take care of the alcohol. And I kid you not, but Kitty has ordered enough liquor to inebriate the whole goddamn town!"

"That's just how I always imagined my wedding reception. A total drunkfest."

"Hell, yeah! Hey…howsabout we go pick up Andy and Daisy from the Kiplingers' house and get some shakes at Baskin-Robbins?" Lily suggested, jumping up and down in her seat.

"I thought you were stuffed?"

"I am, Doll, but it's Baskin-Robbins! And it's my birthday! You can buy mine," she said graciously. "And then we'll stop at the liquor store and get some cheap shit to drink and it'll be just like when we were dumb teenagers! And we can play all my brother's old CDs like Journey and Boston and dance in the living room with all the bozos and laugh about how Aurelia and Dan are stuck at home with their stupid babies when we're all getting down! How fun!"

"That sounds good to me," I told her.

"It's always good to be here, isn't it?" she asked. "Even though when we were kids, we were dying to get away?"

I nodded.

"You'll always come back, won't you, Doll?"

"Always."

She changed Blondie and put in America's greatest hits CD. Together we sang along to the lyrics of "Ventura Highway"—stopping at the same time, for the thousandth time, to ask each other what the hell an alligator lizard was.

Lily turned down Seaward Avenue, the ocean glittering its good-night, the town shaded serenely by the gentle green hills where we would somehow always be children. I looked at the picture she had taped to her dashboard, of her and me and Daisy all done up like the Robert Palmer girls for my Halloween party senior year. We were standing in front of the fireplace at my parents' house, all sultry and seventeen.

Simply irresistible. We knew then we were going all the way. To where, we didn't know. But it was gonna be somewhere *great*. And you know something…with all my bitching and complaining and wondering and questioning and stupid nonsense about this or that…it is pretty great.

And I think it will only get better from here. No…I know it will. I just know it.

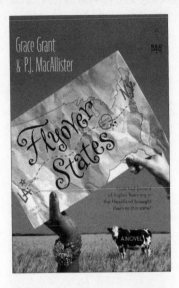

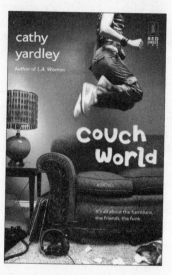